The Forgiven Duke

Jamie Carie

ADVANCE READER'S EDITION

UNCORRECTED PROOF
NOT FINAL INTERIOR

978-1-4336-7323-8

Published by B&H Publishing Group,
Nashville, Tennessee

To my son Jordan,

When I dreamed up this hero, the Duke of St. Easton, I modeled him with two people in mind: King Solomon from the Bible and you. Your vast intelligence astounds me and your caring, loving heart enriches our lives. How blessed we are as your father and mother to know and love you. When people say "the sky is the limit," I think of you. But it's not the sky that will ever limit you. With love, both God's and ours, nothing will stand in the way of your destiny.

A special thank-you to LT Glenn Atherton, USN, and his lovely wife, Jessica Atherton. Glenn patiently answered my many ship-related questions during the writing of this series (any mistakes are mine!). Many thanks and may God bless America!!!

Chapter One

Dublin, Ireland—November, 1818

"Please…let me go."

Lady Alexandria Featherstone pushed away from her fiancé's encircling arm and rushed back toward the railing of the ship. A frantic pulse beat in her neck as she strained to see through the mists that hovered over Dublin's shoreline in a gray-green haze. She looked up and down, back and forth across the rocky beach.

Was he still there?

Why did he care so much? Was it only the prince regent's orders that drove him toward her or something more? Something of gossamer letters and the slashing lines of ink from a man who seemed both haunted and half in love with her.

Her gaze roved over the departing forms on the shore, fast growing into blurry dots of distant friends and family belonging to the ship's passengers. The mist played havoc with her vision, retreating and rolling through the salt-laden air, making undulating forms of dark-clad well-wishers. Had she only imagined him there?

Just to see his face one more time.

There. Her gaze settled on a particularly tall man with jet black hair. If she concentrated hard enough, she could almost see his famous green eyes. But he was turning away, in a hurry, leaving to do something she hardly dared imagine. Would he come after her?

Her fiancé, John Lemon, came to stand behind her. He put his arms around her waist and pulled her lightly against his chest. "What is it, love? Is something amiss?"

Alex turned her face toward him. "It was him. I saw the duke."

"Your guardian?"

Alex nodded. "I'm sure of it. He almost caught up with us." She didn't say how it somehow made her feel safe that he was searching for her, hunting her, wouldn't give up until he found her.

"Well, it is good that he didn't. Did he see you?"

Alex's voice dropped to a low softness. "I don't believe so." She *knew* so. She knew that connection that shook her to her toes when their eyes locked. She saw the confusion, the devastation that she hadn't trusted him, that she'd gone and gotten herself engaged. Her life had gone offtrack so suddenly and thoroughly, she didn't know how to make sense of it. But she couldn't tell John that. John had been her only option, the clear and obvious way to carry out her mission without impediment.

God, You know I have enough obstacles. I need a clear path to finding the truth.

And the truth was, John had offered what her guardian had not. He'd swept out his hand and offered marriage and protection and help in the only thing that mattered to her—finding her missing parents alive. She shivered and crossed her arms inside her red cape. She had to keep foremost in her mind her mission, no matter what she had to do to accomplish it.

Her mind ticked off the events since the day she'd learned that the prince regent had declared her parents dead and appointed the powerful Duke of St. Easton as her guardian. She hadn't believed them dead when the duke's secretary had come to her home on the windswept isle of Holy Island and delivered the news, and she didn't believe it now. Not most of the time, anyway. It just wasn't possible. Her parents had traveled the world for as long as she could remember, solving mysteries and tracking down treasures of all sorts for people. They were famous for it. But the fact that Alex hadn't heard from them in over a year now was worrisome. They were in danger. And the only person who cared and believed, the only person who could find them and save them, was her.

In the months since, she'd tracked every clue her parents had left behind, following their trail through Ireland as they searched for a missing manuscript from the famous Hans Sloane collection. She'd had help along the way, both from new friends and God's guiding hand. And John? She couldn't have continued to Iceland alone. Besides, she was twenty years old, time to think of marriage, and John would make an excellent husband.

Her jaw stiffened with resolve. The duke would only haul her back to London. He had been very clear in his letters that he would follow the prince regent's orders and bring her to his home to protect her, and she knew he just wanted her safe. She would have a London season, her first, and then the matchmaking would begin. And before she knew it, they would have slowly convinced her to go on with her life as any normal person should do and forget about the absurdity that her parents might still be alive and in dire need of her help.

No. She had to fight against these strange and powerful feelings for the duke. They would only lead to heartbreak in ways she had yet to imagine.

"Do you think he will follow us?" Alex asked, unable to help the feeling of hope that he might.

"I don't know. But as soon as we are truly married, he will have no more authority over you."

She should have felt relief in that, but a stab of anguish rent her heart. No more letters from him? Never to see him up close or speak to him again?

There was a slight accusation in John's tone when he'd said "truly married" that made Alex cringe. He'd proposed only a few days ago, and there hadn't been time for the reading of the banns or to elope and find a minister to perform the ceremony with all the preparations for the journey to Iceland. Montague, John's uncle and her good friend, had counseled that they need not rush into it. His knife wound from that terrible stabbing by the Spaniards who had chased her across Ireland would heal in a few weeks, and Montague promised to come to them in Iceland as soon as he could travel. He'd already helped her track her parents through Ireland and he was determined to keep doing so. They could always have a small ceremony once he reached them, couldn't they? Alex had gladly pounced on the idea.

"I don't like this pretending any more than you do, John, but I don't like the rush either. When Montague arrives, then we'll make arrangements."

"And what if the duke arrives before my uncle? What then?"

"We've kept him at bay this long. This ship is sailing to New York, so he might not even know about the stop at Reykjavik. He might already be misinformed."

"Hmm, possible I suppose." John lips lingered by her ear, his warm breath causing goose bumps to form on her arms. "It's just that I'm a little…eager"—his lips brushed against the spot below her ear—"to make you…all mine."

Alex twisted around. "John, you mustn't do that." But there was laughter in her voice. Fortunately, the only other people on deck were far away and not paying the supposed newly wedded couple any attention.

John chuckled. "I have something for you."

Alex turned toward him, brows raised. "You do?"

He reached inside a pocket and pulled out a little velvet bag with a silken drawstring. Alex watched in curious fascination as he pulled the opening apart and reached inside. He took something out and stepped toward her, reaching for her hand. "If we're to be married, even pretend for now, you will need this."

He took her left hand and slid a ring onto the third finger. Her breath stilled as she looked down at the large, twinkling diamond surrounded by dark blue sapphires. "It's so beautiful."

"It was my mother's. She would have approved of you."

Alex gazed up into John's blue-gray eyes. "Do you think so? I wish I could have gotten to know her. She must have had a great love for jewels."

"Oh yes. She had quite a collection. I fear I've had to sell some of the better pieces over the years, but there are still a few left that I have saved for my future wife. They will all be yours, love."

Alex held her hand out and watched the stones sparkle as she moved it. "I don't know what to say. It doesn't seem right somehow."

John drew her close again, pressed his cheek against her temple, and murmured into her ear, "It's perfect. You're perfect."

Alex tilted her face up. His eyes were so adoring, she felt a pang of nausea. "Thank you."

He leaned down to kiss her but she turned her face away. "John...until we are truly wed...you do understand?"

He was saved from promising anything of the sort when a crewman in sailor's garb came up to them. He bowed. "Lord Lemon, Lady Lemon, the captain asked me to inform you that your cabin is ready. He has taken special pains to see to your comfort."

"Cabin?" He only mentioned one cabin. Her face heated as she realized that as an alleged married couple, they would, of course, share a cabin. Her gaze swung to John who seemed very happy indeed. This would be more challenging than she'd thought.

"If you will just follow me, I will be happy to see you settled." The young man lifted his brows.

"Thank you." John turned toward Alex with a teasing smile. "We are eager to get...settled."

Alex shot him a warning glare and took his arm.

She walked into the room, blinking against the darkness while the sailor lit the lantern. He held it aloft so they could see the accommodations. Alex's gaze cast about the sparse furnishings. A small table with a lamp. A wardrobe that would barely fit her three dresses and John's coats. A trunk at the foot of a bed. A single bed. Alex saw another single bed above it attached to the wall. She stilled a laugh and looked askance at John. This would be perfect.

"Two beds, eh?" John's tone was dry toward the sailor.

That poor man mumbled a red-faced apology toward the newlyweds. Alex shrugged at John with a grin. An answer to prayer. She had not been looking forward to taking turns sleeping on the floor.

The sailor left and shut the door behind him. Alex stood still as John came toward her.

"We're not married yet," her voice squeaked.

"I know." He said the words but he drew her into his arms. His face leaned in, toward her hair and cheek and lips.

"You mustn't."

"I know." His lips ran hot against her cheek and jawline, then up her chin to her lower lip. He hovered there for a long moment while she tried to remember where she was and who she still was and what was happening.

With a mighty pull from the dreamlike state back to reality, she reared back, took a deep breath, and chuckled. "I'll take the top bed." For some reason it seemed the safer choice.

Alex watched the slow grin of admiration and something hungry, something she wasn't sure of its meaning, spread across John's handsome face. She wanted nothing more at that moment than to lean in and kiss him. He was so very tempting.

With forced determination, she turned away. "I'll change into my nightdress now. Turn aside if you please."

He cocked one blond eyebrow at her in a way that made her shiver. He was her fiancé, for goodness sake, but he wasn't her husband. And in her heart of hearts, God help her, she wasn't sure he would ever be.

She quickly changed and climbed to the bed.

She pulled the covers to her chin and clinched her eyes shut, hoping she wouldn't have seasickness. Hoping she wasn't the only person on earth who truly believed her parents were still alive.

Hoping *he* would come.

She thought of her guardian and composed a mental letter like the many they had written back and forth to each other over the last several months.

> *Dear Gabriel,*
> *Don't give up. Please...still come for me. I need you, my duke. I need you to believe with me and help me find them.*
> *Love,*
> *Alex*

Chapter Two

What had just happened?

Gabriel Ravenwood, the Duke of St. Easton, turned away from the water, the waves, the ship that was fast taking his ward to a place he didn't know and of which he couldn't foresee all the perils—and well, away from him.

And that man who was with her, who had his arm around her like she belonged to him. Who was he? A deep chill that hummed with anger spread through his veins. He balled his fists against his legs. He had to find out who that man was and what he meant to Alexandria.

Gabriel pressed into the wind as he walked quickly away from the departing ship barely visible amidst the mists swirling across the sea. He stumbled, breathing hard, turned his head, and hoped no one was watching. *God. Dear God.* Hadn't he had enough yet? Hadn't he suffered every public humiliation he'd never imagined? Hadn't he risked everything and just now lost?

Just…get me…through these next few moments.

He couldn't hear his stomping gait as people reared back, faces shocked or glowering with judgment as he hurried through the crowd toward the shipping office. He pulled open the door and plunged forward like a horse at the starting gate. He pressed both hands against the counter where a wide-eyed, skinny clerk stood blinking at him, mouthing some nonsense Gabriel couldn't begin to decipher.

"That ship. The one that just departed, the *Achilles*… give me the passenger list."

The man looked ready to argue and Gabriel snapped. He didn't have time to explain that he was a duke. He didn't have the time or the patience to tell this sniveling youth how he was on the king's business. No. It felt good to lean across the counter, grab the young man by the collar, and heave his terrified face so close that Gabriel could see the red veins running through the whites of his eyes.

"The shipping accounts for the *Achilles*. Now."

The youth nodded, face devoid of all color. Gabriel let loose of him with a harsh sound and turned away while he fetched it. What was wrong with him? What had he become?

Even the knowledge that something was very wrong didn't stop Gabriel from snatching the leather-bound volume from the thin man's grasp and paging through the sheets of handwritten entries like it would engulf in flames at any moment. He pored over the lines of names not finding a Featherstone in the list, nothing that even resembled the name Featherstone.

Then, ignoring the eyes of the room glued to him, he leaned over the book with a sharp inhale. There was one Alexandria.

Not a Featherstone. But a married woman. Alexandria Lemon. Lord John Lemon's wife.

A married woman.

Gabriel gripped the counter with one hand and shoved the book back toward the young man. He pointed at the names. "Do you know this man? This woman?"

The man turned the book further toward him with a shaking hand, looked at the words, and then wrinkled his brow. "Sorry, sir." his lips clearly said.

Gabriel gave him a long stare. "Are you sure you don't know anything about them?"

The man swallowed, his Adam's apple moving up and down a thin throat. Gabriel turned and stumbled from the room.

Lord John Lemon.

Odd name for a nemesis.

He hoped the man had mettle, because he was going to need it. He'd just sailed off with Gabriel's family and he meant to do whatever it took to get her back.

The first thing he had to do was find out who John Lemon was and how he was connected to Alexandria. The thought that she had actually married someone in so short a time was alarming, to say the least. Whoever Lord Lemon was, he might have dire motives for his interest in Gabriel's ward; he might be another form of danger they hadn't considered. A more insidious kind. A clever, calculating enemy more dangerous than the Spaniards following Alexandria could ever be.

11

The thought of it made his blood run cold as he stood outside the busy Custom House, gazing at the scene and trying to decide where to go next. A tall man lumbered past, leading a spotted mare. Wait! The giant! If Gabriel could find the man who had tried to stall him in the streets earlier, causing him to miss Alexandria's ship, he might get some answers.

He rushed to his horse at the hitching post in front of The Custom House and mounted. When he spun around he saw Michael Meade, his secretary, coming around the corner with his men. They must have finally calmed their stampeding horses enough to circle back to the shore.

"Meade!" Gabriel waved to gain his attention.

Meade saw him and motioned to the men to follow him over. Thank God. If he was to search out the identity of Lemon, Gabriel would need Meade's ability to speak in such a way that made it easier for Gabriel to read his lips. The fact that he was deaf still gave him moments of intense despair, embarrassment like he'd never imagined, and a forced humility that still fit like a bad coat. But he was beyond thankful for his secretary. Meade was the person who made his affliction bearable, who made it possible for him to even attempt chasing down Alexandria Featherstone.

"Your Grace! I can't believe you're still here. Did you find the ship? Did you find Alexandria?"

"I watched the *Achilles* sail away, but it was too late. I saw her, though. She was on the deck. Why didn't you tell me?"

Tears threatened at the memory of finally seeing her. Long, dark hair pulled back from a lovely face. Sky blue eyes staring into his. Even at such a distance, he had locked on to those eyes, as if he could pull her back to shore with the intensity of his gaze alone. He'd waited so long, and he couldn't begin to describe how he'd felt when he finally saw her—broken to his core and flooded with emotions: protecting, loving, possessive emotions.

Meade mumbled something as a flush filled his face. He developed a sudden stutter and inability to put two coherent words together when having anything to do with beautiful women.

Gabriel sighed. "Never mind. There was a man with her. He acted very familiar, putting his arm around her waist in a way that said he knows her well. I've just come from the shipping office and seen the passenger list. There was no mention of Alexandria Featherstone, but there was an Alexandria Lemon along with a Lord John Lemon. We have to discover who he is and what he is doing with Alexandria."

"That doesn't sound good. Where do we begin?" Meade asked, brows raised.

"Remember that giant of a man with the cart blocking the street? The one who startled the horses? He knows something. That was no accident, I assure you."

Meade nodded.

"Let's spread out. See if we can find him. Send the men in all directions. You and I will head back to the street where we last saw him. His size will be to our advantage, but tell the men to use whatever means necessary to convince the man to come with them. Tell everyone to meet back at the hotel in a few hours. Hopefully, one of us will have him. "

"Very good, Your Grace."

Gabriel trotted up and down the quay while Meade dispersed Gabriel's hired outriders and soldiers. He'd

hired them to make a big show of his power upon coming to Dublin; now he was glad to put them to good use.
They were trained soldiers with experience. If any one
of them found him, Gabriel was reasonably certain his
men would be able to handle a bumbling giant.

A few minutes later, he and Meade galloped into the
street where they'd last seen him. It turned out to be
ridiculously easy. The man was sitting right where they
had left him, blocking the road, perched on the seat of
the cart and crying like a giant redheaded baby. Gabriel
and Meade stopped and stared in disbelief for a moment
and then dismounted and hurried over to the man.

"Sir, have you gone daft? What is the meaning of
this?" Gabriel demanded in a loud bark.

The man looked up from his hands and, upon seeing
them, burst into another wail, his wide face scrunching
up into a ball of flesh with a giant nose in the center.

"Meade, talk some sense into the man. Get him down
from there."

Meade's eyes widened at the order but he turned
and began to talk...and talk...and talk. Finally, the giant
pulled out an enormous white handkerchief, took a deep
breath, and blew his nose into it several times. Gabriel
gritted his teeth and slapped his gloves against his thigh
waiting for him to finally climb down.

Meade turned to Gabriel and motioned toward a pub
in the distance, mouthing the words, "Perhaps some food
and drink will comfort him, Your Grace?"

"Yes, yes, carry on." Gabriel shot the giant a steely
look that said he'd had enough nonsense and gestured
toward the pub. "Let's get you out of the street and buy
you some dinner, and then you can tell us all about your
troubles."

Gabriel didn't mention Alexandria's name yet; he didn't want to scare the man off, but he had a feeling she was the cause of all this caterwauling. He felt the same way about her leaving.

Meade made arrangements for a quiet table and a midday meal of Irish stew, oysters, smoked salmon, and potatoes to be served while they settled themselves. The man Meade said was named Baylor shoveled in more food than Gabriel could eat in two days. He waited until the man had drained the third tankard before he began his questions. "So, Mr. Baylor."

He shook his shaggy head. "Just Baa-er." He talked with his mouth full, one spoon poised to go in while another was just coming out of his mouth.

"Very well, Baylor. Come now, your little ruse in the street earlier has done its work—I missed the ship. So tell us, how do you know Lady Featherstone?"

His bottom lip started to tremble at the mention of her name, causing Gabriel to sigh with gritted teeth. This was going to take all day and the patience of Job besides.

He pulled out his very used handkerchief and dabbed most elegantly at his eyes and then blew his nose with such force it rocked the table.

"Gad, man, get a hold of yourself. Perhaps it will help if I tell you that I am the Duke of St. Easton, her guardian."

"I mow who you are!" he bellowed, mouth still full.

Gabriel could tell that he bellowed by the way his eyes grew round as saucers, he leaned in, and his mouth opened wide around the words. It was impossible to read the man's lips so Meade repeated what he said.

"Excellent. Then perhaps you also know that the regent has charged me with finding Lady Featherstone and bringing her back to London. It's for her own good," he added hastily upon seeing Baylor's lips draw into a stubborn line. "It's for her protection."

Baylor said something to that, but Gabriel couldn't make it out. He took a deep breath with a prayer for patience, looked at Meade, then nodded toward his coat. "Best to bring out the speaking book, Meade. Let's get the whole story if we can."

Gabriel glanced over at Baylor just in time to see a confused expression cross his face. So, Alexandria hadn't heard that he'd gone deaf. Relief pooled through him. He slid his own untouched tankard toward Baylor and explained. "I have recently been afflicted with a problem of the ears and use a speaking book to communicate. Just converse as you normally would, and Meade here will write down what you say."

A look of pity crossed the giant's face, but this time Gabriel was glad of it. Perhaps it would loosen the man's tongue.

Meade wrote while the giant talked, and after many minutes he slid the book in front of Gabriel. *Baylor met Alex in Belfast. He became quite taken with her and her quest to find her missing parents.*

Of course he did, Gabriel muttered to himself, still looking at the page.

He joined her and the man she was traveling with to help her find her parents. "A sweeter lass has never lived," he says.

Of course he does. If there was one thing Gabriel was sure of about Alexandria, it was her ability to win people to her side and instill in them a loyalty to her that took most people years to accomplish.

He says her parents are treasure hunters and in some sort of trouble and that Alexandria is determined to rescue them.

"Yes, well, so am I," Gabriel murmured aloud. It was the only way to secure her heart. Thinking of her as someone else's wife made him feel sick and angry. Gabriel looked at Baylor and asked the most important question. "I saw her on board the ship. She was with a man. Baylor, who is Lord John Lemon?"

Chapter Three

The chill southwesterly winds pushed against the larboard side of the *Achilles*, flattening the square sails and moving them through the choppy gray water at a brisk twelve knots. The water stretched out toward the horizon, unending in every direction, making the huge brigantine appear more a toy, a mere wooden box with sails made of scraps found in a sewing basket. Great billowy clouds rolled across the sky, lighter gray with puffs of swirling white, pregnant with rain that had yet to spill. And all around them was the eerie sound of a moaning wind that seemed afraid and haunted, aching for relief from some terrible thing it had seen or heard.

Alex stood at the rail soaking in the lonely scene despite her body's shivering inside her red cape. They been at sea a little over a week now, seen the land and the birds slip away into unending wind and water, salt-laden air scented by fish of all shapes and sizes. They traveled northwest toward Iceland's shore, a journey that could take as much as three weeks, but according to Captain O'Mally would take closer to two if they didn't run into any trouble.

Thinking of trouble at sea brought a memory to mind. She had been around twelve years old and her parents had been gone for a very long time. Every day she went to the ruins of the monastery, knelt where she imagined the altar had been, and prayed for their safe return. One day a small ship appeared on the horizon. Alex watched it come closer and closer and then, seeing her parents on board, she ran to meet them.

But her mother was gravely ill and her father barely said a word to Alex, so worried about his wife. Alex remembered how he'd picked up her mother and carried her across the beach toward the castle. She'd looked so thin and pale that Alex just stood and stared, more afraid than she'd ever been.

"Alexandria, run ahead and open the door. Mother needs to lie down and then I'm going to need you to run and fetch the doctor."

Alex shook herself out of her trance, running barefoot and terrified across the pebbled beach to obey. She followed her father inside. "What happened? Is she sick?"

Her father walked up the narrow stairs, turning sideways to make the turn. "Get the doctor, Alexandria. I will tell you what happened after we have done everything we can for your mother."

The sharp words were so uncommon from her father, and the hollow look in her mother's eyes so unnatural that tears burned from behind Alex's eyes.

With a pounding heart, she ran back outside and into the village. They hadn't a real doctor on the island; he was across the causeway in Beal, and the causeway was only traversable twice a day when the tide went out. She didn't want to wait that long, so she ran as fast as her bare feet could take her to Margaret Henry's house, a midwife and known for her herbal remedies. It turned out to be a very good thing as her mother was suffering from a severe inflammation of the lungs. The midwife made an awful-smelling herbal plaster of camphor and stinkweed, then instructed them to keep it on her mother's chest day and night until her wheezing eased and color came back.

Alex hadn't known such depths of relief as she felt when her mother slowly recovered. Her father finally told her the story of the shipwreck they'd had coming back from South America where they had been hired to find an ancient Incan silver mine. They'd been rescued at sea by another ship but not before her mother had nearly drowned.

Alex shivered now as she looked at the cold, harsh sea. She would not want to be floating in its icy depths, clinging to a stick of wood and hoping the sharks and all sorts of sea creatures wouldn't think her toes worthy to nibble on. But her mother hadn't let the fear of it happening again take hold of her as Alex half hoped she would. No, Katherine and Ian had left again as soon as she recovered, on another mission of missing antiquities. And Alex had prayed again for their safety, alone and bereft but determined not to mind too much. It was a pattern that had repeated itself over and over until now.

Now she was going after them, and what she might say when she found them she didn't know, but she felt it building and burning in her chest. Like a volcano waking up and stirring to life. She felt she might explode if she found them safe and well and was a little afraid of what was coming.

Dear God, forgive me for my selfishness. I do want to find them safe and well. But why couldn't they be ordinary people? Why did You put me with them when they don't even seem to care?

There was no answer to the questions, though she'd asked them many times before. She supposed God wanted her to be thankful for her life and to stop feeling sorry for herself. There were many poor and destitute, the plight of slaves and hungry children, the abused and the sick. She had plenty to be thankful for, but the hole in her heart was there nonetheless and she couldn't seem to find a way to fill it.

Alex sighed and turned away from the scene. She would go down to the cabin and find John. He always made her laugh.

⇛ ⇛ ⇛ ⇛

"What are you doing, John?" Alex stood inside the cabin, having just opened the door, shock filling her to see John leaning over the room's small desk, her letters from the duke scattered across it in a picture of frantic disarray.

John reared up and turned toward her. "I, ah, knocked the stack on the floor and was trying to put them back together again."

It was a blatant lie and they both knew it. Alex had a choice. She could pretend to believe him and brush the issue under the proverbial carpet or continue her interrogation. She found she wasn't ready to decide quite yet. She walked over to the desk and picked up the letter that was spread open, the one he had been reading.

John backed away with a wary expression. She held it up, noting to herself the date and that it was the first letter she'd received from her guardian. She read aloud in a clipped and angry voice:

> 10 September 1818
> From the office of the Duke of St. Easton, His Grace, Gabriel Ravenwood
> Madam,
> I deeply regret the cause of our recent introduction and am as surprised as you must be at our ancestral tie. Upon the prince regent's order, I have spent considerable time investigating the claim of your parents' deaths and their current estate. (Do not ever put in writing again what you wrote about our most-honored monarch, do you understand me?) I have been astounded on both accounts. Firstly, your parents have had no contact with anyone known to us in nearly a year. Does this not surprise you? You mention your lack of faith that they are deceased, and I am sure it is difficult news to accept, but a year is a very long time to have someone's relatives come up missing. Please advise if there is something you know that I do not. In the meantime, I think it wise to continue as the regent deems appropriate with my taking charge of your estate and well-being.
> This brings me to the other surprise of my brief investigation into the Featherstone affairs. It would appear that your parents have been hiding, hoarding perhaps, a very large fortune. I tell you this only in the vein of protecting you from fortune hunters should the news come out. You, my dear Lady Featherstone, are the sole heir to lands and moneys

that I must confess nearly equal my own. And my dear, I am among the wealthiest of Englishmen at this time. Do be careful.

She paused there and looked up at John. "Should I be careful, John?"

His face turned a shade darker in the dim light. "Of course not. But why didn't you tell me? If we're to be married, I won't have you keeping secrets from me."

"I hadn't planned to." Alex arched a brow at him and waited for further explanation.

"Alex, love." His mouth turned down in a pout. "It's as I said and innocent. I dropped the pile and then...was curious, I admit. Your relationship with your guardian seems a little intimate and I—I was jealous." He took the necessary steps to reach her and grasped hold of her hands, bringing them to his chest. "Imagine if I had a pile of letters from some rich and powerful duchess. You'd be curious at least, wouldn't you?"

He traced the curve of her jaw with a gentle caress. Alex breathed in and then expelled it in a rush. He was right. She would want to know what those letters said. "I'm sorry. I thought for a moment you were a fortune hunter like the duke warned me against." She laughed and leaned into his chest a little, thinking how good he looked and how he made her feel so many new feelings all at once. "But you don't need my fortune, do you?"

John cupped her cheeks and pressed a light kiss to her lips. "What if I did?" he murmured against her cheek.

Alex reared back. "Are you in financial difficulty? Tell me now if you are. As you say, if we are to be married there shouldn't be any secrets between us."

"The truth?" His blond brows rose and the blue of his eyes deepened. "I haven't told anyone the whole truth of it, not even Uncle Montague."

"You can tell me." If her fortune could help the man she loved, then why not? It wasn't as if she had any idea what to do with so much money.

"Well, it's a sad story to be sure, but not uncommon. My father hadn't any knack for estate management and mortgaged the Lemon land to the hilt until he finally had to sell. He left me with the title and a mound of debt, debt I've worked hard at trying to pay off. I had a little money from my mother's side and invested it carefully." He looked aside and sighed. "It's been a struggle, I can tell you. Robbing Peter to pay Paul, keeping up appearances so I can travel in the right circles to have the opportunities I need and well, doing whatever I can to maintain a decent living in Dublin. I kept telling myself to marry for money, but I just couldn't seem to do it."

He gripped her upper arms and looked hard down at her. "Alex. When I met you I didn't care if you had two shillings to rub together. You have to believe that. And the way you needed to go to the bank and dip into the duke's funds, I didn't think you did! But I knew. I just knew I loved you and wanted you for my wife. The fact that you have this vast fortune? I'd be lying if I told you it didn't make me happy. It makes me breathe easier for the first time in my life. But know." He shook her just a little and glanced at the ceiling as if for help to explain it. "Never doubt that I loved you and wanted you before I discovered this. I'm *glad* I didn't know."

"Oh, John." Alex wrapped her arms around his neck and hugged him to her. In a fierce whisper she added, "I am glad you didn't know at first, for now I'll never doubt your love. But I'm sorry I didn't tell you. I suppose we're rich."

John chuckled and squeezed her against him.

Alex leaned back against his encircling arms and looked into his eyes. "It comes at such a cost, though. If I think of that money, an inheritance, then I have to think my parents are gone. And you know I cannot believe that. I won't believe it until I see their faces. I'll have their graves dug up if they exist. I'll not accept it until I see them for myself. Do you understand?"

John brought her close again and grasped the back of her head underneath her hair. "Of course. We won't speak of it again. Just know I love you and I will do anything to make you happy. We'll find them and God willing, we *will* find them alive."

It was all she needed to hear. It was the only thing that mattered to her. "Thank you, John." She didn't say she loved him. She felt shy about those words, like they were butterflies around her heart, just birthed from their cocoon, still testing and trying their damp wings, still seeing the big, wide world for the first time and trying to make sense out of it all.

A sudden dip and then a jarring motion caused Alex to sway toward the post of the beds. She clung to it, looking at John in alarm. "What was that?"

He shook his head. "I don't know but it didn't sound good. Let's go up and find out."

They threw on their wraps and made their way to the deck where other passengers where rushing to the lee side of the railing, pointing and babbling at the same time. The chilly wind blew so hard across the deck that a shiver rushed through her body. Alex pushed her way to the front and saw the reason for all the excitement. A huge chunk of bluish white ice floated right next to the hull of the ship. "Did we hit it?" she asked anyone who would answer.

"That we did, miss," a sailor responded, pointing. "Look at the end there, it's calving off." A creaking sound and then a big splash sent a spray of freezing water droplets into their faces.

"Oh, my. Did it damage the ship?"

"Naw. That there is a bergy bit, not a real iceberg. Our ship shook it up good though. It will probably break into pieces and then float off toward warmer waters where it'll melt. No harm done. It's pretty, though, don't you think?"

John had finally wrangled his way to her side and frowned at the sailor speaking to her. Alex nodded. She was able to admire it now that she knew it hadn't damaged the ship. "It's so blue. It looks like a crystal from some enchanted land. Isn't it beautiful, John?"

"It is something to see. But it didn't seem wise to hit it. I hope this captain knows what he is doing."

"Oh, he knows sailing. Don't you be frettin' over that." The sailor stood up straighter. "Captain O'Mally has been captaining this brig for ten and some years, and he ain't never had a shipwreck."

"That's a comfort." Another thing to be thankful for. If there was one thing she was certain of, it was that God was watching out for her on this journey. She looked at John and smiled at him.

Thank You, God, for John.

Chapter Four

Baylor crossed his arms over his massive chest and clamped his lips down. "That's all I'm sayin'," his lips clearly said.

Gabriel motioned the hovering serving girl for another pitcher. "Come now, my good man." He began in a deceptively soft voice, knowing instinctively that he would gain more from Baylor with honey than vinegar. "We want the same things. For Alexandria to be safe and for her parents to be found. You want those things, don't you?"

Baylor nodded his big, shaggy head, a worried expression wrinkling his brow. "Aye, but she didn't want anything to do with you. She said you would take her back to London and then she would never be able to search for her parents."

Meade wrote the words in the speaking book as fast as he could. They'd both come to understand how a conversation could become stymied if it took too long to keep Gabriel up to speed and respond.

"I understand why she thought that. I do. I had told her in one of my letters that the prince regent had ordered me to fetch her back to London. But she wrote me another letter, asking me to join her cause and disobey the regent. Baylor, that is exactly what I had planned to do once I caught up with her. Imagine it. With my connections and wealth, I could hire men to travel with us, investigators and soldiers. I could keep her safe."

"She hasn't needed all of that. Why do you think she needs you? Maybe you need her."

Gabriel stopped, his next words falling away. He stared at Baylor, such an innocent and seemingly simple man, but a man who saw the truth. The giant's face remained thoughtful. Gabriel looked away and said in a soft voice, "You're right. I do need her."

Finally Baylor rubbed his knees and said, "Lord Lemon is Montague's nephew. He's a good chap, he is."

Montague's nephew? He hadn't thought of that, anything close to it. "Where is Montague? Is he on the ship with Alexandria?"

"No. Montague is at John's house healing up from a stabbing." Baylor scowled. "A couple of Spaniards are following the lass and they attacked them a few weeks ago. I didn't attend the event so's I wasn't there to help fight them, I'm sorry to say." Gabriel hurriedly read the words, his heart beating a little faster.

The Spanish wanted this manuscript as badly as Alexandria wanted her parents alive. They were probably on that ship with her now. And she only had that John fellow as protection. He looked too pretty to be of much good. Gabriel caught himself clenching his teeth and took a long, deep breath.

"Can you take me to Montague? I have to talk to him." Montague would understand all the nuances to the kind of mission Gabriel had in mind and be more logical than this sentimental giant.

Baylor drained his fourth mug and grinned, foam covering the orange hair on his upper lip. "That, your dukeship, I can do."

Gabriel shook his head, smothering a smile. "Your grace."

"Your what?"

"Never mind."

∾❦ ∾❦ ∾❦ ∾❦

After untangling Baylor's cart from the horses' reins, they made a plodding procession to John Lemon's house. It was a quaint street and well kept, Gabriel reflected as they rode up and dismounted, but nothing compared to his town house in London, nor even a shadow of Bradley House in Wiltshire. The fact that Alexandria hadn't even seen what he had to offer in comparison rankled, even though Gabriel knew she loved a ramshackle castle on Holy Island, a home with a gothic, windswept feel to it that would be hard to replace.

They knocked on the door and stood outside waiting. It took an inordinate amount of time but finally a maid, mop cap askew atop her curly brown hair, flung it open. Upon seeing Baylor her face broke into a wide smile. "Baylor! How did your task go? Were you able to detain the duke?" Her gaze flickered over Meade and then paused on Gabriel. Gabriel raised a brow at her.

"Oh, dear." She swallowed hard with a nervous laugh. "You're the duke, aren't you?" She sank into a curtsy and said some other things Gabriel couldn't make out.

"We've come to see Montague," he interrupted in his best authoritative voice. "He is here, isn't he?"

She looked toward Baylor who started inside. "Come along. I'll show you."

They found Montague seated in a neat sitting room, his feet propped up and a book in his lap. He sat up straighter as they entered. His eyes caught and held Gabriel's for a long moment, and then he nodded in an imitation of a bow. Gabriel took in his bandaged chest under the half-open shirt and understood, especially in a man of his years, why he didn't stand.

A sudden memory surfaced, streaking images of a sea battle from his navy days as he looked at Montague. He'd saved this man's life, long before Montague was an admiral. When Gabriel was just one of the lieutenants, he'd thrown himself on top of him, dragging him away as a cannon blew nearby. The blast had been horrendous. He lost consciousness and woke up in a hospital in Jamaica. He had not been able to recall what had happened until this very moment.

"Do you remember me, Admiral?"

Montague gave a slow nod. "When Alex told me who her guardian was, I agreed to become her champion. I owed it to you, if nothing else, to keep her safe." He looked away. "Though after getting to know her, I couldn't have abandoned her. She has become like a daughter to me."

Meade hurried to write down the words and Gabriel responded. "It appears she needed a protector. I understand you had a run-in with a knife."

Montague's lips curled into a half smile and he shrugged one shoulder. "Spaniards. You might have shown up earlier and helped, Your Grace." They both chuckled. "What's with the book?"

Gabriel took the seat across from him. He folded his hands into his lap, hating to have to say the next words to this man of distinction. "I would like to introduce my secretary, Mr. Meade. Meade will take down what you say in a speaking book as I've had some difficulty hearing of late."

Montague's intelligent blue eyes darted to Meade and then back to Gabriel. He gave Gabriel a small smile, his eyes thoughtful. Meade wrote almost as fast as Montague spoke. "I see that Alexandria's plan was successful and our friend Baylor here has kept you from her ship. Had you planned to board it or take her from the shore?"

"I planned to board it."

"A more dramatic move, but what then?" Montague flicked an imaginary piece of lint from his pants.

"I planned to go to Iceland with her, help her track clues there, and hopefully, though I have personal doubts, find her parents. Then I planned to take her to London and the prince regent."

Montague's head came up, steel gray brows raised. "You would defy the regent's orders for her?"

Gabriel tipped his head to the side. "Something like that."

"I'm sorry, then."

"Sorry?"

"I tried to detain her. I told her you might be trusted and reasoned with. Of course, she wouldn't take the risk, not with your power. She knew the moment you got close enough, she could be forced to give up her

31

search. When I knew I couldn't convince her, I let her make her own plans."

"Tell me about your nephew."

"You saw him, did you?"

Gabriel felt a thunder gathering in his chest. "I did."

Montague sighed. "He's a good fellow. He has a good hand with the sword too, so that should help, though I promised to join them in Iceland as soon as I'm able." A long look of intensity passed through his eyes. "He thinks himself in love with her. Of course, so do most men who cross her path, but he's a charming fellow and handsome. She agreed to marry him before they left."

A stone being thrown into his middle couldn't have more impact than those words. Gabriel swallowed and turned his head away to gather himself. "So they're engaged? Not married?"

He held his breath and watched the words appear on the page.

Not married yet. I asked that they wait until I arrive. I wouldn't want to miss the wedding, you know. They agreed as there wasn't time to wed before they left, what with the only ship headed that direction leaving in two days.

"But she is listed on the passenger list as Alexandria Lemon."

"I suppose they are pretending to be a married couple so she can travel alone with him. I don't like it, but she was determined to lose no time getting to Iceland."

Gabriel remained silent, looking off into the empty fireplace, thinking. What if they didn't wait? He turned back toward Montague. "You approve of the match?"

Montague gave a bark of laughter. "John is my nephew, and you would think I would be ready to dance at their wedding. But"—he shook his head once—"I feel like the father who hasn't met anyone good enough for her. Even John." He rubbed his knees. "And I suspect her heart isn't really in it. Not for John—" He broke off with a humorless chuckle.

Gabriel raised his brows. "For someone else?"

Montague looked right into his soul it seemed. "If you plan to catch her in time, Your Grace, you should hurry."

"Thank you, my friend. Your debt is paid."

ॐ ॐ ॐ ॐ

Montague's words were like a haunting chant circling in his head as he rode back to the hotel. Hurry indeed! Gabriel had to find a way to overtake the *Achilles*. The image of her face when she'd locked gazes with him on the deck of the ship caused a fierce sweetness, a sought torture that burned as if it was branded on his heart. He'd wasted too much time. Montague was right. If he had any chance of talking her out of this marriage, he had to hurry and see that she knew she had alternatives to accomplish her end. That she could have him at her side.

They reached the hotel and dismounted. Gabriel walked over to Meade. "We'll need to purchase a ship. Nothing fancy but something big enough to get us across the Atlantic to Iceland. Something fast. As fast as you can find. Also, hire a crew. Just enough men to handle a small craft but experienced. I mainly want an experienced captain, someone who enjoys a good race perhaps. Hint at an additional reward when we overtake the *Achilles*, which increases with the less time it takes to reach it."

Meade nodded his understanding, bowed, and turned to go.

"Meade." Gabriel stopped him. "Thank you."

33

Meade looked down a moment, his face turning red. Then he looked up at Gabriel. "My pleasure, Your Grace."

Now that Montague had inspired hope that Alexandria was not married yet and might care for him...nothing would stop Gabriel from telling her how he felt.

After seeing that the horses were taken care of by one of his hired groomsmen, Gabriel hurried inside to his room. He had letters to write, had to make sure the regent knew he was still on Alexandria's trail among other business, and his mother was complaining about his lengthy absence and all of the responsibilities he was neglecting at home. With renewed purpose he started up the grand staircase.

"Your Grace, is that you?"

Gabriel stopped, having nearly run the man down but thinking he'd read him correctly. Sudden recognition slammed into him. *Wonderful. Just what I need.*

It was the soldier he'd left cooling his heels in Beal, the little village just outside of Holy Island, on a feigned mission of holding down the fort while the little troop, himself and Meade included, searched for the missing Lady Featherstone. It had been a ruse to rid himself of the captain and his men, and it had worked, up until now. It seemed the captain had tracked him down. What was the little man's name?

"Captain...so...good to see you. Have you found Lady Featherstone and tracked me down to tell me of it?" He watched the man's lips very carefully. Without Meade's presence, traversing the speaking world was a very different matter, and he hadn't wanted the captain to ever know of his inability to hear. When last he'd seen the man, his hearing had been coming back. Now to reveal such a weakness was unthinkable. As annoying and incompetent as the short man was, he did have the prince regent's orders and Gabriel needed to be able to fool him again.

"You know I haven't found her." Gabriel thought he said with a sinking feeling. He continued but Gabriel only caught a few words here and there, words like *regent* and *trouble* and *disobeyed*.

As he spoke the room began to fill with red-coated soldiers. More soldiers than they'd been traveling with to Holy Island to fetch Alexandria. Many, many more.

Gabriel quickly deduced the situation without the benefit of hearing it explained to him. The captain had gone back to the prince regent at some point and been ordered, with reinforcements, to track Gabriel down. He gazed around at the soldiers' faces. A few stared him square in the eyes with a cockiness that spoke volumes. They were enjoying seeing him being taken down a notch.

Since he couldn't make out much of what the captain said, Gabriel tried to stall for time, interrupting the man with a wave of his arm and a steely look. "Captain, I have pressing matters to attend to at the moment. When my secretary returns, we will meet in the hotel's drawing room and discuss this. I must bid you good day."

He started to move around the man toward the stairs but felt a hand grasp his shoulder and then another on his arm, pulling him hard in the other direction. If he could only hear what was going on! He tried to turn and wrench free and then came face-to-face with the captain holding a pistol in his face.

"What is the meaning of this?" Gabriel roared. "Unhand me this instant!"

But they didn't unhand him. They beat him and twisted him and tied his hands together behind his back. The captain stared into his eyes, sure victory and the enjoyment of someone being humiliated and harmed glowing from his beady little eyes. "You can't hear me, can you?" His lips overly enunciated. He laughed.

They hauled him upright and half carried, half pushed him to the awaiting carriage. He was thrown inside, the door slamming shut. "Meade!" He yelled, hoping someone would connect the scene with the duke and tell Meade what happened when he returned.

Alexandria! he silently screamed, the crushing weight of defeat making his heart dissolve into frantic hopelessness. *God, where are You in all of this?*

How would he stop her from marrying now?

Chapter Five

The *Achilles* fought against the winds, beating to windward as it sailed around the coast of Iceland edging closer and closer to its jagged shore, the sails stiff and flat against the constant needle-sharp gale.

Alex hugged her red cloak around her, pulling the hood low over her eyes and peering from under it at the thrashing of the waves. Her heart pounded as she gazed at the edges of the land coming in and out of the foggy haze, revealing sloping black mountains with white-tipped rock faces.

They were almost there. After twenty days of close quarters and dodging moments of intimacy with her fiancé, Alex felt both a sigh of relief and a stab of homesickness. This shore they were nearing, this mist and its lonely feel, made her think of Holy Island and all she left behind. It seemed like so long ago that she'd begun this journey. Was she even the same person?

No. She was certain she was not.

She clasped her gloved hands together and leaned over them, seeing the vapor of her breath add to the spray of the sea. *I need Your light to guide my way. I need Your light to guide my way.* She repeated the simple phrase over and over, knowing that God's love was holding her up, that this mission was hopeless without Him, and that with Him and His light guiding the way, anything was possible. Even finding her parents alive.

A hand on her shoulder made her turn around.

"Is everything all right?"

She nodded at John, wishing for just a few more minutes alone with her thoughts and prayers. He was never far away, but of course they were in the close quarters of a ship and as her fiancé, it was to be expected. Why did it feel so...smothering?

"I'm fine." She turned toward the sea. "Look. We are so close."

John came up close behind her, blocking the shrill wind and creating a space of warmth. He leaned his head into the side of hers and whispered into her ear, "Are you excited? We may find your parents here."

The thought of it never failed to send a jolt of hope blazing through her. "Yes. I pray it is so." Her voice caught on the wind and winged away. She wasn't sure he even heard her, but it didn't seem to matter as he drew a big breath and wrapped his hands around her waist, clasping them against her stomach.

She closed her eyes, floating in the moment and stopping all her plotting and planning, enjoying the presence of his chest against her back and the wind song blowing her hair against the hood of her red cape, feeling warm and ensconced in the whirlwind of an adventure.

It felt right. She was right not to give up.

She imagined sailing around the world like this, with John at her back to protect her and keep her buoyed against life's gale winds and her love holding him up. They could do that—together—couldn't they? She couldn't imagine anything better.

The duke's face, her guardian duke, rose up from behind her closed eyes. As jolting as the sharp wind, she saw his piercing green eyes. Like the screeching cry of an eagle, she saw him snap his head around and stare into her eyes, impaled, caught in a spell she'd never encountered before. Fear and then determination filled her as she stood up to it, met it with the sky blue of her gaze turned to blue topaz.

Emeralds and topaz.

Alexandria looked at John and saw gold—such a golden man. He would hold her and carry her and help her. He would be the setting for her light blue stone, allowing it to glitter and shine. He would support her against the blows of life while her guardian would glitter brighter than her. If Gabriel and she came together, they would have to make God their setting. Her breath caught with the thought.

"Look!" He leaned over her left shoulder and pointed toward the gray-cast shadows in the waves. "Do you see it?"

Alex strained toward where his finger pointed and then inhaled. A whale. She'd never seen a whale before. She watched transfixed as it crested like the moon over the horizon in an elegant arc of sooty skin, shiny and oily, rubbery and firm at the same time. Its back arched and then its tail came up and over the edges of the deep, a grand show that made her press her gloved hands against her face. Oh! The beauty and grace. She blinked hard as the fluke slapped against the surface of the water, creating a big splash. Everyone around them oohed and aahed, two little girls and a boy squealing with excitement as the whale dove back under the water.

Clapping and cheering ensued among the passengers around them. Alex turned a happy face toward John. "That was amazing. Have you ever seen anything like it?"

He shook his head, his eyes lighting on hers. "I've never seen anything like it." His voice was low and deep. He looked into her eyes, his lips so close. The depth of his sentiment touched her in a melting-limb, slow-encompassing way, making her blink and want to turn away.

Gold could be exciting.

She smiled up at him in the midst of the salt spray… thinking how cold emeralds were and how distantly enchanting.

ঽৎ ঽৎ ঽৎ ঽৎ

Alex disembarked in Reykjavik as if in a dream. Stunning. That was all she could think to describe this strange and beautiful land. Where Ireland had been so green with shades of gray and blue and browns, Iceland was even more otherworldly in its stark contrasts of vibrant colors. The sea had turned an icy blue closer to shore, the land green with shades of yellow and rich orange, the mountains surrounding the little village of Reykjavik darkly silver with white streaks of snowy crevasses, all surrounded by a warm mist that swelled with the taint of metals and fish and salt and ice. The land of volcanoes, they'd said in rumors and whispers aboard the ship.

The land of fire and ice.

A feeling of purpose and adventure filled her veins in a thick, throbbing pulse as Alex lifted her single bag and carried it across the dock to the street that led into the village. She stopped and let her gaze sweep over the little town. It was small compared to Dublin and felt more like home on Holy Island. The street led to a row of hodgepodge buildings on either side made from stone and turf. As they walked into town she saw that there were shops and warehouses and a rectangular white cathedral, its tall tower seeming to look over the town and lent grace to the homey feel.

"Tiny little place," John murmured as he pulled his hat lower to shield his face from the constant, bracing wind.

"Let's go there first." Alex pointed to what appeared to be a public house.

They walked through the doors and were greeted by the sounds of someone crying, wailing really. John and Alex exchanged looks and walked toward the sound at the back of the large room.

A woman sat in a rocking chair in front of a stone fireplace, her face buried in her hands. No one else was about so Alex touched her shoulder. "Please, can we help you, miss?"

The woman looked up, startled, and then quickly wiped her tears on her apron. She stood and faced them. "I'm sorry. My son is missing since yesterday and half the town is out searching for him. I fear he has drowned in one of the hot springs." She appeared about to burst into another round of tears but rallied. "Have you come from the ship that just docked? Are you visitors? We are such a small village; we know everyone in town."

"Yes, this is my...friend." There was no use saying they were married if they were to have the ceremony here in Iceland. "John Lemon and I am Alexandria. Is this an inn? We have need of a place to stay."

"Yes indeed. We've rooms here. I'm Ana Magnusson. My husband is out searching for Tomas."

Alex motioned toward the chair. "Please, tell us what happened. Perhaps we can help with the search."

The woman hesitated and then nodded, motioning for them both to sit down. "Tomas is ten years old and always disappearing and giving me a fright, I can tell you, but this time he has been gone all night!" Her lower lip started to quiver. "I'm so afraid he is lying hurt somewhere."

"What does he look like?" Alex knew the feeling and tried to keep her talking.

"He has blond hair and blue eyes. He is tall for his age and has the most angelic smile. Always getting into mischief though."

"What sort of mischief? You've searched all his favorite hiding places?"

"Oh yes. He is usually found at the beach or near the hot springs. He's a good swimmer but the current could have spirited him away. I'm afraid we'll never find him."

John leaned forward. "We've just come from a large ship with a lookout. They would have had a good chance of spotting him if he was lost at sea."

"That's true, isn't it?" Ana's eyes lit up. "I should have Hans alert the captain before they depart to be on the lookout."

"What about favorite games he likes to play? What does he like to do?" Alex clasped her hands in concentration, thinking of places she had enjoyed escaping to as a child.

"He pretends he's a soldier sometimes, making pistols and swords out of sticks." She shook her head as if unable to think of anything else. "He's such a good boy. Oh, I don't know what I shall do if we don't find him." The poor woman broke down again into tears.

"May I see his room?" Alex asked, thinking taking some action would at least help her get through the next few minutes. "There might be a clue there."

"Well, I don't know." The woman hesitated. "We've looked all over his room, of course."

"It may sound a bit strange, but I have something of a knack when it comes to solving mysteries. A gift from my parents, I suppose. They are famous fortune hunters and travel all over the world solving important mysteries."

The woman's eyes widened. "Not the Featherstones? I thought you looked a bit familiar."

"You know my parents? Were they here?"

"They were here months ago. They stayed with us for a time. They were searching for something important, though they wouldn't say what it was. The whole town speculated on it, but we never learned what it was. And then, one day, they just disappeared."

Alex's heart pounded harder with each word. She looked over at John. "As desperate as I am to find my parents and hear everything about their stay here, let us try and help you find Tomas. May I see his room?"

"Yes, of course." Ana led them up a narrow staircase to the sloped ceiling of a small attic room. She lit a lantern and turned the wick until bright light flickered around the room.

Alex went through the drawers, the small box of toys, the clothes hanging on pegs, the pockets of each little pair of pants, and searched under the bed. Nothing unusual. She turned back the blanket and searched under the covers and then, with John's help, lifted the feather ticking and looked under the mattress. She'd always hidden her secret scribbling in a book under her mattress.

Finding nothing, she started to remake the bed. When she lifted the pillow she noticed a fluttering underneath and turned it over. "That's strange."

"What is it?"

"It looks as if Tomas has cut a nice rectangle from the back of this pillow casing. Has this been there long?"

"No. I just washed the bedding last week and a hole wasn't there then. What do suppose he's doing with a scrap of cloth like that?"

Alex stared at the shape of it. "It could be a tail for a kite or…"—she imagined the sticks he played with—"a flag or something at the end of a stick he's using for his make-believe games."

A loud noise coming from the downstairs made them all turn. "That would be my husband. Maybe they've found Tomas!"

They hurried back downstairs where a tall, blond man stood, his head almost touching the ceiling. "We've guests?" he asked his wife in a voice gruff with worry.

Ana made the introductions.

"You haven't found him," she said in defeat.

"Not yet, but we will."

"Lady Featherstone found something in his room. He cut off the back of the pillow casing, and she thinks he may have made a flag or kite with it."

"Another Featherstone, eh? Well, it won't hurt our cause to have you both helping. I've just come in for some rope before heading back out. It will be dark soon and almost impossible to search at night."

"We're glad to help."

"Rope! What do you need that for, Hans?" Ana paled whiter.

"Just in case we need it," he said in a soothing voice. "Could you fill the canteens while I fetch it?"

Ana nodded and filled two canteens from the bucket of water that sat on a long table against one wall. She found a third one and filled it for John and Alex. "I'm coming with you." She reached for a heavy cloak.

The wind had become a gale force as the four of them hurried down the street. Neighbors leaned out of their doors, some joining them and some inquiring the latest news with promises of prayers. Alex studied the buildings, looking for crevices and hiding places where a young boy might have burrowed in and gotten stuck. They called his name, but only the wailing wind answered them.

Alex shivered inside her cloak, thinking she must have some warm furs made up into a better coat for the winter. A road led out of town splitting north and southeast. "Would he have followed the road?" Alex looked in both directions.

"I don't know," Ana moaned.

"We've already searched both routes." Hans shook his head. "I thought perhaps he had gone fishing." There was a catch in his voice as he said it.

John leaned toward Alex. "It's probably hopeless, poor fellow."

"It's not hopeless. We have to pray." Alex turned to the Magnussons. "Might we pray together? God knows where Tomas is."

"I have prayed nearly every minute since I discovered him missing, my lady, but I welcome your prayers." Ana took a step closer and grasped Alex's hand. They all closed their eyes.

"Dear heavenly Father," Alex began in a steady voice, "we beseech You on behalf of little Tomas and ask for Your help. Please, God, lead and direct our steps. Open our minds to new possibilities and clues, light our way. Help us find little Tomas and please keep him safe and well until we get to him. Amen."

John shuffled his feet appearing uncomfortable.

"John, what's wrong?" Alex whispered as they walked a little ways down the road and peered into the brush surrounding them.

"Nothing. I just don't like this. We're losing time and anyway, I don't believe in miracles."

"You don't? Well, I do," Alex stated with heat. She'd been so enamored by his charm and good looks that she hadn't really found out much about his beliefs. How could she marry someone who didn't share her faith? And how could he care that they were losing some time when something so important was at stake?

"Tomas," she called, fanning out and away from the group. "Tomas!" The light of the moon shone bright, helping them search the area around the road that led to a small hot springs. Steam hummed above the surface of the pool as it came into view. It looked inviting to her; might it not have been enticing to Tomas?

"Ana, Hans," Alex called, "is the water too hot? Would he have tried to bathe in it?"

"He might have." Hans walked over. "It's bearable though on the warm side. But we've already looked here. His body…it would float if he had drowned here."

Alex sighed, placing her hand on Han's arm. "You've searched every building in town? Every place surrounding the town? Can you think of any place you may have missed?"

He shook his head, scratching the back of it. "No… we've had the townsfolk looking with us all day. They searched all their houses, the shops…" He stopped. "Wait a minute. The church. The roof was being repaired these last few days and they kept it locked up, but Tomas talked of getting up in that belfry one day. Since it's locked, I don't think anyone thought to check there."

Hope flared through Alex. "Come on." They called Ana and John to follow them and rushed back toward town. Within minutes they rounded a corner and looked up at the church where the tall, square tower of the belfry sat at the top. A perfect place for a child to sneak into and play all sorts of make-believe games.

They ran closer and then around to the other side. "Tomas!" she yelled up at the leaded glass windows. She rounded to the back and stopped. There, plastered against the white stone and hard to see, was a scrap of fabric flapping against the wall. The window looked to have been broken too.

"It's him! It has to be!" she shouted.

John was just behind her. "How are we going to get up there?"

The parents hurried around the corner and gazed up. "It's the pillow casing," Ana shouted. They all ran for the front door, which was locked tight, just as they thought.

"If he's up there, he had to have gotten in somehow. Look for broken windows," Hans shouted. They hurried around the church searching for a way inside. Sure enough, at the back of the building there was a loose board on the bottom of the back door. Hans kicked open the rest of it and they all pushed their way inside.

"Tomas!" They ran through the church to a set of stairs, up the stairs, through a long balcony, and to a little room that held a ladder against one wall leading to the belfry. First Hans, then Ana, her foot slipping on one of the rungs in her hurry, flew up the steps. Alex held her skirt up, waiting for her turn.

"Careful." John came up close behind her, bringing up the rear. "I don't want you getting hurt."

Alex frowned at him. Why was he being so annoying and smothering?

"Oh, Tomas!" They could hear Ana's wail.

A little farther and then Alex saw it too. One of the rafters had fallen on the boy, trapping his leg under its heavy weight. He held the stick over his head with one outstretched arm toward the window. He had somehow managed to break it and get the flag out of the small hole. What a clever boy.

"Mommy," Tomas's voice rasped. "Daddy, help."

John sprang up from the ladder next to Alex. "If you'll take one end of that beam and lift, I'll get the other side."

The father, pale but determined, nodded and made his way around the hole in the floor toward the broken beam. With a big breath he wrapped his arms around it.

"We have to lift at the same time to keep the weight from shifting on his leg. On three."

"Wait, I'll help!" Alex ran to John's side and wrapped her arms around the beam, determined to lend what strength she could, while Ana knelt next to Tomas, tears of joy streaming down her cheeks.

"One, two, three," John counted. They heaved the beam up and over him, lowering it on the other side of the narrow space. His mother wrapped her arms around him, both of them crying.

"His leg must be broken," Alex whispered toward John. "We'll need a split and a litter to carry him out."

"Yes, but not yet." The father rushed to his son's side and gave him a drink of water, cradling his head in his big hands. "Tomas, Tomas, are you in terrible pain?"

"Only when I move it," he said the brave words, but tears streamed from his eyes.

"Tell us where to find a doctor and John and I will get help."

The parents exchanged worried glances but Ana rattled off where to find him. "Hurry," she said to Alex and John.

Alex began to pray, crying out in thanksgiving with her whole being, as they made their way back from the church. "Tell anyone we see, John. Let's have the whole village come to help get him out safely."

John gave her a brief kiss on top of her head. "You never cease to amaze me."

"It was God's grace that led us to him."

"Yes, but you found the flag. Alex, we would have never been looking for that or known what it meant if you hadn't found that clue. I think your parents would have been very proud today."

She didn't reply to that, only hurried down the street. But it was a warm and pleasant thought, gaining her parents' approval. It felt good to use her talent for good. And maybe John wasn't lacking all faith. He had faith in her at least and that might be a start. She should be more patient with him. She could teach him about God and how to pray. Couldn't she?

Chapter Six

Gabriel leaned over and retched into the bucket beside his cot. Not much came up. Bad thing, that. Very bad indeed. He fell back onto the thin pillow with a groan, closing his eyes against the dizziness that had beset him since the moment they'd set sail.

Being back on board a ship wasn't his favorite thing in the best of circumstances, but since his affliction sailing had turned into a rack of torture—the spinning room when he opened his eyes, the dizzy, nauseous, seasick horror of it all. The soldiers had even stopped tying his hands together and guarding the door, knowing he was too weak and sick to leave the cot.

One of them, a youngster named Mick who was still wet behind the ears and looking out of sorts in his red-coated uniform, came into the tiny room. Gabriel blinked hard, trying to keep his eyes open long enough to see what Mick was holding. It was a small bowl, must be dinnertime.

He didn't know how long they'd been on board the *HRH Imperial*, but it seemed like forever. The trip from Ireland to London should only take a couple of weeks, though. Had it only been weeks? They must be getting close. *Dear God, let me last until then, I beg You.*

Mick sat on the room's only other piece of furniture, a spindly wooden chair, and scooted close.

"I just vomited up your last bowl, Mick. Don't think I'm ready for another just yet." Gabriel squinted up at the lad, waiting for a response.

As usual Mick ignored his gloomy predictions and dipped the spoon, holding it to Gabriel's lips. God help him, thirty-two years of age and being spoon-fed like a baby. If his enemies could see him now. He took a few sips and then fell back on the pillow.

Mick pulled something from his pocket that looked like a gnarled piece of wood. He held it out to Gabriel and made a chewing motion. "Ginger."

Gabriel longed for the old irritation at being treated like an imbecile. Mick obviously had figured out he was deaf and so had likely the rest of the ship, but he was too weak to care. He reached for the root instead and brought it to his nose. It smelled pleasant enough and now that he thought about it, he had read somewhere, long ago, that ginger could help ease an upset stomach.

He took a little bite and wrinkled his nose at the strong, spicy flavor. "Can't you make it into a tea or something?" he barked, but he didn't spit it out. If it would help the constant vertigo and nausea go away, he would try anything.

Mick's lower lip jutted out and he nodded as if thinking it over and deciding it was a good idea. He held up a finger and then hurried from the room. "Put some sugar in it," Gabriel rasped after him as loud as he could.

He lay back, closed his eyes, and chewed on a tiny piece, thinking he just might die of this if the ginger didn't work. Then it wouldn't matter if Alexandria married that Lemon fop or not. He grimaced and turned on his side, trying to block out the ache in his heart at the thought of losing her to John Lemon.

An hour later, he was able to sit up and sip the ginger tea Mick brought him. It was helping, a little. His stomach was not revolting, and the tea and the broth he'd drank earlier stayed down. He was beginning to feel like he just might make it through this—thanks be to God!

A dull roaring had begun in his ears, but it was manageable and brought a ray of hope. The last time his ears had changed, he'd regained some of his hearing. The fact that bouts of vertigo actually helped his ability to hear didn't make much sense compared to what the doctors had come up with, but just the possibility that he might someday discover a cure and even have a semblance of his hearing back made his throat ache with longing for it.

The next day Gabriel was able to shuffle onto the deck for some fresh air. He stood blinking into the cloudless gray sky, concentrating on breathing deeply. The captain came up beside him and squinted to look up at him. "London tomorrow," he said twice, overly enunciating the words. Gabriel just nodded and wished he would go away.

While he was eager to get off this floating nightmare he was not eager to see the king. Would they let him freshen up beforehand? He'd lost a weight, a stone or two, and hadn't had a shave since they'd boarded. Nor a bath. After all the sickness and cold sweats, well, he was sure he hadn't smelled worse in his life. And his clothes. They hadn't exactly let him pack a bag before throwing him aboard. Would they let him send for his valet and fresh clothing? What he really needed was Meade.

Thinking of Meade made him glare at the captain. Would Meade discover what had happened to him? He knew his secretary well enough to know that he would turn over every stone trying. But when would he be able to board a ship to London? It might take weeks before he sorted it all out. "I would like to be taken to my town house to prepare for my visit with the king. Can you at least give me that?"

The captain looked him up and down, the decision wavering in his eyes. He gave a slow nod, then turned and marched away. Clever man. The captain knew if the regent pardoned him, a show of kindness after this ill treatment might not go unnoticed. He was hedging his bets and it was something Gabriel planned to use to his advantage.

≈ ≈ ≈ ≈

Five days he'd been home.

Five precious days of resting, recuperating, and reconnaissance gathering. It appeared the captain hadn't done him any favors after all. The news hadn't reached them yet in Dublin, but Queen Charlotte was dead. London was a black shroud of mourning—windows darkened, the people draped in black. She had died November 17, the year of our Lord 1818, at seventy-four years old in residence at one of her favorite places on earth: Kew Palace with its lovely gardens the queen had tended herself over the years.

The old king was in deep mourning—blind, deaf, lame, and insane, at least that was the word, fading away. No one really knew how much the king even understood about what had happened. The prince regent had been at his mother's side and to Gabriel's knowledge didn't have any idea as to the missing manuscript and all that was going on with Alexandria.

Gabriel paced back and forth across the rug in his elegant drawing room and pondered the possibilities. The queen's death would certainly delay any conversation he would have with the prince regent. As sad as the queen's death was, it might just have saved his neck.

His butler, Hanson, appeared at the entry to the drawing room. He strode forward, leaned over the desk, and wrote on the speaking book.

Gabriel walked over to read it. "You've a guest, Your Grace. The prince regent himself." His butler looked half frightened to death.

"Well, don't keep him waiting in the hall!" Gabriel barked. "I'll need you to stay and write down what he says if he'll abide it."

The butler hurried away, coattails flapping. How he wished for Meade's steady presence. He had looked into that too since being home and discovered that his stalwart secretary was well on his way aboard a ship he'd hired, a little schooner named *Mary-Ann*, probably some fisherman's long love. It wouldn't be a comfortable ride aboard such a small craft, but Gabriel could just picture Meade enduring it with those gritted teeth and calm-eyed surety he had when it came to getting a job done. Especially a job concerning himself or Alexandria. Gabriel expelled a breath with a smile. Meade would do just about anything for Alexandria Featherstone.

The prince regent walked into the room, chin up and glaring down his nose at Gabriel.

Gabriel swept into a low bow. "Your Highness, I must first tell you that I am having an affliction with my ears and cannot hear well. My butler will have to write down what you say in a speaking book so we may converse."

Gabriel turned to the butler. "See that His Majesty has anything he needs before we begin." He turned back to the regent, who appeared deep in consideration of this turn of events. "My deepest condolences on your blessed mother, the queen."

The regent started to say something and then stopped, appearing confused. He nodded instead and sat on the edge of one gilt-edged crimson chair. It looked to creak under his ponderous weight. Gabriel threw out his tail-coat and seated himself across from the man, wary and watching. As soon the regent seemed settled and the butler had the speaking book, seated in the chair next to Gabriel, they began.

The regent started on a long and animated discourse about something that his butler was obviously having a hard time keeping up with.

Oh, please God, help me. This is going to go badly indeed. Gabriel pressed his fingers against the bridge of his nose while watching a bead of sweat trickle down Hanson's temple. He finally passed the speaking book over and Gabriel tried to read through the scratching lines.

He says thank you for condolences, et cetera, et cetera. He mentioned something about the Sloane manuscript and your guardianship, et cetera, et cetera. He's here to check up on it and discover what's what. More, but I didn't catch it.

There was no reason under heaven that Gabriel would tell the regent that his butler had missed most of what his esteemed Royal Highness had said. Time to improvise.

"Your Highness, might I tell you a story? It's about this mysterious manuscript."

Like a child come to life, he brightened and nodded.

Gabriel told him of the last six months, trying for his best tone of voice, though he couldn't know how he sounded, but he tried to let the emotion of the story color his voice as he explained about Alexandria. He told it from her point of view and from a child needing her parents as much as a government needing a manuscript. He told of Hans Sloane's collection and the hidden mystery that men like his the kings of Spain and France had reason to believe could be valuable to their country.

Then Gabriel glossed over his part, how the regent had appointed him guardian and he was doing his best to complete the task, but Alexandria, God bless her, just wanted her parents found. He painted her more a pretty child than a woman. He painted her like him, the regent. Impetuous, a little reckless maybe but so full of heart, someone who needed guidance and help...support.

"So you see, Your Majesty, while it is of the utmost importance that we find this manuscript before Spain and France do, don't you think we should also help Alexandria find her parents, dead or alive, so she can put this to rest and go on with her life?"

The regent sat back, the heavy folds of his boyish face rapt and considering.

Gabriel pounced on the moment. "If I could find out what her parents are really looking for. If *we* could"— Gabriel lifted an elegant hand and moved it to encompass the regent—"we could help Alexandria find her parents if, God willing, they are still alive. You would do anything to bring your dear mother back, would you not? Think of it, Highness. Alexandria is like that, doing anything to bring both her precious parents home—safe and alive. And," Gabriel nodded sideways, "we might find what this thing is that means so much to Spain. It would be good to know, don't you think?"

The regent's face hardened from compassion for Alexandria to determined ambition. "Yes, I think so." He rose, looking at the butler and giving quick instructions.

Gabriel hoped Hanson got it all.

When the regent left, Gabriel read the note.

Meet him at St. James Palace tomorrow at noon. He will show you the part of the manuscript they have.

Gabriel took a deep, shaky breath. He was walking on water now. There would be no turning back from this day's work, and if things didn't go well, if this alignment with the regent turned sour on him, well... He put his fingers inside his cravat and pulled it away from his neck.

Chapter Seven

The story of Tomas's rescue spread through Reykjavik like the flow of lava from one of their many volcanoes. An outpouring of love and support for the Magnusson family and admiration for the smart, pretty Lady Featherstone swept through the inn with days of visiting and celebration. Tomas's leg was broken, but the doctor said it was a clean break that would heal and not the crushed bone that would make him lame for the rest of his life.

All rejoiced at this news, especially Tomas. He lay propped up by various pillows on the cushioned bench in the main room, receiving his visitors and their gifts of toys and sweets like a young prince. He had been so afraid, pale and weak after two days without nourishment, but now the color was back in his cheeks. His mother hovered, tears in her eyes much of the time, making certain her son had anything he could think to ask for.

As for Alex, she was treated like a heroine, a personage of awe, an angel some even called her. As the townsfolk visited with the Magnussons, they spent a few moments ogling and thanking the young sleuth from England and her handsome Irish fiancé.

Even now the room had two families visiting. Alex looked down at the pretty little girl who had come in with her parents to visit Tomas and saw her staring wide-eyed in wonderment. Alex smiled encouragingly at her. The girl took a couple of skipping steps nearer and smiled back.

"What's your name?" Alex asked.

"Asa." She smiled up at Alex revealing two missing front teeth. "And you're Lady Featherstone. I like your name."

"Thank you, Asa. I like your name as well."

The little girl reached out and took ahold of Alex's hand, swinging it a few times, her face nearly bursting with shy excitement. The girl's mother was talking to Ana and another girl, Asa's older sister, stood beside her, darting glances at Tomas. The mother was wearing what Ana had explained to Alex was a spaðafaldur cap, and it still gave Alex a start when she saw it, it seemed so odd. The woolen cap fit snugly on the woman's head with a flat, white tail of sorts that had been stiffened somehow and came up and over her head toward her face. Her dress was quite beautiful though, black wool with a few horizontal blue stripes on the bottom. The bodice was red wool that had wide, embroidered ribbons crisscrossing from the waist to the neck. Around the neck was a circular ruff that made a pretty frame for the lady's face. The other women in the room wore similar dresses but less formal hats. Alex liked the tail-cap, a simple woolen cap with a long silk tassel. Ana had jumped at the chance to knit one for her when she'd admired one aloud, and the man's striped version for John, as one of many gifts of thanks she and her husband seemed determined to honor them with.

"Lady Featherstone, do come and meet Ila Jóhannsdóttir. She and Phin Jóhannson started our library and might have some information for you. They spoke with your parents while they were here," Ana said.

Alex patted Asa on the head and hurried over, nodding in a bow toward Ila Jóhannsdóttir. "I should love to ask you a few questions."

They all settled around the kitchen table and Ana poured tea. "It would be my honor, Lady Featherstone," the woman said in a thin voice full of importance and in perfect English. "I am sorry to hear that your parents are missing."

"Thank you. I am determined to find them. When did you see them and what sort of questions did they ask you?"

"They were here many months ago. They came to see me and my husband at our home on one occasion. Very elegant people, your parents." The woman looked around as if to share a great secret. "They wanted to know about a man who came to Iceland a long, long time ago. He is mentioned in the sagas of our people."

"Sagas?"

"The sagas are the stories of our people from the old days when the Vikings settled here. They were written down on calfskin pages and called the Icelandic Sagas. We have carefully preserved them."

"Who was this man they wanted to know about?" Alex held her breath waiting for the answer.

"His name was Augusto de Carrara. He was an Italian inventor and scientist who visited our island."

Alex inhaled. The same man she'd heard about in Ireland. "Did you find him in the sagas?"

"Yes, his name is in one of the books, but alas, the only thing we found was a mention of him at a feast in the sixteenth century. He attended a celebration at a farmstead in the southeast part of Iceland."

"What were they celebrating?"

Ila shook her head and waved a hand as if that were unimportant. "Something about a sunstone. The sagas mention a stone that could tell the direction of the sun to help the Vikings navigate their ships. They were very excited about it, but of course today we have more advanced tools for navigation."

Alex paused in thought. Did Augusto come to Iceland for this sunstone? "Nothing else? That seems strange. A foreigner visiting here would have been curious back then, wouldn't he?"

"Not really. Iceland may seem remote, but the Europeans have been visiting since the Vikings settled here. Your parents said they were looking for a book of his, I believe, not one of our sagas. They seemed sure he was here, and the saga confirmed that indeed he was, but they wanted another book."

The missing manuscript. That's what they wanted. Alex frowned. "Did my parents ask about anything else?"

"Just one other thing. It was rather humorous." Her smile was thin and her eyes held a tinge of condescension.

"What's that?"

"They asked about the Black Castles of Iceland."

"Yes, of course. In Ireland an expert of antiquities told me that the last known place where the manuscript my parents were looking for, was heard to be in the *Dimmu borgir*—the Black Castles of Iceland. They must have gone there. But what was so humorous about it?"

"They thought that the Dimmu borgir was an actual castle or castles, but they aren't." She smirked. "They are huge black pillars, the remains of volcanic lava. They do, however, have a look of castles about them if one has imagination. Some say"—she leaned in, her voice just above a whisper—"it is connected with the infernal regions of the earth and that when Satan was thrown down from heaven, he made it his home: the catacombs of hell."

Alex shivered under the woman's steady gaze. "But if there isn't a real castle, then why would the manuscript be there?"

The woman sat back and shook her head with a look of doom in her eyes. "I don't know the answer to that, Lady Featherstone. After your parents left Reykjavik, we never saw them again."

Alex cast a frightened glance over to John who had come to the table and joined them. "We have to go and see it; something may have happened to my parents there."

"Yes, but we need not go until Montague has arrived." John gave her a look full of meaning. He wouldn't want to talk about their plans to marry in front of anyone any more than she did, but he hinted at reminders when the occasion called for it.

"But what if they are still there, in trouble or injured? What if they've fallen in a crevasse or those boiling mud pits we've heard of? We can't wait." Her voice rose in worry.

"Alex, they would have been here nearly a year ago, right? If something like that happened to them"—he shook his head—"they would be long...gone."

"We don't know that! I won't give up that easily. John, you knew I would have to go there when you agreed to accompany me." She turned away from the staring women with a sharp-eyed glance toward John, eyebrows pulled together in a frown.

John sighed and looked at Ila. "Is the route to these Black Castles dangerous?"

"It could be. Any number of accidents can occur. You should be careful of the mud pits. They can suck a person in and boil him alive."

"Oh, ya." Ana's eyes grew round. "Take great care when traveling in Iceland. I've heard of more than one poor soul lost and never found again." The memory of how close they had come with Tomas made them all pause, Ana's eyes filling with tears. "Do be careful, Lady Alex." She patted Alex's arm.

"All the more reason to wait for Montague." John frowned.

"No." Alex stood. "Even if he does heal quickly, it could be weeks before he can book passage here. We have to go. We'll hire a guide to help us. Ana, do you know of anyone who would take us there? I have money. I will pay him well."

Ila and Ana exchanged glances. "Svein," they said together.

"The Black Castles are in the northeast. Svein has family there and knows the way," Ana explained.

"Excellent." Alex smiled. "Where can we find him?"

"Oh, he's only three doors down from here. He is the town's blacksmith. A strong, single man." Ana cracked a grin. "All the girls have been vying for his heart for years."

"Excellent," John muttered.

The women laughed but Alex quickly cut the laughter off when she saw John's scowl. He always seemed touchy when she spoke about another man. "Let's go and see him, shall we?" She reached out and tugged John toward her. He pulled her close to his side with a smitten look.

A dreamy sigh came from Ana from the other side of the table. "Oh, to be young and in love again."

Ila snorted, which for some reason made John laugh, and then they were all laughing about it.

They put on their heavy wraps, John helping Alex into her new fur coat, and stepped out into the long rays of twilight. Iceland was near the lands of the Arctic Circle where the winter days were short and the nights were long. In the summer months they might get twenty hours of sunlight, but it was approaching December and already getting dark by dinnertime. That would make their journey more challenging for certain.

The cold wind blew at them once they stepped away from the building. John must have been thinking the same thing as he said, "It's going to be a tough journey, Alex. Darkness comes so early and the weather...more snow as we travel north, I would think."

Alex reached for his hand and squeezed it as they walked down the street toward the blacksmith's sign. "It was around this time of year when my parents were here. The weather didn't stop them."

John leaned over and kissed the top of her head with a chuckle. "Yes, I know. I didn't think that would dissuade you. I only felt the need to point it out."

They reached the door, finding the top half open. Alex peeked inside and realized why. A fire roared from the stone forge in the center of the room. Tools lay strewn everywhere, and a shirtless man, with his back to them, pounded on a long, black rod with heavy whacks of his hammer.

John leaned around Alex and pounded on the bottom half of the door. "Sir, might we have a word with you?" He shouted to be heard over the ringing metal.

The man turned around, wearing an apron that covered his large chest. He had long, blondish-brown hair, the same color mustache, and a small beard that covered his chin. "You must be the Irishman and the English lady I've heard tales of." He bowed, extending the hand holding the iron poker out to one side, the other hand crossed his stomach with a graceful flair. "Please, come in."

He directed them to sit at a scarred worktable while pulling on a long, white shirt with ruffles on the sleeves and down the deep *V* collar. All of his movements had an elegant grace to them, as if he were brandishing a sword and certain of victory, Alex noted with a curious smile.

"To what do I owe this honor?" He poured tea into mismatched cups and passed them over without inquiring if they would even like any.

Alex got straight to the point. "We have need to travel to Dimmu borgir, the Black Castles, and Ana said you might be willing to take us since you have family up there and know the route."

"Dimmu borgir. There is nothing there but the lava rocks. What need have you of those?"

"I am looking for clues to help me find my parents, Lord and Lady Featherstone. They were here about a year ago, and I believe they went to Dimmu borgir. I'm not sure what I might find, but it's the last clue I have. I must find out if there is anything there connected to my parents or the manuscript they were searching for."

Svein rubbed his chin, eyes gazing off in thought. "I remember your parents and the rumors after they disappeared. I suppose it's possible there might be such a clue." He turned to Alex. "It won't be a pleasant trip this time of year."

"That's what I've been telling her, but you have yet to see her stubborn side," John murmured.

"We'll need horses. There are no roads for part of the journey. Do you ride well, Lady Featherstone?"

"Yes." She quickly exaggerated her horsemanship. "Please, call me Alex and this is John. He is an excellent rider." She had no idea if that was true or not, but no need to give the man reasons to turn them down.

John frowned at her. "I'm a fair hand at riding. Actually, I've heard the Icelandic horses are something to see. I admit to be looking forward to seeing them for myself."

Svein stood back a little and surveyed the two of them, one hand back on his chin, the other arm across his stomach. "I have orders to fill before I could leave. We can purchase you a couple of horses from a nearby farmstead. Icelandic horses are the best in the world. I think you'll like them." He turned his eyes to John. "You're funding the expedition?"

"I am." Alex cut in. "And I will pay you well." She held his gaze firm as he still seemed to be deciding.

"Very well. We will leave in three days. Meet me here in the morning. I will have the horses and our supplies ready."

Alex reached beneath the fur and took out a bag from her inner pocket. She poured out some coins into her hand and laid them on the table. "Will that be enough?"

Svein quirked a brow. "Not even close."

Alex felt her face flush and looked at John. He motioned for the bag, shook out several more coins, and pushed them over. "That should be more than sufficient."

Svein shrugged. "I will do my best with it." And then he winked at Alex.

After they left, Alex laughed. "What a colorful character he was. Do you think we can trust him?"

John squeezed her hand. "We've little choice, love. He seems harmless enough, but I will watch out for you."

They had slowed as they neared the inn. John stopped and then pulled her close to the shop beside it, out of the wind, and wrapped his arms around her. He leaned down and murmured into her ear, "The waiting is killing me. When can we get married?"

Alex thought of the different meanings behind his words. She liked his kisses, but she wasn't at all sure she was ready for the wedding night. What if she became pregnant? She knew enough about how babies were made from working with her sheep. What would happen to her search if that happened? And was she even close to ready to be a mother? She still wanted her mother's notice. There was so much at stake.

"I know. It is not the best of circumstances and I... John, I appreciate your patience, but I don't want to rush if we don't have to. No one has commented that we are traveling together. Perhaps it is not so frowned upon here in Iceland."

"I hope you are not marrying me for my escort." John's voice was low and serious, causing a lodge of dread in her throat.

"Of course not!" But she couldn't look him in the eyes when she said it.

He held her a little away from him and gave her a searching look. "Alexandria, do you care for me?"

"Yes! Of course I do. It's just that it all happened so suddenly. I need some time to accustom myself to the idea. And you know my foremost desire, my most important ambition, is to find my parents. I can't let anything come before that."

"I know, and I want that too. For all of us." He took her back into his arms and held her tight against the wind.

She thought of how he would feel if she someday broke it off. *Dear God, am I just using him as a means to an end?*

When did I become a woman like that?

She thought of the duke and a deep longing to hear from him filled her. What if, before they left for the Black Castles, she wrote him a letter? Might he get it? If he wasn't coming after her, then he would be back in London at his town house, wouldn't he? She had his address memorized. She looked at John and her cheeks burned. She would have to smuggle it out. Perhaps Ana would help her. She was so kind and would do anything for Alexandria after her help in finding Tomas.

Yes, that is what she would do.

She would put her confused emotions in a letter and let her guardian advise her. It was the right thing to do.

Chapter Eight

The prince regent was with two of his cabinet ministers and the lord chancellor when Gabriel arrived at St. James Palace. He entered the royal palace to find a servant waiting for him, been led through the Guard Chamber—a grand room with tall, narrow windows; twenty-foot ceilings; and a ten-foot-tall fireplace that a man could stand inside. There was an intricate design of swords fanned out across the wall like a work of art and every kind of weapon imaginable hanging on every inch of the other walls. An impressive display of England's power.

Gabriel was then taken to a magnificent drawing room done floor to ceiling in white plaster work with gold ornamentation. The furniture and rugs were also white and gold. Thousands of candles from two massive chandeliers lit up the golden hues so the whole room seemed to glitter. Gabriel noted all of this in an instant as the servant bowed and left him at the door. He hesitated and then pulled himself up with a determined air and walked over to the group of men.

The regent caught sight of him and waved him over. "St. Easton!" he clearly stated, probably in a booming voice.

The other men turned and bowed but scurried away when the regent spoke quick words to them. Gabriel tried to maintain an air of confidence that he knew what was going on when really he felt like a drowning man, unable to find his moorings. *God, help me find Your way through this madness. I've thrown my lot in with a reprobate.*

After the other men left, the regent gave him a thoughtful stare and then waved Gabriel to follow his ponderous form from the room.

They weaved their way through the palace's maze of wings, dark passages, backstairs, and suites. A person could get lost for days and had, or so the stories went. Finally, they came to the long and deep room full of books—the queen's library.

Sunlight streamed in from tall, arched windows on one side of the cavernous room, lighting the rows of bookcases overflowing with books. The walls held more bookcases, connected by arches near the ornate molding of the ceiling with busts of famed personages perched on the highest point of each arch. The queen's desk, looking rather small in such a huge room, sat in the middle, a neat piece of furniture that was more practical than ornate.

The regent led Gabriel all the way to the back of the room where shadows overtook the corners. He pulled forth a key and opened a small cabinet. Inside were drawers, small compartments, and a safe. With another key he unlocked the safe, pulled something out, turned, and handed it to Gabriel. He had not said a single word since his greeting. Now, he looked into Gabriel's eyes with a small smile.

King George, the prince's father, was deaf, Gabriel realized. The regent knew how to communicate without many words. Gabriel felt a new respect for the man grasp hold of him.

The regent motioned with one arm to a chair and a desk holding ink and pen. On the desk was a note that read, *I looked at it and can't make any sense of it. See what you can find out. I will come back in an hour.*

Gabriel bowed and watched him go. If the regent didn't come back, Gabriel wasn't entirely certain he could find his way back to the outdoors. With a deep breath, he seated himself and opened the faded black leather cover of the manuscript.

Mathematical calculations, advanced calculus, a new math he'd seen a little of, and mechanical drawings leapt out from the page. He tried to make sense of it for a moment, shook his head, his brows drawn together in concentration, and then turned the page. Page after page, over every inch of the pages, squeezed together in corners and boxes, some sideways, some diagonal, running off the page and then, with the slashing lines of a brilliant mind trying to get it on paper as fast as he imagined it, they continued onto the next page.

Gabriel's brain whirled with images, impossible images that the pages evoked; astonishment and a pooling dread caused a cold sweat to break out across his body.

Oh, God, what is this?

He swallowed back the knot in his throat and started over, more slowly and carefully. There were sixteen pages of new thought, sixteen pages of plans for etchings, as on glass or crystal. There, in one corner was a drawing of crystals with the words *Icelandic Crystal* scribbled underneath.

Iceland. The crystal mines. He remembered it now. The only kind of crystal in the world that was completely transparent with double refraction capabilities. Dutch mathematician and physicist Christiaan Huygens and even Sir Isaac Newton had discovered uses for it, optical instruments and such, when this man, Augusto de Carrara, was alive. That had to be the connection with Iceland.

And Alexandria was there—heading right for whatever this proved to be.

Gabriel closed his eyes and pressed his fingers against his forehead, then looked back at the last page, imagining the thing being built, but it abruptly ended. It was only half the plans, if even that. But even with this much…it looked fantastical, futuristic, impossible. A thought that had never been thought before stared at him from the pages, making his mind open to all the possibilities of its design.

His mind strained, gaining a slight foothold of this new thought, and then he felt it slide away. But it was there, and it asked a question he didn't think mankind had ever asked before.

What if light could be used as power?

And then it struck him. Not just power—the ultimate power. What if this could be used as a weapon, the most powerful weapon in the world?

He rose and paced to the corner of the library, his stomach sick. This was so much bigger than anything he'd imagined. *Dear God, Alexandria!* The vision of her blithely traipsing about Iceland with that young fop— they would eat her alive! They would do anything to have the other half of this knowledge. Kings, powerful leaders…who knew how many knew of this and wanted the rest of these plans.

Could the Featherstones indeed still be alive? Did they know what they were searching for? The impact it could have on the world? Of course, the regent could have invented any number of stories about the manuscript, because only a person educated in the latest mathematics and science could begin to understand these plans. The Featherstones probably had no idea what they were sent to find. But there were others who did. The Spanish and possibly the French.

The thought of Spaniards after Alexandria in Iceland made his hands curl into fists. He had to get back there. He had to get her home.

With a shuddering breath, he leaned against the bookshelf at the back of the library. A hollow vibration touched his back. He stood away and then leaned back against it again. It felt different when his shoulder pressed against it, lighter and almost as if it was resonating. He stood upright and knocked his fist against it, not hearing it, but feeling…something strange about it. Without his hearing, touch had become keener. Sensing vibration through the air, through furniture, through the floor, had become a quiet language to gauge action by. Something was not right with this wall.

Gabriel backed up and studied the bookshelves lining the walls. They were ten feet tall and filled with books.

These shelves were connected to the walls, unlike the other free-standing bookshelves in the room. But when he looked closely enough, he noticed the one in the corner was not connected to the wall. He plucked some books from the shelf and saw a different back than the other shelves. It matched, almost perfectly, but it wasn't the same. It was a false back.

With little, precise movements he was able to scoot the shelf out and away from the wall, books falling to the floor as he did it. He pushed them aside and then pulled the shelf free of the others enough to squeeze behind it. It was dark but he ran his palms up and down the wall, looking, hoping for anything.

Nothing. Only the smooth panels of wood. He was being silly. Augusto's manuscript had cast a spell on him. He shook his head. He was just backing out when his foot caught on something near the bottom of the wall.

He reached down and ran his fingers along the edge, feeling a protruding lever hidden by the molding near the floor. He pushed it, feeling sudden vibrations as something clicked or sprang open. Gabriel leaned back, awash in astonishment as the panel in the wall moved, revealing a dark space behind it.

The door was only about five-feet tall and four-feet wide, but Gabriel stepped nimbly through, a strange foreboding overwhelming him.

It was dark, only a pale dimness from the library where Gabriel stood, and then a deep, cavernous darkness ate up the room. When his eyes adjusted, he saw the shadowy legs of a table. He went over to it and felt along the top. There. A lantern and flint to light it with. He fumbled with the flint, nearly dropping it, his heart pounding in his ears. He struck it once, twice, and then a bursting of flame fired the air. He held the flame to the wick and watched it glow to life.

Gabriel lifted it high and turned toward the room.

Dancing light from the lantern's glass flickered like yellow diamonds across the walls. Gabriel looked toward the center of the room.

God help us all.

There it was. What he had just been reading and imagining. It sat in the middle of the floor, like a giant ice sculpture.

The half-completed invention of Augusto de Carrara. The weapon of the future.

With shaking legs, Gabriel stumbled from the room, rushed from behind the bookcase, and found himself standing face-to-face with the regent.

"What is the meaning of this?" The folds of the regent's face quivered as he thundered the question, fire in his eyes.

Gabriel bowed his head, knowing he had no choice. He didn't have time to consider whether it would be advantageous that the regent saw what was in that room. No, he had to tell him.

Gabriel motioned toward the bookcase. "Your Highness, I beg your indulgence for a moment, but I think I have stumbled upon something very important. If you would follow me?"

The regent scowled but motioned that he go on. Gabriel scooted one end of the bookcase farther away from the wall to allow for the regent's girth and then carried the light ahead of him, illuminating their way. Once inside he held the lantern aloft and nodded toward the center of the room. "Your Majesty, the machine."

The regent gaped, looked at Gabriel in shock, and then looked back at the massive structure in the room.

"As you can see, someone has been building the plans in that manuscript. I believe we are seeing something very dangerous."

The regent shook his head at the massive machine, walking toward it and touching it. He turned toward Gabriel and appeared to be shouting, but Gabriel was able to make out the words. "And very valuable. This must be the work of Brooke."

"Yes, I believe he must have hired someone to decode the partial manuscript I was just studying. Someone who is an expert in mathematics and science. Considering the manuscript was written decades ago...it's astonishing really. Augusto must have been a genius."

"Come." The regent beckoned him back into the library. He motioned toward the desk with pen and ink and sat down at it. He wrote quickly, passing the paper to Gabriel.

I owe you a debt, St. Easton. Now that I know the full importance of it, I will include you in the mystery of this manuscript. I haven't told anyone of our alliance, but I expect utter compliance. Do you agree?

Gabriel looked up at a man he'd always thought rather worthless and countered. "Only if you allow me go back to Iceland and bring Alexandria here to safety."

I've already set that ship in motion, literally. The regent wrote. *She should be in London within the month.*

"And then?" Gabriel asked.

"And then you will see to her welfare while I see to finding her parents and the missing part of this manuscript."

Gabriel nodded. Alexandria wouldn't like it. She would chafe at being pulled from her mission. But none of that mattered anymore. It was too dangerous. And if the regent's soldiers reached her soon, they would demand she come straight to London, which might keep her from marrying John. It would be better if the command came from the regent. That way, if she thought herself in love with John, she couldn't blame Gabriel.

He had to force her to remain with him in London.

It was the only way to keep her safe.

Chapter Nine

Alex breathed in the cool afternoon air and closed her eyes, amazed by her horse's easy gait. It was so smooth it felt as if they were sailing across the uneven ground. Sturdy and strong, the Icelandic horses were the prettiest animals she had ever seen. Baen, as Svein called her horse, and the entire Icelandic breed had two additional gaits no other horses in the world had. It was heavenly compared to that tall beast Missy had loaned her back in Carlisle.

"Svein, what is this gait called?"

Svein turned from his stocky, caramel-colored horse and grinned. "The *tölt*. It is very comfortable over long distances. You like it, yes?"

"Yes, very comfortable. She's such a pretty horse too." Her horse was dark cream with a white mane and gentle brown eyes.

"I picked her for you because she is so pretty. And for her name." Svein bellowed back to her.

"Her name? Baen?"

"It means 'prayer' and I think you have many prayers inside you."

Alex shot John a smiling glance and he rolled his eyes. "It's perfect, Svein. Thank you," she stated, thinking that her continual communication with God, both thanksgiving and pleading, was the rock of her foundation that gave her the courage for this journey. How anyone traveled through life without that she could hardly fathom. She thought about that over the next hours as they climbed hills and picked their way across hardscrabble valleys.

She looked over at John, his bright head pressing into the constant wind, looking like a foreign prince from some long-ago day in his striped tail-cap and dark furs. His horse was called Blakkur, a dark brown horse with a black mane and a white star between his eyes. They both fit perfectly her imaginings that they were exotic people in a strange country on a mission of great danger. It wasn't far from the truth, she supposed, shivering with excitement. She'd never felt so alive.

They'd been on the road from Reykjavik for a couple of days. The road had ended hours ago and now they traveled over rough, patchy ground, passing the occasional turf farm, roaming sheep, and hamlets dotted with cottages made from wood and peat. There weren't many trees in this land. The wind roamed freely over the rocky soil and blew strong and constant, making her nose red and achy, but she wasn't complaining. It felt as if she'd been dropped on a distant planet where the earth was dry orange and brown, with tuffs of snow-covered grass. The loose dirt crunched under the mare's feet, and Alex felt a rumbling beneath the surface, like any moment the rolling unease underneath them would explode and crack, pulling them beneath the surface of the crust. So strange—alien and exciting somehow.

Here, she was no longer Alexandria Featherstone. Here, she could be some otherworldly creature with kohl around her eyes and a strange headdress that reached toward the sky. She closed her eyes as the horse sailed across the choppy ground and imagined herself an Egyptian warrior queen, come to conquer an alien race.

"Are you sleeping?" John's voice was low and quiet with humor.

Alex's eyelids fluttered open. "No. But if we keep going much longer, I might fall asleep."

"I think I could sleep while riding these magnificent animals. I wonder if we shouldn't take them with us when we leave."

"If you take them with you, they will never be able to return," Svein informed from in front of them. The man had good ears. "Icelandic breeds are protected by law. No horse can be brought here. It might taint the line. And if an Icelandic horse leaves, it can never return."

"Is that why they have special gaits and look so different?"

"Yes. And we plan to keep it that way." The usually smiling Svein sounded more serious than he ever had.

The sudden sounds of pounding hooves from behind them caused Alex to spin around. A crack of sound exploded from behind them with shouts. Good heavens, they were being shot at!

The three of them hauled to a stop. John reached over and grasped the reins of Alex's jumpy horse. "What's happening?" she shouted. "Who are they?"

"Whoever they are, they will be upon us in moments." John looked over at Svein. "We need to take cover."

"There. Those stones in the distance." Svein pointed toward the only possible place in the area. "Hurry!"

John let go of Alex's reins and nodded that she go before him. Alex kicked the sides of Baen's belly and yelled for her to go as another shot whizzed through the air. Had the Spaniards caught up with her?

The pile of stones off to one side of the path were hardly large enough for the three of them to crouch behind. Alex worried for the horses, who stood taller than their cover. If only there was something she could do. She really did need to learn how to shoot a pistol.

John had one that he pulled out and loaded with powder and shot. Svein pulled out a long, gleaming knife and a short sword. Alex grasped a large rock that was lying on the ground beside her. It was better than nothing.

Her heart thudded as the men drew closer. They reined in their horses and pointed their pistols toward the rocks where they crouched.

"Alexandria Featherstone," one of them shouted. "It is she that we want. No harm will come to you if she comes willingly with us."

"Over my dead body," John murmured, leaning around the stone to aim at the men.

Svein slanted a look at Alex. "Do you know these men?"

Alex peeked over the stone and studied their faces. They were dark skinned and had dark hair—good-looking men. Possibly Spanish but she didn't think so. The man's accent sounded different. She sank back down. "I've never seen them before."

"What do you want with Lady Featherstone?" John shouted.

The sound of a pistol going off answered.

John growled low in his throat, leaned around the side, and shot back at them. Alex heard one man howl and the sound of the horses' panicked whinnies. She peeked over the top again and saw that one man was down, still moving but injured. The other man was trying to keep his horse under control while keeping his pistol aimed at them.

"You should not have done that," he shouted with a heavy accent. "Now, you must die."

"John, shoot the man on the horse. I will charge them."

John nodded, aimed, and shot while Svein waited for the retuning fire and then ran from around their stone cover so fast that it took Alex's breath away. She peered out again, seeing Svein charge the man on the horse. John reloaded and ran from the other side, toward the man on the ground.

Alex watched in awe as Svein tore the man from his horse. He had pulled out a sword, though, and looked to be quite good at wielding it. She bit down on her bottom lip, her gaze darting from John, who was holding his pistol on the man on the ground and seemed to have him under control, to Svein, who was not faring well at all against the darker man.

A sound escaped her throat when Svein's foe backed him toward her, the tip of his blade at Svein's throat. He seemed about to run him through! They turned, the man now with his back to her and getting closer.

Without thinking, she rose up as tall as she could and flung the large rock in her hand at the man's back. It hit him in the head, made him totter and grip at the sword. Alex screamed as the sword slashed down across Svein's chest, leaving a well of red.

"John, help him!" she shouted. Thinking to hold the pistol on the other man she ran over and ripped it from John's hands while the other man turned, rage in his dark eyes. Svein stumbled and dropped to one knee on the ground.

John let Alex take hold of the pistol and pulled out his sword, turned to the foe, and hissed out, "Don't get too close to him, Alexandria. Just hold it on him." She nodded, keeping her gaze trained on the man, who lay still looking at her with narrowed eyes, but seeing John fighting the other one from the corner of her eyes.

John was good. She could see the difference between Svein's and his heavy movements. So, too, could his opponent, it would seem, since he started backing away. It wasn't long, a flash of quickly executed movements and then a sickening sound, the blade going through flesh and the groan of the man. He slumped to the ground.

The man lying at Alex's feet made a harsh sound in his throat and turned his face toward her. He spit at her, gasping out, "Stupid girl. You are undeserving of the Carbonari—" He paused, his breathing coming in short puffs, his face grimacing with pain. "You do not deserve...what your parents—"

Alex crouched beside him. "My parents? You know my parents?"

He turned his face away and breathed his last.

"No, wake up." Alex turned his face. "Who are you?"

Nothing. The man was dead. She turned to see John coming toward her. "They are both dead then." He held out his hand to help her up.

"Who were they? Oh, John, he mentioned my parents. What have we done?"

⁂ ⁂ ⁂ ⁂

Twilight deepened into the long darkness. The creak of the saddle leather, the whistle of the wind, and the crunch of loose earth under Baen's hooves made an oddly calm melody that fit so well here. Alex tilted her head back and breathed in the cold air, watching a million stars come dancing out, the edges of light still lingering around the circle of the earth.

A strange and fantastical beauty here, Father. Is this what my parents love so much? This...everlasting adventure? But what of the men they had recently buried? How could any adventure be worth the loss of lives?

She looked at Svein and took a breath of relief, glad his wound was only a long scratch down his chest that they had easily bandaged up. She didn't know how she would have gone on if he had been killed too.

She looked at John's moonlit silhouette and felt another twinge of doubt and fear. He always made her laugh, made her feel like they were on an adventure together, but now, things seemed so serious between them. He'd killed two men for her. And when she thought of the life marriage promised, she shrank inside. Everything in her strained for this...what they had now—adventure and danger and...meaning, but that seemed so wrong. Life lived in a house in Dublin, a normal life like the one John promised seemed the right path, the right choice, but then why did the thought of it smother her? What was wrong with her?

Svein held up his hand to stop them. "We're nearing Lake Mývatn. Stay close. Many hot springs are coming up."

The little path they were on meandered near the dark waters of Lake Mývatn. They wound around it for another hour, hearing bird call and the forever wind that pushed against their faces. As the trail dipped south, the wind turned sharper, moaning with an unease that made Alex shiver inside her furs. She nudged the mare closer to Svein and felt a tingling crawl of fear. "Will we stop for the night soon?" Her voice was quiet in the darkness, afraid to shout and wake up the ghosts that seemed to be hovering about.

"Yes." He grinned back at them, his white teeth lit by the moon, his eyes gleeful. "We are almost there. Just stay close. We must watch for fissures. Some are deep and could cause great injury to the horses and ourselves."

Alex looked back at John, her brows drawing together, and shot him an anxious glance. John just shrugged, motioning to keep up. They stepped around pools of dark water, some bubbling, some with steam coming from them, a sharp, sour smell in the air. Alex wrinkled her nose but said nothing. It was too otherworldly to speak aloud.

Sudden dark towers rose from the earth in front of them. Was it a castle? A fortress? Alex peered through the dim moonlight, leaning forward and breathing deeply in and out. Great towers rose into the night sky with oddly placed round windows. Closer and closer until Alex saw that they weren't buildings at all, but twisted, bumpy lumps of gigantic pillars and arches—all black.

Silently they rode up a slight hill and under a massive arch into what seemed to be a courtyard. Alex took a sudden inhale and stopped Baen. "Oh my," she whispered.

Not a courtyard and yet one. Tall, uneven pillars, like black sand castles, surrounded them. It was as if the earth had burned down and this was all that was left. Hellfire and brimstone. She could smell it and taste the sharp metal tang on the tip of her tongue. No wonder they said when Satan had been cast down from heaven after rebelling against God, he'd landed here and made it his home on earth. She could almost believe it.

Alex shivered, but from a deeper cold than any she'd known as they rode through the dark fortresses in utter silence. Even the wind had fallen off and quieted. No bird sound or animal sound, only the soft crunch of the horses' hoofs, and even those seemed too loud. It seemed as if eyes were watching them all around, making their presence known.

Her flesh prickled with fear as they rode deeper into the maze of pillars. They seemed to go on forever. Would they ever come to an end? She bit her lip as her breath deepened. Yes, they would. She would not be overcome with wild and dark imaginings. She would be brave.

Svein slowed down to ride even with her. "We camp just on the other side. Come on."

Alex reached over and touched his arm, her eyes on the cloth tied around his chest. "Svein, I'm so sorry about those men. I never intended for you to have to fight for me. I feel so bad that you were hurt."

He shrugged. "'Tis nothing. I would have done any-thing to protect you."

Alex shook her head. "I would not ask that of you. Please know that."

A clearing throat from behind them made Alex look back at John. He was frowning at her and shaking his head. When she looked back at Svein, he winked at her, causing Alex's face to fill with heat. She shrank back from Svein and slowed her horse, putting an even dis-tance between both men.

She was noticing that John's easy manner could turn demanding. More and more he seemed to feel like he had the right to order her about and it chafed. She sup-posed husbands held that right, but she was used to being independent and wasn't so sure she would ever come willingly under any man's thumb. One of many reasons never to marry.

They nudged their horses forward to a place where the ground was flat and the black towers of lava rock loomed behind them.

The sensation of watchful eyes still pressed against her back as they dismounted and set up camp. She doubted she would be able to sleep in such a place and wished they could ride on to an inn, but she knew better than to voice that aloud. John was always looking for a weakness in her, something to send her more thoroughly into his arms and marriage. She would have to pretend courage even if she didn't really feel it.

She huddled in her sleeping furs close to the fire Svein had built for warmth and prayed God would send angels to protect them from the eyes, the evil, the hovering doom that clung to the black lava and her heart.

ᕭ ᕭ ᕭ ᕭ

Alex woke to the sounds of birds and ducks from the nearby lake. The dawn was creeping over the land, a light that felt different from the night before but appeared only a little brighter all morning. She stared over her shoulder at the Black Castles. In this light, in the daytime, they looked more like what they were: twisted shapes of hardened lava but still spooky enough to put a shiver down her spine.

John brought over a steaming cup of tea and held it out for her.

Svein joined them, passing out dried salmon and some reindeer grass. Alex wrinkled her nose but took a bite, chewing and then spitting it back into her hand. "Oh, that's awful."

The men chuckled. John didn't even try it, only shook his head with his mouth pressed shut.

"Svein, I don't know where to begin our search. Should we go back into the Dimmu borgir and look for clues?"

Svein shook his head. "No one lives there, I am certain. My village is just north of here, called Reykjahlíð and I have explored all these places as a boy. There is one place I am thinking of that has been an odd home from time to time." His eyes lit up as he motioned them closer. "Long ago, Jon Markusson, an infamous outlaw, hid there for a time. It is a cave with a hot spring inside. Many have used it for bathing. Come, I will show you."

The sunlight strengthened as they wound their way northeast toward the cave. The land rose in elevation, the ground changing from orange dirt to black rock.

"Look!" Alex pointed ahead at a plume of exploding white smoke. "What is it?"

"Hverfell, a volcanic crater. Would you like to see it?"

"I would love to." She couldn't come so close to an actual volcano and not want to look inside.

The trail up the side of Hverfell became steep and rock covered. The horses were steady though, and she never feared they might lose their footing. At the top they stopped and dismounted. John took her hand. They crept together up to the edge and peered down into the vast, circular bottom, a nub of rock in the center. Austere and strangely beautiful. Alex couldn't fathom the power of its fiery underbelly.

Svein motioned for them to follow him around the upper edge, walking their horses toward the opposite side. He pointed to the north. "These areas can be very dangerous. There are boiling mud pots where the earth is soft and underneath the mud so hot it can scald your skin. And places like that mountain there, Krafla, do you see it?"

John and Alex stopped with him and nodded.

"In the early 1700s the fissures opened and lava flowed to the valley. Three farms near our village were destroyed and the village too, but none were killed. The story goes that as the lava was headed toward the village, the people gathered in the church and prayed. A miracle happened when the lava flow stopped right in front of the church and flowed to either side. The village was burned, but all the people survived and rebuilt it." He winked at Alex. "Another prayer story for you."

A chill raced down her spine. Was God trying to tell her something?

The descent on the other side was not so steep, and before long they were down on the flat ground and traveling at a faster pace.

"Here we are." Svein pulled on his reins and leaned over the pommel, pushing back his hat. The sun shined more brightly than Alex had seen it shine yet in Iceland, and the wind died down to a low breeze. She pushed off her fur hood and looked around. There was no cave that she could see.

Svein laughed. "Now you know why it makes such a good hiding place. Come." He dismounted and led the horse to a place where the ground looked to be solid rock in earth shades of brown and tan.

As they neared, Alex saw a great fissure that wound like a snake's back in the earth. "Look, John. It's down there, inside the ground."

They dropped the reins allowing the horses to graze on the meager plants in the area while the three of them knelt at the widest edge of the crack. Alex peered down and gasped. Turquoise water shimmered from a great pool, steam lightly rising. "Is it very hot?"

"It is perfect for bathing."

"But how do we get down there?"

"Alex, I'm not so sure we should." John frowned at her.

"We have to. It's the only way to look for clues to see if someone is staying there. And besides, I want to bathe in it."

He gave her a little shake of the head and then seemed to reconsider. "All right. Svein, how do we get down there?"

Svein showed them the way to climb down, hanging on to crevices and ledges. It was a short drop, and then there were plenty of rock ledges along the pool to walk around it. Sunlight poured in from the hole brightening a streak of water and making it paler blue. Alex looked around, found a nice ledge to sit on, and took off her shoes and stockings.

With her dress hiked up to her calves, she dipped her toes into the water. "Heavenly," she murmured, shifting on the ledge until her legs dangled over the edge submersing them in the warm, bubbly water. "The water feels so light. My feet are floating."

John crept over to her side and did likewise, putting his bare feet in the pool and reaching over to kiss her temple. "I think I might like the idea of swimming."

What would they would wear? It was too cold outside to get their clothes wet. But oh, how she longed to dip her whole body in the magical waters.

Svein crept over to the other side, poking around the nooks and crannies of the cave. After a little while he turned and grinned, his white smile lighting the dark recesses like a candle. He was holding something aloft. "I think I've found something."

Alex scrambled up. "What is it?"

"A blanket. And there are some clothes and other supplies stashed over here. Someone is indeed staying in this cave."

Alex looked around with some fear. "I wonder where he is."

"And when he might return," John added.

"We'll wait here and find out." Svein settled himself on a rock.

They didn't have long to wait as a short time later a sound from overhead startled them. Alex craned her neck. An old, wizened face peered down at them. He grinned as his rheumy eyes settled on Alex.

"Might you be lookin' for me, perhaps?"

Chapter Ten

"So you see, Mother, you'll have to move in for the season while Alexandria is here."

Meade wrote what his mother said and passed the speaking book over. Thank God Meade was back. Gabriel had hardly been able to function inside his own household without him.

I cannot possibly stay the entire season. I have my own social activities and won't be tied down to an unprincipled debutant for the season. I'm sorry, Gabriel. It's quite impossible. Perhaps one of your sisters can come. Or…you could always hire her a companion. The girl has caused so much trouble already. It will be a struggle to like her at all.

Gabriel ground his teeth. "Very well, I'll ask Jane."

Jane was the only sister without children and therefore, had more than enough time on her hands. Plus, she was closer in age to Alexandria and would get on well with her. He should have thought of it before. "Meade, send a note off to her. I would like to get this settled sooner rather than later."

Meade nodded and scurried off to obey.

After his mother left, Gabriel paced about the drawing room like a caged panther. Would the king's men really find her in Iceland? Knowing her luck and the way people rallied around her and her cause, it wouldn't surprise him if she remained hidden from them. Within a month, the regent had said. Gabriel doubted he would see her within two.

And what was he to do in the meantime? This sitting and stewing was stretching his nerves to the snapping point. He needed to *do* something. He'd thrown himself back into his regular activities, but even the hard physical labor of sword fighting hadn't lessened this constant pressure that made him feel like he was teetering on insanity.

In desperation, he knelt beside an elegant damask-covered chair and laid his forehead against the embroidered cushion. *Dear God, I am trying to do as Alexandria bade and look to You, but it only feels terrible. There is no relief from this pressure bearing down upon my soul. If only I could escape into the opera. The powerful notes of a musical score. Anything. I am cracking from the inside out and You don't seem to be anywhere around. Help me!*

He actually broke into a sweat. Even though it was the dead of winter and there was a lively fire to try and take the chill from the far corners of the enormous room, he shook with an awareness of hot and cold. Why was it costing so much of him regarding Alexandria?

A sudden thought that he was shouldering her trouble, protecting her somehow even though he wasn't anywhere near her, made him sit back on his heels and rub the bridge of his nose. He stood, went over to a bookshelf, and took down one of the many copies of the Bible in the house.

Turning to Deuteronomy he paged through it until he found the verse. There. "Be strong and of a good courage, fear not, nor be afraid of them: for the LORD thy God, he it is that doth go with thee; he will not fail thee, nor forsake thee." What if he was supposed to pray this for Alexandria? What if this pressure was to goad him into an intercessor's prayer for her?

He immediately bowed his head and prayed the verse. As he said it under his breath, he had the distinct impression that he should sing it.

Sing it? He'd never been a very good singer when he could hear. What would he sound like now?

The pressure increased as he considered all the risks. What if someone heard him? He would sound ridiculous. What if God was asking him to do this and he disobeyed? Would it have any impact on Alexandria whether he sang or just recited the verse? Was he losing his mind?

The pressure increased as he pondered the idea until his chest felt leaden. With a deep breath he closed his eyes and very quietly sang the words. *"Be strong and of a good courage, fear not, nor be afraid of them: for the LORD thy God, he it is that doth go with thee; he will not fail thee, nor forsake thee."*

A little chuckle came from his chest. It did feel good to sing it, better than good. He sang it again, a bit louder. *"Be strong and of a good courage, fear not, nor be afraid of them: for the LORD thy God, he it is that doth go with thee; he will not fail thee, nor forsake thee."* This time the words behind his closed eyelids turned to color. He saw the letters and the notes of the music with colors combining the two in an oddly jubilant musical score.

He sang it again and again, louder and louder, no longer caring who heard or what they might think. He opened his eyes and sang—the blues and silver, purples and gold, reds and yellows and orange, dancing about the room in front of and around him. An unimaginable joy filled him and the belief, so strong and sure in his heart now, that God was with Alexandria, His love that Alexandria spoke so passionately about upholding her and guiding her—it all overwhelmed Gabriel.

He stopped, fell back on the settee, and closed his eyes, a peaceful exhaustion coming over him. And he suddenly saw that what used to cure his ennui, the opera, was just a shadow of what God could do inside him if he trusted enough and took a leap in faith like he just had. Walking with God could be far more exciting and fulfilling—abundant life—than trying to take care of his own needs with earthly means as he had always done. And helping Alexandria didn't necessary mean he would be by her side, though he still longed for that. It might mean prayer and singing and things he had yet to imagine.

God's ways and thoughts were so much higher than man's ways and thoughts that he couldn't begin to fathom Him. Walking with God meant just that—leaning on Him in every way, every minute of the day. He hadn't been doing that at all, though he prayed more. He'd still been leaning on his own understanding.

God, forgive me. I've been so shortsighted. I want to walk with You like that. Help me to know how.

He looked around, sensing a commotion, to find his mother bursting in the room. Her eyes were wide with shock and tears stood out on her cheeks. Jane came in after her, more tears, more shock.

Jane ran to Gabriel and threw herself into his arms. Her body shook as she soaked his shirt in tears. Meade came in just behind them.

"What has happened?" he asked Meade, who also looked as if someone had pummeled all the air out of him.

He mouthed the words Gabriel could feel Jane was saying against his chest, "Lord Rutherford is dead, Your Grace." Meade's lips trembled as he said it, so he clamped them together in a quivering line.

"Oh, Jane." Gabriel gathered his youngest sister tighter in his arms. He looked at his mother, sitting stiffly now on the sofa staring off into space and holding her wrinkled hand against her mouth. He turned back to Meade. "How did it happen?"

"Horse." Meade made a motion of sitting a horse, something Gabriel and he had done a lot of over the last months.

"Was he racing?"

Jane leaned back and shook her head. "Jumping."

"Hunting accident," Meade added.

Gabriel pieced it together in his mind. His brother-in-law, Matthew Rutherford, who had been as kind and loving a husband for Jane as any he could ask for, had gone hunting, jumped a wall or something, and been thrown. Matthew was a good horseman, so it must have been just bad luck—a senseless tragedy. *God, why do You let these things happen? To Jane? It's so unfair.*

He was too confused to even continue the line of thought. Taking Jane's hand he led her over to the sofa, sat her next to their mother, and handed her a snowy handkerchief. She dabbed at her plump cheeks whose dimples when she smiled were such an endearing quality. They wouldn't be seeing those for a very long time.

Blasted senseless tragedy. He wanted to fall on his face and beg God's help, but that would have to wait for later. If he flung himself on the floor and cried out like he wanted to do, his mother would think he'd gone mad. Instead, he rang for his butler with whispered directions to call in the doctor. Dr. Bentley would know the best thing for Jane right now.

Gabriel sat across from the women, leaning toward them with elbows braced on his knees. "I can't begin to express my sadness for you, Jane. For all of us. Matthew was the best of men. I can't believe he's gone."

Jane spoke and Meade hurried to the desk to write down what she said. *They've brought his body to the house. I don't know what to do with it. What do I do next?*

His mother answered before Gabriel could, and he supposed she was giving Jane directions as to the funeral arrangements; it was what she would do in this case. But Jane needn't worry about all that. "Meade and I will take care of everything, Jane. You must stay here where we can care for you. I'll have some footmen go to your house and pack up your things. Does that sound all right?"

She sniffed and nodded, looking at Meade with tear-filled eyes of gratitude. "Thank you, Mr. Meade. You have been so kind…"

"I've called for Dr. Bentley to come and call on her," Gabriel said to Meade. Their family doctor was almost exclusively theirs. He had known Matthew well and would be as devastated as the rest of them. "Alert the rest of the family to come. We must surround Jane with our support."

It was only two weeks until Christmas with all the family celebrations and events. Now he wasn't sure they would have a Christmas this year. Perhaps something small, for the children.

If only Jane had some children. The thought came from seemingly nowhere, making a terrible event deepen in despair. He banished the thought.

Jane leaned back against the sofa cushion and closed her eyes. Silent tears continued to trickle down her cheeks, but her breathing had evened out and she looked a little more in control of her emotions. His mother rose, her face looking to have aged a decade in the last few minutes.

"I will call on you all tomorrow. I feel the need to lie down now."

"Are you all right, Mother?" The strain on her was unmistakable.

She nodded and waved him away, but Gabriel didn't feel much better. She was more fragile than usual. He must treat her better, he realized, spend more time with her. Life was a fragile thing indeed.

ᴥ ᴥ ᴥ ᴥ

"A letter, Your Grace."

Meade walked into his study a week later, waving a piece of paper, the first note of happiness since Matthew's death lighting his eyes.

Gabriel's heart leapt. Could it possibly be? A letter from Alexandria?

Meade passed it over the desk and settled himself across from Gabriel, looking as if he fully anticipated reading it himself. Gabriel was too excited to dissuade him. He lifted the cream-colored paper, smudged on the outside, and looked at the address. The moment he saw the elegant scrawl of that familiar handwriting he knew. It was from her. The Icelandic postmark made it certain.

He carefully pried up the wax seal with the Featherstone coat of arms and turned away from Meade. "A moment, Meade, and then I promise I will tell you everything."

Meade blushed scarlet and hurried from the room. Gabriel sighed. He hadn't meant to chase him away entirely.

> *My dearest guardian duke,*
>
> *I have smuggled out this letter in secret as my now fiancé, John Lemon, would be devastated to know I am writing to you. When I saw you had come for me on the docks of Dublin's shore and I was finally able to see your face, I was overcome with feelings I have never felt before. I do not know what you planned to do should you have me within your grasp, but I think because of my lack of faith, both in you and in God, I have made a terrible blunder. When John presented the idea of marriage, I was desperate to continue my journey to find my parents. He is so encouraging and helpful on that account that I confess I leapt at the chance, not due to feelings of everlasting love for him, although I do care for him. Oh, I am not saying this as I wish to! My dear duke, I think I have made a terrible mistake. I desperately need your advice and I miss your letters dreadfully. I confess that I hope you haven't given up on finding me. I just need more time to find my parents. Please trust me in this.*

You can still write to me. Please write to me in
Reykjavik.
Yours,
Alexandria

The breath whooshed out of him and his heart thudded as if he had been running. She wanted him to find
her. She asked him not to give up. And she didn't even
realize that he had decided to discard his duty and choose
faith instead—faith in her, faith in God. Something he'd
never done since knowing the responsibility of his family line, the St. Easton motto *Foy Pour Devoir*: "Faith for
Duty" ever before him. If she had known that, she would
have waited for him. She would have never accepted
Lord Lemon's suit.

Gabriel wiped new tears from his cheeks realizing,
as if awakening from a dream, that they were there. In
the aftermath of Matthew's funeral, the stark minute-
by-minute reality of Jane's grief ever before them, he
had hardly known what he felt toward God.

And now this gift.

So undeserved and yet its value undid him, laid bare
and stripped him of every shred of pride and rebellion.
Overwhelmed, he fell to his knees. "I can't make sense
of it! Help Alexandria. Help Jane. Help me. I don't know
what else to pray."

He clutched the letter to his chest and hoped Meade
hadn't heard him. Just a few more moments basking in
the wonder that she needed him as he needed her.

Chapter Eleven

The aged man was surprisingly nimble as he scurried down the rock face of the cave like a pale monkey. He landed with a little grunt and hobbled over to where Alex and John stood. His eyes were such a pale blue that Alex wondered if he could see. His hair was sparse and white, sticking up here and there, making him appear as if he'd just rolled out of bed, and he was holding something under his arm. He peered up at them and gave Alex a toothless grin.

"I know who you are," he said in a voice that creaked with age. The words caused a shiver to run down her back. John took a step closer. The little man matched John's step and stabbed John's chest with a wrinkled finger. "Don't know *you*, though." He looked over at Svein, squinting his eyes. "So Svein Stephensen led you here. Wondered how she found me. She couldn't have found me by herself. No, no, Svein did it. Svein Stephensen." It was as if he was talking more to himself than to any of them.

"Is your name Enoch?" Svein asked in a gruff voice. "I've heard of you."

"Rumors and nonsense. That's what I say."

He pulled a paper wrapped object from the place tucked under his arm and stared at it, turning it over and over in his hands and mumbling some incoherent phrases. "Must do it." Alex finally caught. "Must, must, must."

As if he had made a decision, he thrust the package out to Alex. She took it, looked down, and saw through the dim light of the cave that parts of it were soaked in blood. An involuntary squeak came from her throat as she dropped it on the cave floor.

The little man groaned. "What did you do that for?" He leaned down, his back rounding in a stoop, and picked it up. Dusting it off, he looked sideways at Alex. "Aren't you hungry?"

"What is it?" Alex shrieked.

"Lamb for dinner right here. You cook it up nice for us, eh?" He held the package out toward her with a hesitant, suspicious gaze. When Alex reached for it a second time, he pulled it away and cackled with glee. He held it back toward her. Again, she reached for it and again he snatched it away. Goodness gracious, the man was stark, raving mad!

"Come now," she coaxed, "if you'll just show me where you keep your pots and where to build a fire, I'll help you cook it."

He grumbled some more under his breath and waved them all to follow him. A little ways into the cave he picked up a lantern, lit it, and led them deeper into the cave. They twisted and turned down and around rocky outcroppings and low arches. "You'll find what you need in here, you will, you will, you will." The cave opened up into a vast space, the pool behind them. He stood aside and held up the lantern.

All three of them gasped. The space, as big as her bedchamber back home, was filled with every kind of imaginable item. There were tools and furniture, mostly old and broken, dishes and pots, bottles and jars, ragged and dirty-looking clothing, blankets and bedding, papers and books, even a broken wagon wheel still attached to a wooden axle the size of small tree.

"You'll find what you need in here," he repeated.

Alex turned and looked wide-eyed at Svein and John. Compassion filled her for the man but she wasn't sure what to do.

There was a little path running through the middle of all the objects which he hobbled down, digging through this pile and that, until he came upon a large metal pot. He turned toward them with glee, brandishing it high above his head. "Told you so, I did."

Alex took the pot and placed the paper-wrapped meat in it. "I think we should build the fire outside, don't you? We wouldn't want to harm your things."

"Smart!" He grinned at her in that vacant way that made her flesh prickle. "Wait, we'll need some of these." He went to one corner and on a broken-down table leaning against the cave wall sorted through some food stores. He brought back two big turnips and a few dusty potatoes. Without a word, he led them back again toward the pool and then outdoors.

Alex lingered at the back, her gaze darting among the piles for books. Her heart sank as she noted how sadly kept they were. If there were any of the sagas with a mention of Augusto de Carrara in this mess, she didn't know how they would find it.

The light faded as the men moved away, so she hurried to catch up with John's shadowy form. Soon, they came into the brighter area of the pool. John took the pot from her while she climbed up, then handed it up to her while he came up last to the top where they all stood outside again.

Bright and cold after the warm snugness of the cave, Alex pulled her fur tighter around her. The three of them lingered in a group as the old man took off toward some spot to build a fire.

"Is he mad?" Alex whispered to the men.

"Quite." Svein nodded. "He is a hermit and moves about from place to place in this area. I hadn't remembered him or thought to connect him to the clues you are looking for, but perhaps he has spoken with your parents."

"That might explain why he thinks he knows you," John suggested. "Didn't you say you resemble your mother?"

"Yes, that might explain it." Alex bit her bottom lip in concentration, looking at the old man's back getting farther and farther away from them. "Let's go along with him, try to ease into a conversation."

"He might be volatile, even dangerous."

Alex frowned at John. He didn't seem dangerous, just touched in the head.

"And that might not be lamb in that package," Svein said in a teasing, scary voice. "We might be dining on his last visitor."

Alex paled but gave a weak laugh.

"Stop it, Svein. There's no use frightening Alexandria," John warned, then added with unease. "You were joking, weren't you?"

Svein chuckled low and waved them to start after Enoch. "We'll know after the first bite, won't we?"

They all pitched in to make a fire and get the stew going over the low flames. It would be some time before it was ready, so they crept back down to the warmth of the cave and sat around the pool.

"Enoch," Alex began, "you said you know who I am, but we've never met. How can that be?"

He made several motions of his hand toward her, huffing and smiling and turning aside as if embarrassed. He almost turned pink, but Alex couldn't tell for sure as he hid his face against his shoulder.

"Did you meet my parents?"

His rheumy eyes turned suddenly toward her, his chin uplifted, his toothless smile alight with joy. "She saw me."

He was like a child. A newborn in an old shriveled body. Alex blinked back sudden tears, the meaning slamming into her. Her mother *saw* him? How? How had she seen this man and not ever seen her?

"I'm so glad." Alex stretched out her hand and clasped his frail one. She squeezed, gently, his withered hand. "What did she say to you?" Alex's voice was careful and soft.

"She said a great thing is hidden in my things and we must find it...together. She said if we find it, we will change the world together. She looked at me and said...I have the key."

Alex leaned in, very calm and still. The men remained as quiet as statues in the background. "Did she say what it was they were looking for? Did you find it?"

He gazed at the crevice overhead, a streak of light in the stone-bound ceiling. He looked around the cave and at them, up and around again, and then he leaned toward her, his bushy white eyebrows raised. "I have the key." He chuckled with a low sound—mad but alight with joy—then he quieted, still rocking.

"Enoch." Alex leaned toward him. He looked at her afraid, shaking his head and backing away. "Enoch, I am her daughter. She would want me to know."

Everyone sat still, breaths held. Everything stopped as they awaited a madman's answer, their minds suspended as to what it might be.

Enoch. Please. Alex silently begged with her eyes. *Trust me.*

"We eat first," he rallied. "And then I will show you the book I showed your mother."

ॐ ॐ ॐ ॐ

The lamb stew, and she was sure it was lamb stew having grown up on the staple, tasted like dust in her mouth despite the ravenous hunger the overland march had placed on her stomach. There was just so much to think about. Who was this mother who could tame madmen from their hiding places? Who was this woman who knew of keys and mysteries and held within herself the wherewithal to solve them?

The world as Alex knew it, the world she had created for her child's self, stretched like an oddly shaped bubble around her, ill-fitting and threatening to burst, asking her to question everything she'd built in her mind. She looked over at John as an anchor, but he seemed adrift in this place too, skidding along against the craggy lava rock and wildly blue bubbling pools with an increasing air of desperation. Where had his easy camaraderie gone? The teasing answers and quick smiles of confidence? The feeling that their few kisses would stay them for a lifetime?

Did anyone know what they were really doing? She had been so sure…but not now.

Alex exhaled and bit down on her lower lip. She sat on the rocky edge of the cave's bathing pool, took off her boots and stockings, and plunged her feet into the pool. Swishing her feet back and forth and closing her eyes, she dangled in the hot, bubbly water. She'd let the old man get to her. She needed to remain steadfast in her mission.

Taking a deep breath, she let it all go in that moment, at least, for a moment. She didn't worry about the next movement and what they needed to find. She just leaned back her head and reveled in the warm bubbles against her toes, trusting God to show her the way.

Something touched her shoulder.

Her eyes fluttered open. Enoch stood next to her, holding out a book. It was in very good shape. Perfectly kept. She opened it and turned through the beautifully drawn pages in the artistic Celtic script similar to the script in the Lindisfarne Gospels. The language was Icelandic and impossible to read, but she kept looking through it, looking for the clue he was trying to show her.

She turned to the last page, so blue, with a pool drawn below the walls of a cave, and there sat a girl with her feet dipping into the pool. It was newer. The ink recent.

Alex inhaled and looked up into the pale blue eyes of a half-blind madman. He tapped his finger against the page. "I know you." He smiled deep into her eyes.

"This is how you know me?"

"Yes." He reached into a pocket and drew out an iridescent green and blue feather. Then he reached into the other pocket and took out a stone of black lava. He placed them in Alex's hand, closing her fingers gently around them. "I've been waiting for you to come." He tapped again on the picture in the book. "Featherstone. She drew it here for you."

Alex looked up at him in question, her blood roaring in her ears.

"The key," he touched the book with a gnarled finger, "is there."

Chapter Twelve

"Jane, how are you this morning?" Gabriel came into the breakfast room, seeing his sister staring off into space, her breakfast untouched. He placed a hand on her shoulder as she turned, looked up at him with those stricken eyes she tried to hide, and gave him a wobbly smile.

"I'm all right," she clearly mouthed.

It wasn't true, of course. The clear fact that she was trying to keep her pain from him caused a pang in his chest. What Jane needed was something to do. Something to take her mind off of things for a while. Wandering around his town house, alone much of the time, wasn't helping her at all. She dreaded callers except from family. Didn't want to go out into society. Hmm.

Gabriel bent down and kissed her cheek, then went over to the sideboard where platters of food were set out. "You know, Jane, I was thinking of going to the British Museum today. Would you like to accompany me?"

She rose to fetch the speaking book, one of many that lay about in each room of his house now. She returned to her chair and patted the seat next to her, which Gabriel took, thinking it was a good sign, even though he usually sat at the head of the table.

Jane wasn't confident in her ability to converse through lipreading and preferred to write it out. *What are you looking for? Does this have something to do with Alexandria?*

His family had heard about the reason he had gone to Holy Island and then all the way to Ireland, but he'd told only Jane the full story. Her eyes had filled with shocked laughter and admiration when he told of waylaying the captain in Holy Island, then being shot before sailing off to Ireland. She'd shaken her head in amazement at Alexandria's ability to stay one step ahead of him and clasped her hands in romantic glee when he told of the masquerade ball. She had been won by Alexandria's steadfast quest to find her missing parents and admired the young woman already.

"Yes." He hesitated, not sure how much to tell her about what the Featherstones had been hired to find. "There is an important manuscript that has disappeared from the collection Hans Sloane gave to the British Museum. I find myself rather curious about it and the British Museum seems a good place to start asking questions."

Jane arched a brow at him and took back the book. "You're worried about her, aren't you?"

Gabriel let out a breath, his attempts at being glib about the matter dissolving with her forthright, questioning eyes. "Well, yes I am. There are some very powerful men looking for that manuscript, and she has placed herself right in the thick of things." He looked off into the far corner of the room. "I'm chafing at the regent's bit here. Biding my time isn't a specialty of mine, if you must know."

He turned a grim smile upon her. "I find if I don't do something, at least *feel* like I'm doing something useful to help her, I will go mad." He rubbed his chin, elbow propped on the table beside his plate, shooting her a side glance. "Would you care to join me on this wild adventure?"

Jane laughed. The first real laugh since Matthew's death. Even though Gabriel couldn't hear the sound of her laughter, he could see it on her face and he was glad for that, so glad.

"Well, eat up then." He took a bite of eggs. "We'll need our strength if we're to skulk about London today."

She put her hand on his forearm. "Thank you, Gabriel, for everything."

He could only nod at her around the sudden knot in his throat and then motioned for her to eat. Which she finally did.

    ᘒᣔ ᘒᣔ ᘒᣔ ᘒᣔ

Gabriel and Jane took the formal coach with the St. Easton coat of arms on the sides, pulled by four grays as it would be the most comfortable for Jane in London's dreary cold, at least that was what Gabriel thought would be best. But she only sent him a small smile and a slight shake of her head when she saw that he'd ordered it.

Charlotte, the oldest of the sisters, would have insisted on it. Mary, the middle sister, would have been embarrassed by the grandeur but too caring of his feelings to call him on the carpet about it. Jane rolled her eyes and hopped inside. Ah, women. Who could understand them?

It wasn't long before they pulled up to the elegant Montagu House where the British Museum was housed. Gabriel had sent word that he was coming and would like to meet with the principal librarian, so it didn't surprise him when they were met in the front entrance hall by a man who promised to lead them to Mr. Planta.

They passed rooms full of sculptures and busts, paintings and drawings, bookcases filled with every kind of book from the King's Library, and every imaginable earthly curiosity from Captain James Cook's objects of the South Seas to the foot of Apollo from Greece. They were finally led to the Manuscript Salon where Mr. Planta rose and came over to meet them. He was an old gentleman but thin and agile with deep set, intelligent eyes. He bowed to Gabriel and Jane, taking her hand and leaning over it.

Gabriel waited while Jane explained the need for the speaking book as they had decided she would do. He could employ Meade with other tasks this day as Jane had a fair hand and a quick mind when interpreting what someone was saying, though she did go into much more detail than Meade, which slowed the process at times. Never mind; she needed to get out of the house and have a task that made her feel needed.

They were directed to a seating area by the long row of windows and served tea.

"How may I be of service, Your Grace?" Planta asked with kindness in his eyes. Older gentlemen, Gabriel was finding, had more compassion with "afflictions" and thought of them less as a weakness than an occurrence of change in one's life.

"Are you aware of the missing manuscript from Hans Sloane's original collection?"

"Yes, of course." He nodded vigorously.

"When did you learn it was missing?"

"We catalog and inventory every spring. It was discovered missing about five and a half years ago. May of 1813."

That would make sense. The Featherstones were hired in October of 1817, time for all the players to learn of it and begin searching for it. But someone had managed to get ahold of a partial copy of it, and that copy must have been copied, sold perhaps, and now it appeared there were three partial copies, one in England, one in Spain, and another in France, if Brooke was to be believed. Did Mr. Planta know of the existence of the partial? Gabriel wasn't sure he should tell him if he didn't.

"Where there inquires about it?"

Mr. Planta launched into a lengthy description while Jane wrote furiously, trying to keep up. She finally passed it over to Gabriel. *Yes, over the years there have been many, many inquiries since the manuscript was stolen. The Antiquities Society had been in an uproar, of course, and that had led to all sorts of speculation making the manuscript the most-talked-about item in the collection for a time. There had been questions from foreign dignitaries with speculation as to what exactly the manuscript had been about. There was even one time when Mr. Planta was quite sure he was being followed home each day, but seeing his routine so regular and perhaps, boring, they gave up. But he did start to carry a walking cane with a knife blade that popped out of the end. His wife had thought he'd lost his wits, but they had eventually left him alone. The most he knows about the manuscript is that it has a design for some sort of machine written in it, but no one to his knowledge had ever attempted to build it. He had told anyone who asked exactly that. Did the duke have new information?*

Yes, the duke did, Gabriel thought dryly, but he dared not breathe a word of what he'd seen in the palace. "Not really, just a matter of some treasure hunters hired to find it, and now they've come up missing. Nasty business, that."

Jane wrote as Mr. Planta talked. *Oh, my. No one knows who might be behind their disappearance?*

"Sadly no. They've vanished from the face of the earth it seems, and I've been appointed guardian to their daughter. She has a keen desire to find them, as I'm sure you can understand. I thought you might know something useful." Gabriel braced his elbows on his knees and rubbed his chin with one hand, looking off into the distance, deep in thought.

Jane started writing again. She passed the speaking book over with wide eyes. *He says there is one thing he always thought odd about the whole affair. A letter came to the museum one day. He hasn't shown it to anyone because he thought it must be a prank as it wasn't signed.*

"May I see it?" Gabriel asked him.

Mr. Planta nodded and went off to fetch it.

They waited, sipping tea that had gone cold as the gray light of London's skies hovered around them. Jane shivered, looking at him with a mix of worry and anticipation. *Wonderful.* She was smitten, he could see it. She would end up like Alexandria, taking on cases of mysteries to be solved and getting herself in the middle of trouble. *Never mind. If it chased the shadows from her eyes, it would be worth it.*

Planta returned and held out a small note. Gabriel looked at the address on the outside and his heart began to thud. It was Alexandria's handwriting. He was sure of it. He lifted it closer and studied the postmark. It was from Italy. Tuscany, Italy. How could that be?

"How long ago did you receive this letter?"

"Six months ago, give or take. It was the end of June, I believe."

Could Alexandria have been in Italy in June? It seemed impossible, but he had learned long ago that when it concerned her, nothing was impossible. Gabriel opened the letter and read the one line, etched out in that same flowing hand.

We're very close to finding it, but they are watching us. Send help!

He looked up at Mr. Planta who raised his eyebrows in silent question. The realization hit him like a bludgeon to the head. This wasn't from Alexandria; it was from her mother. If she looked like Alexandria, then couldn't they have similar handwriting? He imagined Ian and Katherine Featherstone in Tuscany, in trouble.

God help them. Alexandria was right.

The Featherstones, if they were still alive, were in great danger and needed their help.

Chapter Thirteen

Astonishment, perplexed and angry astonishment, filled her. Why was she angry? Alexandria stood and thrust the book back at Enoch. "Can you read it? Tell me this story."

So many thoughts swirled through her mind. Had her mother known Alex would follow them? And was she trying to tell her something? Something about this book? What did that mean? Why would her mother do such a thing? That letter, the last one from her mother that she'd written from Ireland...she had done it purposefully, leaving that clue in Alex's hands, knowing she would follow them here. But why so mysterious and strange? Why couldn't they have just taken her with them?

"Please, Enoch. Tell me the story in this book. There might be a clue."

Enoch nodded his old, white head and sat down cross-legged beside her. "This is not an Icelandic Saga, no, no, no. This is a tale more recent but still hundreds of years ago. This is a tale of a man named Augusto de Carrara told by his only friend, a monk called Oswald."

"How did you come by this book?" She wondered now if her mother had given it to him.

But he shook his head and frowned at her. "Listen."

He opened to the first beautifully illuminated page and read in a clear, sane voice.

Once upon a time, there was a man, a brilliant and cold-hearted man, who lived in the hills of Tuscany. No one dared go inside his house, nor visit his blacksmith shop unless the need was desperate. It wasn't that he lacked the skill to fix a wagon wheel or straighten a bent sword, no, he could do those things very well. It was because of his furious temper.

One day two boys crept into his shop and hid behind some wooden boxes of tools. They watched Augusto work for a long time unnoticed, then escaped unharmed. The story they told the village instilled even greater fear and was wondered at by all the people for many years to come.

The boys said he took out a music box and wound it up as far as it would go. A strange music came from the box, making the boys feel peculiar and frightened, but they sat transfixed as Augusto threw himself into his work. The fire raged from the brick furnace; the hammer pounded on silver so bright it hurt their eyes to look at it. They crept closer until they could see what the craftsman was working on.

Enoch held his hands wide and stared at Alex in a way that caused a chill to run down her spine.

A very great machine stood in the middle of the room. It whirled and turned inside and light flashed from it. Terrified, the boys ran away thinking the man was no man but an angel or a demon with supernatural powers. The townsfolk were frightened and decided to rid themselves of this creature. So in the darkest part of night, they burned down his shop and the house where Augusto slept.

The villagers thought they had put an end to Augusto and went back to their quiet lives, but Augusto knew the boys were watching him and he knew the small minds of the townsfolk so he prepared himself. After the boys left, he had gathered his most precious books and manuscripts, his plans and paintings, and fled his home. He roamed the hills of Tuscany for many days until he found an enormous cave, the marble caves of Carrara, where he started over, building his furnace and making his tools, living in hiding.

One day, a very great man from the Medici family, whose riches and power extended over all the world, heard of Augusto's inventions and asked him to come to Florence and be his military engineer to invent all sorts of armaments and the *trace italienne*, star forts to withstand their enemy's cannons. Augusto did not want to live in the city—he was afraid of what people thought of him and hated being in society, so he said he would send weapons and the plans to build them to this man for a price. They agreed and for many years Augusto worked in his caves, making the Medici family a strong military force that helped the empire flourish.

But Augusto's heart grew cold and dark as he invented these death machines, and his mind became twisted with evil thoughts. The only thing that tied him to the innocence of his childhood and kept him sane was a special music box. The music box he always played while inventing.

One day his music box wouldn't work and in a rage he threw it against the cave wall, breaking it into many tiny pieces. Augusto roared with anger and despair, looking at the broken pieces on the floor of his cave. And then he had a terrible memory come back to him.

119

"Augusto, come inside." His mother had called to him from the open doorway of their little cottage in the town of Massa. Augusto turned from his latest obsession, a delicate building of sticks, and ran through the sprinkling rain to his mother's side. He had been playing for a long time and was hungry and his mother was sure to have dinner waiting for him.

He hugged her legs through her skirt, his love for her bursting in his young heart, and sat at his chair beside his sister, Maria.

Suddenly, his father burst through the door. His eyes were wild and his face looked as if he'd put on a mask of rage.

Augusto froze in his seat, his heart pounding with terror. "Papa?" his little voice murmured, but no one heard him.

His father roared and rushed over to his mother and grasped her by her hair. He jerked her head back while she screamed. He lifted his arm high in the air shouting, "You whore. You filthy, rotten harlot! I'll kill you! I will kill you for this!"

She screamed again. "No! Whatever you mean, it is not true."

His father didn't listen. He plunged the knife into her chest. Blood spurted out making red drops on the table.

Augusto looked down at his sleeve and saw the red dots there too. The next thing he remembered was waking up at his grandfather's house — alone. He never saw his sister or father again.

His grandfather was a very old man who rarely spoke to him, but he showed Augusto the power of fire and metal and gave him the one thing that meant everything to little Augusto — his mother's music box.

So Augusto became an old and bitter man, a man with hands covered in the blood of thousands. With the music box gone, his mind snapped and his soul crushed him. He stared at the broken pieces, remembering everything, and broke into great sobs. For three days he railed against God, shaking his big fists at the sky and daring God to kill him. For three days he worked on putting the tiny pieces together and could not. On the third day he lay on the hard floor of his cave and cried out for God to save him if He wouldn't take his life and end his pain.

And God did. God sent a peace so great into Augusto's heart that it melted the anger and grief and gave him new hope.

The next day Augusto packed up his things and vowed not to work with the Medici family ever again. He wanted to go home, so with God strong in his heart, he conquered his fears and bought a house in town. Back in Massa the townspeople were astounded that he was alive and so changed. They were careful of him at first but soon grew used to his odd ways.

Looking for answers, Augusto visited the town church where he met a monk named Oswald. Oswald was very glad to call Augusto friend, and they had spent many hours together reading the gospels and talking about God and His Son, Jesus. They ate together and talked of things that Augusto had kept in his heart and never shared with another person. They laughed together and became very great friends, the only true friend Augusto ever had.

Augusto began working on another invention. He would tell no one what it was, and he made many journeys around the world for special materials to build it with. He worked day and night to create his most intricate machine. When he finished it, he asked his friend to come and see it. Oswald was very curious to see what Augusto had been working on those past years and knew it was a great privilege to be invited to see it.

On the night Oswald went to Augusto's house to see the invention, there was no moon and it was very dark. As he came to the door, he felt the earth vibrate and shake so that he could hardly stand. He was very afraid, but he opened the door and saw something he could hardly fathom.

A huge crystal machine stood in the center of the room with Augusto standing before it, his hands outstretched on it. A whirring of wheels and gears shook the little house as a low sound started to hum from the machine.

Oswald's heart raced. He took a few more steps into the room, seeing that a hundred or more candles made the crystal so bright, he had to turn his eyes away and shield them with his hand.

"What is it?" he shouted to Augusto, but his friend didn't hear him.

He was concentrating so hard, his hands moving over the crystal, that he didn't even see Oswald in the room. Before Oswald could walk over and touch his arm, another sound came from behind him, a loud racket of horses and men.

Oswald shrank back as soldiers poured through the door toward them. The machine was humming and moving, so bright they all stopped and gaped at it, their faces drained of color, their eyes bulging out with terror. They pointed their swords and shouted at Augusto, but he seemed to be in another world, as if a trance had come over him. He did not even notice the soldiers and ignored their warning.

In a frenzy of fear, the soldiers rushed to Augusto and grasped hold of him, torches flaring, lighting the walls on fire and knocking over the candles. Flames burst to life in every corner as the soldiers flew at the man and the machine.

Oswald shrank back, fear so great he shook from head to toe. The soldiers hauled Augusto up and shouted that he tell them what it was. Augusto looked like a frightened child. He shook his head and stared at them but did not speak. The soldiers hauled him up, yelling in his face.

Oswald watched in horror as one soldier thrust his sword through Augusto's chest. Augusto howled with pain but did not fight back. They pulled him up, blood dripping from his chest. His hand reached back toward the machine, his throat roared with raging panic as they dragged him out, leaving a trail of red on the floor.

After his friend's death, Oswald was taken to Florence where the Medici family had him imprisoned, thinking he knew what Augusto had made, but he did not. He only knew this story, and so he wrote it down in his prison cell during the long weeks before they finally freed him. When he returned to Massa, he saw that Augusto's greatest fears had come true. All that remained of his house and invention was a pile of charred wood. The townspeople would not even speak his name for fear that something horrible would happen to them. There is only this story that remains of Augusto de Carrara.

Enoch stood and rubbed his hands together. "Go to Helgustadir in the southeasterly fjords of this island. There you will find the crystals. It is where your parents went." He turned away but John hurried toward him, took him aside, and whispered something in his ear.

Enoch shook his head. John reached for the book but Enoch held fast to it. What was John doing? Trying to take the book from him? Alex looked away, a deep unease filling her. He was acting so desperate lately. On edge and jumpy. He needed to trust that she knew what she was doing, and making Enoch angry was not a good idea.

Thinking back to the story, Alex took a long breath, wonder and dread filling her. Augusto de Carrara had written the manuscript her parents were hired to find. Nations, rich and powerful men, were searching for it, desperate to have it. The manuscript could hold the plans for one of his many inventions, perhaps his last one. It had to be something of great worth.

Like a weapon.

A weapon that held the hearts of kings.

Chapter Fourteen

A deep disquiet settled around Gabriel's heart as he led Jane from the library. That note from Alexandria's mother rang with desperation. He could picture her writing it in secret, looking behind her as if someone was just around the corner...waiting to capture them, kill them even.

Lord, send Your angels to protect them. Keep them alive until we can get to them, I beg You.

They came to the waiting carriage and Gabriel helped Jane inside. Strong winds gusted with rolling, dark clouds overhead. He peered up into the sky, pulled his hat lower, and lifted the collar of his coat to cover his neck. "Jane, I find the need to walk and think. Go home. Tell Meade what we've discovered. I shall follow you shortly."

"But it looks like rain." She gestured toward the sky. "You could catch a chill." She stopped him with a hand on his arm and anxious eyes.

Gabriel patted her hand. "Don't worry, Jane. There are plenty of establishments to get out of the rain should it start pouring. I will be fine." She was so emotionally frail these days, so much more easily worried about accidents and injury. Gabriel hoped it would fade in time. Matthew's death had left quite a mark, as expected, but he hoped the change was temporary and she would return to the strength of her faith that had always come so naturally to her.

After sending Jane home in the carriage, Gabriel walked along Great Russell Street, thinking about what he had learned from Mr. Planta at the British Museum. Alexandria would be ecstatic about the note, there was no doubt of that, but therein lay the problem. If she learned of the clue in Italy, she would do anything to get there and go after her parents. And he couldn't let her do that. Much too dangerous. No, the best solution would be to hire his own investigators to search the Tuscan area. He imagined the joy on Alexandria's face when he found them for her. The love she would feel toward him.

God, I miss her. I miss her letters.

As he contemplated the yearning in his heart, he came to St. George's Church and decided to go in. He went up the wide steps to the Roman-inspired portico with its stately columns and opened the doors. Inside, it looked quiet and empty. Gabriel sat in the back on one of the pews and bowed his head. He could feel the thunder vibrate against the stained-glass windows as he closed his eyes.

Quiet. His quiet world gave him too much opportunity for introspection, leading to morose moods and a feeling that he was coming out of his skin at times.

He needed peace, but it seemed aloof and distant. Impossible to have.

Seeing Alexandria's face, he buried his face into his hands. Her dark hair that came alive in the sun when she'd pulled back the hood of her crimson cloak, the sunshine lighting up her face. Blue eyes in a face of creamy skin with a blush of pink on her cheeks where the wind had whipped color into them. Lovely but more… It was as if he knew her spirit and it matched his. The rib taken from *his* side.

It hurts to think of her. And with him! Pain like he'd never experienced slashed through him as he saw John's face, his arm around her, his head leaning down toward her. It was all Gabriel could do not to commandeer a ship and sail back to Iceland to fetch her himself. But if he did that, the regent would have his neck. Gabriel had no choice but to wait for the regent's soldiers to bring her back.

Lord, bring her safely to me, I beg You. I will guard her with my life. You know that I will.

With a burst of frustration, he expelled a breath, stood, and walked quickly out of the church. He plunged down the walkway in the soundless pouring rain. He was soaked through in minutes. Looking about, he noted a public house up the street and hurried toward it. He could sit by a fire to dry out, get something warm to drink, and hire a carriage from there.

As he crossed the street, sudden arms grasped him from behind and yanked him into a dark side street. Gabriel grunted as a heavy object came down on his shoulder, but he was able to spin around and free himself from the hold.

He looked into the face of a dark-skinned man with black hair and a mustache that curled up on either side. He was tall, an inch taller than Gabriel, but thin and wiry. The other man with him was short and squat, swaying from side to side with a leering smile—he was holding a pistol.

Gabriel backed away, reaching for his short sword he always wore at his waist. The tall man was speaking, but of course Gabriel couldn't make it out. He only knew one thing for certain—they appeared Spanish and two Spaniards had been following Alexandria; Montague had told him all about them. This could be them. It had to be. And if that was the case, they wouldn't want to kill him. They would want to know what he knew about the manuscript…and they would want to know where Alexandria was, if they didn't have her already.

He reasoned through this in seconds and then charged the short man, thinking he wouldn't shoot and the tactic would surprise them. He was more nimble than Gabriel thought. The little man scurried back and climbed onto a ledge protruding from a storefront. Gabriel stretched up and slashed his sword against the man's legs. He threw back his head in agony and dropped the pistol. Gabriel kicked it, spinning it like a gleaming black top down the street.

Gabriel turned just as the thrust of the tall man's blade came within an inch of his chest. He parried the move in defense, stepping closer to counter the attack. The Spaniard's sword was longer, thinner, and after a few movements, Gabriel knew that he was fighting an accomplished swordsman. If only he could hear what the fat man behind him was doing, but he dared not look around.

127

The cold rain made the street slippery as they rushed back and forth, parry and riposte, slash and stab. He just avoided a slash across his forward thigh and then leaned in with a mighty thrust. The Spaniard's sword flashed like the lightning around them. Deflecting it, Gabriel panted, starting to panic. Thank God he had kept up with his practices, but the fact that he couldn't hear was a definite disadvantage. Where was the other man?

Just as he thought it, he felt something crash across the back of his skull.

Oh no.

His eyes rolled back into his head and darkness closed in.

🅝🅢 🅝🅢 🅝🅢 🅝🅢

Gabriel dreamed he heard music.

The most beautiful opera he could ever imagine. Sweeping notes trilled in and out with sound as if they were breathing, as if alive, seeming heaven borne in their perfect accord with each other. Harmonious sounds. Yes, that was it. He drifted in that place…floating and peaceful…drifted there forever it seemed.

Eons later, his eyes moved against the black wall of his eyelids as a wave of searing pain jolted him into shadowy awareness. A throb of heat burned from the top of his head down to his chest, down farther where his stomach rolled in rebellion. He turned to his side and emptied the contents of his stomach, sweat breaking out over his whole body. He lay back down, gasping for air, some part of him realizing that had he not crept from unconsciousness for the event, he would have never woken up.

My God, do not forsake me. Jesus's words rang through his being until he settled back into the darkness.

Next when he awoke it was to a hard tapping on his shoulder. He turned his head away, wishing for sleep and silence forever, but the tapping turned to shoving so he opened his eyes. Flashes of light streaked across his vision. He closed his eyes against it but was roughly shoved again. He yelled out and pushed the hand away, opening his eyes and peering through the dim light.

A slovenly, dark-looking man stared down at him. His lips said something beneath the thick growth of hair, but Gabriel couldn't begin to make it out. The man held out a tin cup and shook it at him. Gabriel was to drink, was he? He understood that much.

Lifting his head made his vision swim. The dull ache in the back of his head pulsed with his heartbeat. Ah yes, the fight. It was coming back to him. He blinked heavily as his hand shook, spilling water across whatever it was that was covering him. The bludgeon to the head. That explained the feeling that his skull was cracked. But where was he?

The tilting of the room combined with the familiar nausea jogged his senses toward the answer. A ship. Dear God save him; he must be on a Spanish ship.

He took a sip of the water tasting the cool, clear goodness. Well, at least they wanted him alive. They wouldn't go to the trouble of waking him to drink if they didn't. Little good that it would do him, what with being unable to keep anything down. He should warn them of his impending doom, should they not locate some ginger.

"Terrible seasickness. Ginger root if you have it."

He could almost see the man's scowl beneath the heavy, black beard, but Gabriel shut his eyes and tuned him out. He was too tired to care if they found it or not.

129

All through the night, great waves crashed against the ship causing it to dip into deep troughs and then rise, as if taking off for flight onto the swell of a wave. Gabriel sweated it out with fingers gripping the side of his cot and teeth clinched together. He clung to sanity against the constant heaving of his stomach and prayed for it to end. But it did not end. It went on for hours and hours and hours.

In the morning, the stillness felt like he'd stepped into another world. He woke with a start and sat up. Were they still here or in some heavenly place and hadn't realized it yet? With shaking legs like a newborn calf, he stumbled from his room and up the ladder to the deck. As soon as a sailor saw him, there was a great commotion, men running toward him.

Before he had time to make it to the railing, seeing sea all around him, he was tackled from behind and taken down to the planks of the deck. Three men attacked him, pummeling him and holding him down. His head reeled anew as they tied his hands and hefted him up, stretching him from limb to limb as they carried him back to his cot and threw him on it.

He curled onto his side, hands tied behind his back, the aching of his shoulders just beginning, and watched them leave.

This time they locked him inside.

Chapter Fifteen

They traveled east from Svein's hometown of Reykjahlið. Svein stayed behind with his family giving Alex and John strict instructions for the route to Helgustadir and the crystal mines that lay in the southeastern fjords on the coast of Iceland.

They crossed mountainous land, the rocky soil rich orange where the snow was sparse. Every few miles they saw various sizes of volcanoes and pseudovolcanoes with their round crater tops and pools of snow in the centers, others filled with the bluest water Alex had ever seen.

And then there were the boiling, bubbling mud pools and steaming mud pots Svein warned against, where they had to dismount and carefully tread across this liquid world with its thin earthen crust, like tiptoeing across a bubbling pot of soup by treading on floating dumplings. She inhaled and closed her eyes, her face against the wind, basking in this alien land that sparked strange currents of disquiet and excitement through her veins.

By noon, the road turned south and the landscape flattened into a rocky ice desert. It looked like what she imagined the face of the moon to be like, but she didn't say that to John. They maintained a mutual silence through this extraordinary world as if by unspoken agreement that mere words would ruin the magical quality, that they wouldn't be able to hear the land speak to them unless they were still and silent inside.

As the day waned into afternoon, the land changed again, became greener the farther south they went. Alex could begin to smell the sea in the air. They passed homesteads, as they were called here, farms with sheep and horses mostly since the land was poorly suited for crops. The volcanic mountains were ever in the distance before and behind them. They crossed little trickling steams and a rushing river, pausing to see cliffs where waterfalls gushed over the tops, spraying clear droplets toward them.

It was growing dark when they finally came to the little town of Reyðarfjörður where Svein had told them to stay for the night. In the morning, they would track down the people of the Helgustadir Mine and ask questions about Augusto and the famous crystal. But now both she and her little horse were near exhaustion. Alex's stomach growled in anticipation as they trotted down the street and saw the inn Svein had mentioned. It would be good to get out of the constant wind for a hot meal to warm their insides.

"Here it is." John's voice sounded strange and clipped after hearing nothing but the moaning wind for the first time in hours. Alex glanced over at him. "Are you as tired as I am? I'm not sure I can swing my leg around to dismount from this horse."

John chuckled. "We should find a hot springs to soothe the aches from our bodies. Wait there and I will come and help you down."

Alex did as he instructed and waited until he dismounted and looped his horse's reins around a post before coming over and pulling her down into his arms. She tottered a moment, adjusting to straightening her legs after so many hours in the saddle, clinging to his shoulders and laughing at herself. "My legs don't seem to want to come together."

John looked to be choking off a laugh. "Let's get you some dinner and find someone to take care of the horses, shall we?"

They went into the inn and spoke with a jolly faced fellow who nodded and assured them of providing everything they needed. "Sit yourselves down here now." He directed them to a low table in the common room. "And my wife, Heidi, will bring out some food. Did you come by ship?"

"Originally we came by ship to Reykjavik, but we've been in Iceland for a fortnight and have most recently traveled overland from Dimmu borgir."

"Oh, you saw the black castles, did you? I've not been there in an age. Sightseeing on our island, are you? A newly wedded couple, I'm guessing. On a wedding trip?"

Alex blushed, not sure what to say. The man was certainly nosy.

John winked at him. "She has always had an interest in Iceland, haven't you, love?"

"Uh, yes, and a recent interest in the famous Icelandic crystals. We've come to see the mine."

"Oh, the crystals now?" The man beamed. "I know just the man to see about that. I will take you to him in the morning."

"Thank you, Mr....?"

He stretched out a meaty hand to each of them. "Johannes Kristinsson, pleased to meet you."

"We are Lord and Lady Lemon of Dublin. I am John Lemon."

Alex frowned but didn't say anything to correct him. He was going along all too easily with the man's misconception that they were married, and she wasn't sure why. They had told the truth in Reykjavik. The thought that all of this dishonesty was going to get her into trouble pounded like a little hammer against her temples. And John was worse than she was. He didn't even seem to feel guilty over it.

A slight woman with thin blond braids came forward and introduced herself as Heidi, then brought out a meal of fish and potatoes with thick slices of hearty rye bread. After only a few bites, Alex had to fight off the urge to nod off over her plate, exhaustion overcoming her as the warm food settled in her stomach.

John leaned over and chuckled in her ear. "We had best get you to bed before you land face-first in your fish."

"Sorry," she mumbled, nodding.

They were shown to a small room with hardly enough space for the bed and one chest of drawers. Alex plopped down on the soft pallet and fell back against the pillow. "Here, let's at least take off your shoes," she heard John say over her.

She drifted off to sleep with the sound of them hitting the floor with a distant thud. She felt John lift the blanket over her and tuck it under her chin. Such a nice man, she thought as he kissed her good night on the forehead.

🙰 🙰 🙰 🙰

The next morning, she opened her eyes to the smell of bread fresh from the oven and coffee in the air. Coffee? She'd not had coffee in an age. Her stomach rumbled as she turned her head and saw John, turned toward her, still asleep and lying right beside her. Goodness gracious, they'd slept the night through in the same bed together!

She sat up and rubbed the sleep from her eyes. She looked back down at him. With his hand curled under one cheek, he looked boyishly sweet, younger than his thirty-some years. She started to lean toward him to give his cheek a kiss to wake him and then reared back. Thoughts like that would only get her into trouble.

Instead, she eased from the bed, slipped on her shoes, and crept out the door. Perhaps she could attend to her morning routine somewhere else. Heidi had been shy but helpful the night before. Perhaps Alex could borrow a brush and some soap to wash her face in another part of the inn. At least she wouldn't be here beside him when John awoke. Knowing John, he would try to take some liberties.

Her cheeks burned as she thought about that and hurried down the stairs to the common room. Heidi was busy in the kitchen making breakfast.

"You can tidy up in here." She gestured toward another bedroom. "I'll have my daughter bring soap and water. Will you and your husband be wanting breakfast?"

Alex couldn't meet her eyes. "Yes, please. Thank you. He should be awake shortly."

After hurrying through her morning routine and feeling refreshed, Alex made her way back to the common room to find John awake and looking ready for the day in a fresh suit of dove gray coat and trousers.

She sat across from him and shot him a big-eyed look, muttering, "I can't believe you've said we are married. We're in quite a jam now. Can't tell them the truth after we've spent the night through together."

He shrugged. "It simplifies things without Svein. Why did you tiptoe away this morning? I was looking forward to waking up with you beside me."

"Exactly." Alex leaned forward and whispered, "We aren't married yet and we're not going to act like we are."

The teasing light that was becoming so familiar came into John's blue eyes. "You can't blame a fiancé for trying."

Alex rolled her eyes, her annoyance with him draining away. "Oh, yes I can." But there was laughter in her voice now. She could never stay mad at John for long.

After breakfast they rode a short distance with Johannes to the Helgustadir farmstead on the northern shore of Reyðarfjörður Bay. It was surrounded by rocky cliffs and mountains, the fjord frothing blue water and beating against the cliff heads. Sheep grazed all around them and the call of seabirds filled the air. It reminded Alex a little of home.

They dismounted and knocked on the door of the long, rectangular house covered almost entirely in some kind of green moss. It had a thatched roof that hung deeply over the sides of the house and a whitewashed front door.

A young girl, two dogs hugging her skirts, opened the door. "Father," she called back into the house. "Strangers are here."

An older man with curling gray hair came to the door and surveyed them. "Hello, Johannes, and who have you brought this fine day?"

Alex breathed a sigh. He didn't seem as fierce as his face made him appear.

"Come in, come in. Sit down."

They settled in a comfortable sitting area of the large room.

"I've brought Lord and Lady Lemon, Valdi. This is Valdi Adamsson, the owner of the mine." He looked at Alex and John. "They've come to see the crystal."

Valdi turned his head toward Alex and scratched at a spot. "You want to traipse about in a mine cave, girl? 'Tis not a pleasant experience."

"If you please, sir. I'm not afraid." She wasn't sure how true that statement was, but it seemed the right thing to say. The old man huffed with a doubtful sound.

He got up and went over to a table and lit a lantern. Opening a drawer he took something out, carried it over to her, and placed a large, cube-shaped chunk of crystal in her hand. "This is what's down there, Lady Lemon. Only covered in mud." He frowned at her then, wrinkling his face. "What interest do you have in Icelandic crystal?"

Alex held it up and looked through it. It was as clear as glass. "It's just so beautiful."

"And useful." Valdi motioned them over to the kitchen table. He pulled a book off a nearby bookshelf and opened it. "Now, place the crystal on the page."

Alex did as directed and then she and John leaned over it. Valdi held up the lantern so the light would shine directly on the book. "Do you see that?"

Alex peered through the crystal at the words. "But how is that possible? It's amazing! There are two of every letter." She looked at John. "Do you see it?"

He nodded. "I've heard about this. The crystal bends the light. It's doubly refracting, isn't it?"

"That's right, and why it became so useful. Over the last two centuries, scientists have used this crystal to study light, build prisms, and develop all sorts of different types of optics tools. We are very proud of our crystal."

"Have you heard of a man named Augusto de Carrara? He came here in the sixteenth century for this crystal."

"How do you know this name?" The man's face changed to suspicious again.

Alex exchanged glances with John, not sure how much to say. John hurried with an explanation. "Near Dimmu borgir, an old hermit told us a story of him coming here for the crystal. We were curious about him is all," John shrugged, "so we came here to see if anyone knows what he might have wanted with the crystal."

"Perhaps I should show you the cave after all," Valdi said in a voice that held a slight note of menace.

A shiver prickled across Alex's skin. John took a step closer to her, standing just behind her, and put his hands on her shoulders. "Perhaps that isn't necessary. We were only curious. Is it dangerous?"

"Not dangerous, just uncomfortable." Valdi waved at them. "Of course, if you're afraid to get a little wet and muddy, I understand."

"I'm not afraid," Alex stated in an even voice. "I want to see it."

Johannes took a seat and clasped his hands together. "I will wait for the young couple here. Don't like getting wet and cold myself." He nodded. "Go on then. I'll take you back to the inn when you return. Might have a little nap here by the fire, where it is so warm and comfortable."

Alex wrapped her coat closer around her neck and shivered. *Lord, protect us,* she prayed as they followed the man out toward the caves.

Chapter Sixteen

The sun shone bright against his eyes and seagulls soared over the port city of Santander, Spain, as Gabriel Ravenwood, the Duke of St. Easton, was pushed and prodded onto dry land. He stumbled at the end of the gangplank, felt hands on one side grasp him and hands on the other side shove him, throwing him off balance into the dirt. They hauled him up, his arms long past numb and burning sinew of aching shoulders, his feet bare and filthy, someone having stolen his shoes, his face covered in beard and grime. But he was alive.

For good or bad, whether he wished it or not.

He was still alive.

The city sparkled under the sun like a winter haven of pale sand and cool breezes. Soft waves of blue water sparkled around them. He squinted at it—the light too bright after the last weeks of hellish nightmare in the dark hold, gnawing on the dirt-encrusted ginger root for all it was worth and keeping down enough water to yet breathe.

He'd lost weight and muscle strength. He could feel it in his blood and his breath, how winded walking up this hill was making him. Weak and spindly, easily snapped by a stiff wind or whatever they had planned for him, a mere shadow of the strong and capable man he'd once been.

God, how did it come to this? I don't understand…anything anymore.

He saw himself six months ago and nearly retched on the side of the carriage they were cramming him into with their rough hands and harsh-mouthed faces. He slumped against the corner and closed his eyes. He'd been another person six months ago, six months when his life had been ordered and perfect and his brand of normal. The ennui he'd felt, that he had complained and railed against, dear God, how he wished it back again. Anything numb. Anything but this constant agony.

It's her fault. It's Alexandria Featherstone's fault.

The thoughts dogged him as he licked his dry lips. Was it? What if he'd never gotten that letter? Would it have made a difference?

No. Shut up. It was never her fault I got dragged into this nightmare.

The argument rattled around in his feverish mind over and over, off and on, for days or weeks even, it seemed. He sometimes felt a very real stab of fear that this was the end for him. That he would die trying to be the guardian duke to this mysterious and lovely woman he loved beyond all reason.

How could he love her? He didn't know. But if he closed his eyes during the worst of it and thought of her, if he remembered every line and curve of her face as they kicked him and shoved him and belittled him, spit in his face and stole his clothes…he got to the next moment still breathing. There had to be something in that.

The carriage drove on and on for hours and days. They untied his hands so he could eat at the public houses and take care of his personal business behind trees along the way. He thought of running many times while shielded by a bush, but they would be on him in minutes. He didn't have the strength to outrun them and they knew it, or they would never untie him and give him those few precious moments of human decency.

No, they knew it and scoffed at him for his weakness. Those dark eyes and faces with varying amounts of facial hair. They took pride in that, Gabriel could see, so groomed and impeccable in their uniforms. He hated their pointed beards and groomed mustaches. He hated their haughty, laughing eyes. He hated his enemy.

Love thy enemies and pray for those who persecute you. The Scripture kept coming to him but he turned from it, shaking his head at the voice, an outer rebellion that exposed his heart. *I cannot. I cannot. I cannot.*

Jesus did.

Gabriel took a great, shuddering breath at the thought.

I cannot.

On the third day they came into a large city. Madrid. It had to be. He had never been there, but if they were taking him to Ferdinand VII, the king of Spain, as he suspected, then they would be entering the capital city. His suspicions were further affirmed when they passed an enormous iron gate with marble towers on either side.

He could see inside to the rectangular courtyard and royal palace. Rows upon rows of windows as far as the eye could see outside the carriage window. Columns and scrolling stonework made up the palace facade. In the center, the building rose into the blue sky—a wide section of stone with an enormous clock, statues, and flags. Fit for a king, to be sure. But they did not turn into the courtyard, instead circling around to a street behind the palace.

The street darkened under the shade of enormous trees lining either side. Darker yet with a chill that settled in the interior of the coach. They turned and stopped in front of a large, plain building. Gabriel braced himself, an internal tightening of his stomach and ribs as the door swung open and his captors reached inside and hauled him out. He looked up at the gray stone walls and saw the iron bars on the windows. Of course.

The *Carcel de la Inquisición.*

A chill swept over him as the horrors of the Spanish Inquisition crossed his memory. When Napoleon had ruled Spain some scant years ago, he had ended the dark practices of the inquisition that for centuries had eradicated all religious beliefs save Catholicism from Spain, but Ferdinand had been reinstated after Napoleon's defeat and restored the practice.

Gabriel agreed with the belief that the crown's way of singling out the wealthy citizens as detractors and the subsequent confiscation of their property was nothing more than a convenient way to incur wealth for the crown than to force papal rule on its citizens. It might not be used in abundance these days, but the place was still standing and, more telling, they'd brought him here where tales of harrowing torture cried from the stones.

They meant to have answers.

His captors roughly pushed and pulled him through a dark hall devoid of furnishings or ornamentation. One of them stopped suddenly, reached for an iron ring in the stones of the floor, and opened a door revealing cold steps. They prodded him down into further darkness and dank air. Gabriel's stomach tightened into knots of dread. A large room of stone lay at the bottom of the stairs where dim light drifted from a skylight above. He was hurried across that chamber, but not before he saw iron rings seven-feet high mounted on the walls and a wheeled contraption against one wall.

He swallowed a sour taste from his throat, recognizing the rack of torture.

They continued through another stone chamber and down another set of stairs, farther and farther down into the earth. One soldier disappeared, only to reappear moments later with a lantern to light the way. The next chamber held an iron door that was unlocked. Inside were rows of cells separated by iron bars. Gabriel didn't know if he was glad or not that no one else appeared to be inside them.

They opened one of the cell's doors and thrust him inside. A little light came from a very high window, which must mean this chamber was at the far end of the building and faced an outside wall. That he wouldn't be left in complete darkness left him reeling with relief. He did not know if he could have endured being deaf and blind in this place.

The soldiers spoke but he didn't know what they said, and they seemed used to him not answering. One of them thrust a canteen of water at him, which he grabbed before the man could change his mind. The other motioned that they should leave. Gabriel was left wondering when and if he would ever see anyone again.

Upon further inspection, Gabriel found a cot attached to the wall as the only furnishing. He sat upon the straw ticking, the smell of mildew heavy in the air. *God help me. I could go mad here. I have only You now.*

He chuckled, feeling half mad already that he'd even said he *only* had God. He took off his coat, rolled it into a lumpy pillow, and lay down to sleep. Fitful sleep with hours of waiting in between and then more fitful sleep. When would they come for him?

☙☙ ☙☙ ☙☙ ☙☙

He was awakened with a rough shove of his shoulder. For the first time since being attacked, he saw the tall Spaniard again. He was with two other men, soldiers from the looks of their uniforms. They hauled him up and took him up the long passageways to the first chamber of the dungeons.

He began to struggle as they led him straight to the iron ring and chains on the wall, an involuntary reaction of terror. It was no use; he was too weak. Thirsty too. They hadn't fed him or given him anything after that first canteen for two days.

One man held him while the other chained his wrists to the ring, stretching his arms high over his head until his shoulders felt as if they must come from their sockets. Sweat poured down his back despite the cool, dank air. His breaths hissed from his clenched teeth.

"I am deaf," he told them for the first time. "I will not be able to answer your questions unless you write them down." He wasn't going to let them torture him because he couldn't hear what they said, but shame filled him at the desperation he felt to be free of the irons. What might they want to know that he wouldn't willingly say?

The tall Spaniard eyed him curiously as if trying to judge the truth of his words. He spoke orders for paper and ink to be brought. Gabriel hung there, sweating and panting, stretching to the tops of his toes to lessen the pressure on his wrists, arms, and shoulders. The muscles of his upper back quivered, his arms numb and prickly at the same time. Finally, a page was thrust toward him.

Tell us what you know of the manuscript of the Hans Sloane collection sought by your king.

One of the soldiers stood ready by the chains, hand lightly pulling and increasing the tension on the lines. Gabriel swallowed the bile in his throat. "There is a partial copy of a manuscript missing from the collection. The prince regent has one of the copies."

The chains tightened a little more. Excruciating pain made him groan, his back bowing in an arch as nerve endings screamed from Gabriel's wrists. The Spaniard took the paper back and wrote another question, seeming to take his time while Gabriel tried not to cry out again.

Does your sovereign know what the plans are for? Has he tried to build them?

Gabriel groaned as the chains tightened so he dangled from the manacles, his toes barely touching the floor. "Yes, he built what he could, but no one knows what it is. It..." he took small breaths and sputtered out, "doesn't make sense."

With a nod from the man, the soldier pulled again. Gabriel cried out as his feet left the floor. He dangled in abject misery, sweat pouring from his head and dripping onto his bare chest.

The paper was thrust at him again. *Where is Alexandria Featherstone?*

He shook his head. "I don't know."

Again the chains tightened. The Spaniard shook the paper at him. His lips asked the question in a shouting, enraged face. "Where is your ward, Lady Alexandria Featherstone?"

"I lost her in Ireland. Just...as you must have. I don't know."

He screamed as the chains tightened yet again, then blessed blackness overwhelmed him and he slumped into unconsciousness.

He jerked awake to freezing water being thrown into his face. In slow measure, he began to notice his whole body's pulsing pain—from the barely healed wound on his head to his shoulders and arms, wrists and hands, his back. God help him, his back felt stretched too taut, like a rope unraveling. With a grunt he turned over and tried to sit up. They had released him from the chains and he lay like a puddle of flesh on the stone floor. The Spaniard came toward him.

God, they will kill me now and what good will I be to Alexandria then? Give her a good life, Lord. With or without her parents, keep her safe within Your love...like she claims You have for us. Give her a joyous, happy life, I pray thee.

The dark man leaned over him and peered into Gabriel's eyes, an evil smile curving his lips. "You will tell the king...tomorrow...where she is."

Gabriel nodded, willing to promise anything to buy more time.

He was hauled back to his cell, given another flask of water and broth with a few floating chunks of meat in it and a lone carrot, which he slurped down too fast, making his stomach churn in rebellion. He drank the water slower. Savoring it, saving it in case it was the last they ever gave him. After his meal he knelt on the cold stone and cradled his head in his hands.

Silent sobs racked his shoulders, increasing the agony with each movement, but he couldn't help it. He thought of his sisters, *Jane*, his mother, *Meade*, his friend Albert. How would their lives be if he never came home?

Alexandria.

He saw her face, saw it break into a glorious smile, the sun lighting her dark hair and the life within her lighting her blue eyes. If he told them she was in Iceland, they would go after her. The thought of them bringing her here and doing this to her was more than he could stand to dwell on. He turned his thoughts back toward King Ferdinand and the meeting on the morrow. If he didn't tell them where Alexandria was, they would kill him. He saw it clearly in the Spaniard's eyes today. Only the meeting with the king was staying his hand.

What Gabriel needed was to convince the king that they needed him. That even in knowing Iceland as the place she was last headed for, that she was extremely difficult to track, as his men could attest to. His mind spun with the thoughts, grasping any plan he could come up with. Yes, if he could convince Ferdinand that the only way to find Alexandria was through him, then he just might have a chance.

He felt for her last letter, took a shaking breath to find it still in the inner pocket of his waistcoat. It was the only thing he still had after he'd been ambushed and taken. They'd taken everything else down to his boots, but somehow they hadn't found this.

It was still there.

It was his only chance.

Chapter Seventeen

Alex took shallow puffs of the damp air as they followed a narrow path down, down into the mine, deep
into the earth's depths. The single light from Valdi's lantern swung back and forth in a reckless way. What if it
should go out? She shivered at the thought of complete
darkness in this place. They could be lost forever and no
one would ever know what had happened to them.

She paused, clinging to the rough rock wall with one
hand. What if her parents were down here, decaying
in some hidden crack or hole? What if Valdi had killed
them and was leading her and John to that same demise?
She looked over her shoulder at Valdi. He scowled at
her and motioned her to keep moving. Oh, dear. What
had she gotten them into?

A little farther and she heard the dripping of water.

"Here now," Valdi stayed her with his arm, "watch
your step. We've come to the veins of crystal, but there's

a pool of water under them and mud so thick you would never get out if you had the misfortune to step in it."

Alex shrank back against the cave wall, points of jagged rock piercing into her back and shoulders. She suppressed a small squeak, pressing her lips together in stubborn determination instead. "If only it weren't so dark. I fear I can't see well enough to see the crystal veins."

She pressed harder against the cave wall as Valdi passed her on the narrow path. He fumbled around with something and then a flash of light came from his hand. He held it up and lit a rush that had been bored into the wall. He circled the pool, lighting three more. Light flooded the area as it caught fire, a thin trail of smoke drifting toward the cave's tall ceiling.

Alex looked around and gasped.

A muffled word of exclamation came from John.

All around them the walls sparkled and flashed as the flickering light made the crystal veins come to life. Against the dark, wet cave walls, veins of crystal weaved like roots of a plant, some thick and some thin, twisting and twining together and running the length and breadth of the space around them and up and over their heads. In the middle of the cave lie a dark pool, silent, still and deadly with its thick muddy bottom. They clung to the narrow path that hugged the wall, looking up and around, avoiding that pool with every step.

"It's so beautiful."

"Many have thought so," Valdi said to Alex with a note of pride in his voice. "It is mined with small pick-axes and chisels that take much concentration and time. This crystal comes off in cleavages, lines so straight and pure that when you find them, it is easy to separate. We take the crystal out in blocks, like ice, that way."

"I wonder what Augusto wanted it for?" Alex asked aloud, not thinking what she was saying.

John gave her a sharp look, but Valdi flashed a glance over at her, eyebrows drawn down over his eyes. "The legend speaks of a machine. A very great invention he was building."

"What sort of machine? Do you know anything else?" All fear fell away in her curiosity.

"No." His tone was harsh. "We should return now."

Alex took a deep breath, knowing she wasn't going to get any more answers from him. She turned rather quickly, too quickly. The rock beneath her foot slipped out from under her. "Ahhh!" She reached for the wall but it was too late. Her arms windmilled as she teetered on the edge of the pool.

"Help!" She reached out into thin air as her other foot slipped. Moments later her back hit the pool with a great splash. Her heart pounded with the flailing of her arms.

"Alex!" John screamed, going down on his stomach on the path and reaching out his hand toward her.

He was too far. Alex's head went under the dark water.

"Don't touch the bottom!" She heard Valdi roar.

All thought left her except the command not to let her feet touch the bottom, not to do everything her instincts wanted her to do—use the bottom of the pool to push herself to the surface.

She keep her knees tucked up and pushed her arms up and down until her head popped up from the surface, treading water with hands circles and the small movements of peddling legs.

Taking a giant breath, she paddled in the smallest space she could make, her skirts heavy and working against her.

"Grasp this!" Valdi held a long, gnarled stick out to her. She swam toward it, keeping her feet high, and grasped hold with one hand. John joined Valdi as they pulled her toward them. As soon as she was close enough, John reached down for her, clasped her wrist, and dragged her up onto the rock floor.

He held her there, both of them breathing heavy, his arms around her dripping form, his head pressed against her wet head. "Thank God," he kept saying, over and over. "You silly fool, thank God."

"I warned you," Valdi barked in a rough voice. "You're as foolish as your parents. Let's go."

With slow and careful movements, Alex stood. She was soaked, cold and dripping…afraid, shaking from head to toe, her teeth chattering. "I-I-I'm s-s-sorry." So her parents had been here and had asked to see the mine too. But now didn't seem a good time to question Valdi about that.

"Keep hold of her until we get out of this area," Valdi ordered John and gestured with an angry sweep of his arm that they go before him.

John clung to her hand as they crept by Valdi, leading her out of the inner circle where the pool lay and up the steep incline toward the top and outside. Once outside the cold, stiff winds hit Alex like a bucket of icy water thrown into her face.

"Hurry to the house." John took her hand again and ran with her toward Valdi's house.

They burst through the door together. Johannes jerked awake, sat up, and rubbed his eyes. He took one look at them and grumbled, "Now what? What has happened?"

"Alexandria fell into the pool. We have to get her out of these wet clothes and warm and dry."

Valdi came up from behind them. His voice shook as he called out, "Ashanti, take her to your room and help her find something to change into that is warm. One of your mother's robes perhaps."

The girl paled, eyes widening, but nodded at her father and waved Alex to follow her.

Her room was small and crowded with furniture. Alex took off her sodden coat and let it drop to the floor where it lay in a wrinkled heap, the fur collar looking like a wet dog. With shaking hands she worked the buttons of her dress free and pushed it down to the floor also.

The girl held out a blanket, eyes wide. "You can dry off with this. I will go and fetch my mother's robe."

"My thanks." Alex tilted her head. "Is your mother here?"

The girl shook her head, a gaunt look of grief filling her deep brown eyes. "She died in the mine many months ago... Father hasn't moved her things yet."

She died in the mine? No wonder he hadn't wanted to take them there. And the fact that Valdi would allow her to touch her clothing, something they held so sacred, made Alex's eyes prick with tears. He wasn't a monster; he was a complicated man plagued by the grief of his wife's passing. She mustn't let her imagination run away with her so and misjudge people.

"I'm so sorry to hear that," Alex said to Ashanti.

When the girl left, Alex stripped off the rest of her clothing and rubbed life back into her cold skin with the woolen blanket. She was drying her hair and turned away as Ashanti entered with the robe. She felt the soft folds on her shoulders and grasped it, wrapping it around her and tying it with the long ribboned belt. It was a lovely robe of dark blue with a high collar and reaching almost to her ankles. Her hair hung long and wavy down her back as she turned a gentle smile on the girl. "Thank you. I'm feeling better already."

"You look pretty in it."

Alex smiled. "Shall we go in by the fire? I find myself in dire need of something warm to drink."

"I'll bring you a mug of warm goat's milk."

"That sounds perfect."

Alex took her hand and followed the thin frame of the girl back to the sitting room.

"Thank God. How do you feel?" John rushed to her side as if she were on the brink of death and guided her to a chair by the fire.

"I'll be fine, thank you, John." She looked over at Valdi who was staring at her in the robe with an ashen face. Sorrow and sympathy filled her chest until it ached. *Lord, help me say something gracious and kind, something with Your love in it for him.*

"You saved my life. I thank you."

He looked down and frowned at his feet. "I shouldn't have taken you there. I knew better. My wife...when your parents were here...she took them to the mine and fell into that pool. She didn't know how to swim and they were not able to save her as I saved you today."

Alex inhaled with shock. "You must hate them, my parents. Why would you let me see the mine?"

He shook his head, his eyes full of pain. "It was an accident, a terrible accident, and they were devastated to

be the cause. But their mission must have been important and that's why I showed it to you. After the funeral,
they purchased some crystal to take with them, paid
a great deal for it, but I don't know where they were
going. They didn't answer questions, just asked them."

Alex took a long breath and closed her eyes, suddenly
bone weary. They must have been horrified by such an
accident. And she was at another dead end. Had they
left Iceland after buying the crystals? If so, where would
they go? It could be anywhere in the world but one
place. The one place she longed to be.

Home on Holy Island.

ୡ ୡ ୡ ୡ

The next day, Alex and John rode along the southern
shoreline going west, the fjords of blue water and sailing
ships to the south and the hills and valleys of farmland
to the north. They passed fishing villages, little hamlets
with their churches, markets, and townsfolk's cottages,
mostly thatched-roofed huts in various sizes.

They rode slowly back toward Reykjavik where Alex
would have to decide once and for all if she would marry
John Lemon. Montague, unless something dire had happened, would certainly be there waiting for them. She
had run out of excuses. She had nearly run out of time,
and so she rode at a snail's pace, saying it was to rest the
horses so they wouldn't have to change them out. She'd
grown rather fond of Baen and was loathe to return her
to her owner.

Rubbing the soft spot between the mare's ears, she
sighed. A sad weight filled her chest and bowed her
shoulders. She'd failed. She didn't know what to do. She
had no idea where her parents might have gone next.

Dear Lord, I was so sure I was the one. The only one who would find them. Can't You give me some clue?

Nothing but the wind, softer and warmer here on the southern shores, answered her.

"You've done your best, Alexandria." John reached over and clasped her hand, giving it a tight squeeze. "You've done everything possible. You can't blame yourself."

Alex stared into his blue eyes, blue like the crater pools, like the sea that held this island in its palm. He would make a good husband. So why didn't she love him?

"I can't let them go."

John's mouth turned down, his eyes sincere in their regret. "You don't have to."

"But I do," Alex said so soft she felt the words more than heard them. "I can't go forward without letting them go."

John just squeezed her hand again and together they looked down the road ahead.

૎૎ ૎૎ ૎૎ ૎૎

Hours later, they came to a lonely looking farmstead and dismounted. It was growing late, the day ending in winter twilight. John tied the horses to a rail and led the way to the door. "Perhaps we can beg a bed for the night."

"And some food." Alex patted her stomach. "I'm ravenous."

"Yes, and some food. Take out some shillings in case."

Alex dug into her pocket and pulled out the ready coins. John knocked twice and then a third time. "I don't think anyone is home."

They backed up and noticed there wasn't any smoke coming from the fireplace, nor any animals in the pens. The fences were broken down and the place had a dilapidated look about it.

"I wonder if anyone even lives here." John tried the door. It was not locked and easily swung open.

Cobwebs and dust greeted them, but there was still a table and chairs and a fireplace ready with wood.

They worked together to feed the horses with some old hay and water them with a well that still had a half-broken pump handle. After lighting a fire, they cleaned off the table as best they could and took account of their supplies. They had a loaf of bread and some smoked salmon wrapped in a cloth. Alex had three little potatoes she washed and shoved into the coals. John had a round of goat cheese and a tin of crackers. When it was ready, they spread it out and gazed across the table at each other. "We'll not starve this night," John said with a wink.

"No indeed." Alex grinned and took a bite of fish.

"I must say, Lady Alex, you are looking fine this evening. Are those new jewels around your neck, or is it your skin that is so luminous?"

Alex hooted a laugh. "La, my lord. If your tongue was any glibber, there would be notices out for your capture. Have you broken many hearts with such talent?"

John lifted his brows. "None that can shine a candle on the present company, my lady." He leaned toward her and traced his fingertips along the side of jaw. "I've never met anyone like you."

His voice was suddenly serious and intent. Alex held her breath, trapped beneath his gentle exploring fingers on her face. She closed her eyes and drifted on the feeling, drifting and floating and…seeing another's face.

The Duke of St. Easton.

Tears struck from beneath the cloak of her closed lids. She saw his raven's hair, short and close to his head. She saw his startling green eyes, penetrating, looking deep into her through his black demimask at the masquerade ball. She felt his strong hands clasping hers in the dance, moving her body around the crowded ballroom in an arc of grace that made her float, and yet at the same time feel safely moored to something stronger than herself. She felt John's breath as he leaned closer. She felt John's lips touch hers and imagined they were *his*.

She reared back, breathing hard. "I can't marry you."

John's face turned dark and thunderous. "What? Why not?"

"I'm so sorry…but I…can't go through with it. I just can't marry you."

She rose, knocking over her chair in her haste, turned from the pain in his eyes, and fled into the night.

Chapter Eighteen

*Blessed Father, holy God, I implore You to act on our behalf.
I will do anything You want if You will only save her. Even
unto my death. I will keep my silence and die if it will protect her. Anything. Please. Save Alexandria from evil, save
her from harm in whatever form it comes. And if it be Your
will that she marry John...ah, even that, all knowing and
merciful God, let it be done according to Your will.*

Gabriel stood outside the king's throne room praying while he waited to be called inside for his audience
with the king. He balanced on one foot and then the
other, trying to ignore the aching and bruised body that
spasmed and bled and hardly seemed his anymore. He'd
never been so thin and weak and could hardly recognize the broken man he'd become. He prayed he would
remain upright for this audience, this test with the king
of Spain. King Ferdinand VII had a volatile reputation,
and Gabriel could only hope he was having one of his
better days.

At a signal from a liveried footman, he was ushered into the ornate throne room. Walls of crimson velvet, gilded frames and furniture, gold everywhere. The ceiling was covered in fresco paintings of gods and goddesses and the sprawling kingdoms of Spain.

Ferdinand sat in one of two thrones on a raised dais, enormous bronze lions on either side of the stage. He watched Gabriel enter with narrowed eyes, toying with the scepter in his hand.

Gabriel came forward and grimaced as he bowed low over his leg. He would not be able to hear the king give him permission to rise so he hurried out the explanation, gaze trained at the carpet. "Your Highness, I must confess to being unable to hear and beg use of a speaking book to converse with you."

Gabriel peeked up from beneath his thick lashes and saw the man wave him up. Standing made a wave of pain radiate down his back causing him to suck in a bracing breath, beads of sweat forming on his upper lip. He steadied himself, holding his back straight with little but pure vein-pumping terror and gritted-teeth determination, waiting, ever watchful of the other men in the room while Ferdinand ordered a desk to be brought in and for one of his attendants to be seated next to where Gabriel stood with paper and ink.

The king's first words were a new kind of shock. "The Duke of St. Easton indeed. I am shocked by your appearance. Are you always so ill kept?" The king's brows rose high on his forehead, almost touching the long, brown, curling wig he wore.

Gabriel craned his neck to read the words and then ground his teeth together. "I apologize, Your Majesty. I was not given time to…freshen up before our appointment."

"I shall have to speak to Didacus about that." Ferdinand flicked a piece of lint from his golden sleeve. "No sense treating our prisoners like animals." He clasped his hands together around the scepter and leaned forward, staring hard at Gabriel. "They tell me you know something of this manuscript of Augusto de Carrara's. Is this true?"

Gabriel read the last words thrust out to him and then bowed his head in acknowledgment of the fact. "I know of it. I've seen the partial manuscript King George has in his possession. To my knowledge the partial plans have done little good for anyone. No one knows what sort of machine they are meant to create."

"Precisely. And that is why I must have the original." He banged the scepter on the floor in a child's fit of anger. "There is a rumor that treasure hunters have been hired to find it and that they are the only ones who have gotten close. My men tell me they have gotten very close to its discovery. What do you know about that?"

Gabriel took a breath, his heart roaring, the only sound he could hear. "If you are referring to the Featherstones, then yes, I know they were hired to find it, but I have heard no rumors that they did. I only know they are supposedly dead. They have not been heard from in over a year."

"And you believe this is true? That they are dead?" Ferdinand steepled his fingers and stared at Gabriel over them.

"I have no reason to believe otherwise." He held his breath waiting for Alexandria's name to be brought up.

"But not everyone shares your view, do they? What of their daughter? Their only child and heir."

"I was given the wardship of Alexandria Featherstone, that is true. More proof that the regent believes her parents are dead."

"But what of Alexandria? She seems to believe them alive, doesn't she?"

Gabriel shrugged. "She is young and doesn't want to believe the truth. She will accept it sooner or later."

"I have reports that she is talented like her parents, that she is following their trail, hoping to catch up to them."

Gabriel scoffed, letting the doubt and his disdain of the idea fill his level green eyes. "The imagining of a child."

Ferdinand narrowed his eyes. "Or she knows something that we don't."

Gabriel's stomach flipped over. He closed his eyes briefly to focus himself, stretching out internally for God's presence and wisdom. "That is unlikely since the regent has ordered her back to London under my care. She is to have a season and pick a husband. If England thought she knew something, the regent would let her continue her search, don't you think?"

"I think you have smooth tongue, St. Easton. I think you have more at stake than a girl's fantasies, and I think that will become very useful to me."

It was as if the floor had dropped out beneath him. Ferdinand had seen into his heart. He somehow knew that the Duke of St. Easton had fallen in love with Alexandria Featherstone. It was time for the letter, the one letter she had sent him from Iceland that hinted of an attachment toward him.

"I will tell you where she was last known to be if you allow me to lead the search and go after her."

"Impossible. You will tell me where she is regardless. You were on the verge of it last night so I hear."

Gabriel ignored the barb, reached into his pocket, and pulled out the letter. "She hasn't been easy to run down, Your Majesty, as I'm sure Didacus and your men will tell you. But she will come willingly to me. I am the only one she will come to. I am the only one who can find her." He held out the letter. "Here is the proof."

At the king's nod, one of the attendants took the letter and passed it into Ferdinand's hand. Everyone in the room stood as though statues, waiting while he read it.

Gabriel read it along with him, having memorized every line.

> My dearest guardian duke,
> I have smuggled out this letter in secret as my now-fiancé, John Lemon, would be devastated to know I am writing to you. When I saw you had come for me on the docks of Dublin's shore and I was finally able to see your face, I was overcome with feelings I have never felt before. I do not know what you planned to do should you have me within your grasp, but I think because of my lack of faith, both in you and in God, I have made a terrible blunder. When John presented the idea of marriage, I was desperate to continue my journey to find my parents. He is so encouraging and helpful on that account that I confess I leapt at the chance, not due to feelings of everlasting love for him, although I do care for him. Oh, I am not saying this as I wish to! My dear duke, I think I have made a terrible mistake. I desperately need your advice and I miss your letters dreadfully. I confess that I hope you haven't

*given up on finding me. I just need more time to find
my parents. Please trust me in this.*

*You can still write to me. Please write to me in
Reykjavik.*

Yours,

Alexandria

The king's eyes dipped down to the last line and
then hovered there. "Pretty, is she?" Gabriel didn't have
to look at the speaking book to understand that comment. The king flicked the letter back toward the attendant who brought it back to Gabriel. His fingers closed
around it, like a man starving, its sustenance as food to
his soul.

"Of course." There was no sense denying it.

The king chuckled. *"Amor!"* He clapped his hands
in an overly dramatic way. "What would the world be
without it? And it can be so very useful." He stared at
Gabriel, eyes dark with power. "Very well, St. Easton.
You may accompany my men to this place where she
has gone. You are to bring her back to me and I will
equip her to continue her journey to find her parents."

"You won't harm her?" Gabriel asked, lips drawn
down and scowling for good measure. He had no intention of bringing her back to Ferdinand, but if he had to,
he would ask such a question. He would demand her
safety.

"Of course not. She is my prize. I shall treat her with
every"—he waved a hand in a circular pattern in the
air—"dignity." He smiled a humorless smile.

Like the dignity with which Gabriel had been treated?
He clenched his jaw at the thought.

"And where, exactly, did you last see her, St. Easton? You've kept us on tenterhooks long enough."

"Last I saw her she was on a ship…a ship sailing to Iceland."

He threw back his head and laughed. "That is the last place on earth I would have thought to look."

Gabriel shrugged. "I have no idea why her parents went there, but she discovered that they did."

"Well, see that you dress warmly, St. Easton. It sounds like a ghastly place."

ॐ ॐ ॐ ॐ

Back on a ship.

God help him.

Gabriel felt for the ginger root in his pocket that he had paid one of his jailers a silver button to attain for him days before they had boarded the *San Cristobel*, a twenty-gunned galleon of clean lines and hearty hull. Didacus, the tall Spaniard who had been following Alexandria, and his stubby companion, *El Gato*, stood to one side watching the loading of the ship, watching him most especially.

Gabriel swung a dark look on them, his hair, having grown longer since captivity, swinging in his eyes. He shook it away. How he would like a sword to thrust through their wicked chests, but he had to play their game to its bitter end. He had the king's permission to lead the excursion to find Alexandria, but that didn't mean he had any power. No, they still treated him like a prisoner. At least he'd convinced them not to tie his hands. Why, he'd asked in his most condescending tone, the purr of the panther in his eyes, would he attempt to escape when they had the same goal in mind? A man in love would do anything for his beloved, wouldn't he? It wasn't far from the truth.

But he mustn't turn into a sniveling invalid because of the blasted seasickness. If he lost any more weight... well, it didn't bear thinking of. *God, I know I've already asked for so much, but I really could use a miracle here.*

Sometimes he thought he was going mad, not really knowing if God was hearing him or if he was just talking to the wind. God's way of answering his prayers thus far seemed to be not helping at all. He supposed Jesus's disciples must have felt that way when they saw their rabbi murdered on the cross. They must have doubted everything they had done for the past three years with this man who they thought was God. How could something turn out good, perfect even, when it looked like everything was failing so miserably?

As if to validate his thoughts, an unknown sailor shoved him hard from behind and sent him sprawling on the deck. He looked up from the weathered boards to see laughter erupting from the faces around him. He turned over and sprang to his feet, wary of a trap forming in the glittering eyes of the seamen circling him.

One man pulled forth a wicked-looking cutlass and sprang toward him. Did they mean to kill him? What was happening now?

Gabriel swung to the right, just dodging the blade. He turned with a neat twist, got behind the man, and pulled his sword arm back so hard and fast that he felt the pop and then watched with both pleasure and dread at what was to come as the weapon fell. The man slumped to the deck in agony. Gabriel turned, looking back and forth at the crowd, his heart slamming in his chest, ready for the next one.

A sudden movement from one side brought Didacus to the center of the crowd. He was shouting at the men, his eyes burning with rage. They fell back while he grasped Gabriel, and Gabriel let him, gambling on the fact that Didacus was protecting him from a mob beating. Didacus hauled Gabriel to the foremast and directed him to be tied to it.

As they set sail, the punishment for injuring one of the sailors sank through Gabriel's frantic mind. A big man, dark with hair all over his body, came forward. Gabriel swallowed as the man stripped off his shirt, grinned a slow, evil grin at him, and took up a long, leather whip.

The wind pushing against the sails, they floated out toward the open sea, and Gabriel gazed up at the clear blue sky and tensed his body as the first of his twenty-five lashes began across his back.

Fresh pain—tearing, ripping flesh pain—flashed in bright, agonizing lights of white behind Gabriel's closed eyelids. His throat worked and his whole body cried out to God—a silent, writhing, pain-cry song. He was drowning. This beating would end him, he knew it. He clinched his teeth and cried out in a loud voice, "God, where are You?"

Sing.

Sing? It made no sense and made him so angry he bucked against the ropes. *Sing? That's the best You have for me?* He shouted it from every part of his being.

Yes, sing.

Another hiss of the lash, agony spreading through his whole being and he complied. He sang the first song that sprang to his mind.

Be thou, O God, exalted high;
And, as thy glory fills the sky,

So let it be on earth display'd,
Till thou art here, as there, obey'd.

To take me they their net prepar'd,
And had almost my soul ensnar'd;
But fell themselves, by just decree,
Into the pit they made for me.

He laughed at the words and bellowed them as loud as he could, the sting of the whip pushed to the back corners of his mind.

O God, my heart is fix'd, 'tis bent,
Its thankful tribute to present;
And, with my heart, my voice I'll raise,
To thee, my God, in songs of praise.

Awake, my glory; harp and lute,
No longer let your strings be mute;
And I, my tuneful part to take,
Will with the early dawn awake.

Colors burst around him...so vivid, so bright that he wondered that they couldn't see them. Like light shields they held his spirit—a resonate, humming being that wept and shouted praise—in a sacred place that felt little pain.

Thy praises, Lord, I will resound
To all the list'ning nations round;
Thy mercy highest Heav'n transcends;
Thy truth beyond the clouds extends.

Be Thou, O God, exalted high;
And, as thy glory fill the sky,
So let it be on earth display'd,
Till thou are here, as there, obey'd.

Gabriel clung to consciousness, singing the words of the old hymn over and over as the whip lashed bloody lines of murder into his bare back. He couldn't hear the words and he didn't know if anyone else could hear him, but as he sang he basked in color, all the colors of the rainbow.

He closed his eyes and felt his cries of agony seeming from a faraway place, interposing the song in waves of red, like the blood dripping down his back. Yet he sang. To stay alive. He sang and survived with the colors.

Chapter Nineteen

"Alexandria! Alexandria!"

She jerked awake to the early morning light, the rushing waters of the nearby waterfall where she had stopped to rest and think about what she had done gushing like music in the background. It was John. And he sounded panicked.

She stood and mounted her horse, heading back toward the road. There was no sense in running from him. She had to face what she'd said. They had to decide what to do next.

With the dawning light she could just see him come around a bend in the road. She took a deep breath, watching him gallop up to her. "Thank God." He reined in and stopped. He was hatless and his blond hair was wind tousled. His face was tight with a pained reserve that made her heart ache. He reached over and grasped her arm. "Don't ever frighten me like that again. I've been looking for you for hours. I thought I'd lost you to some horrible misfortune!"

"I followed the road. There was nothing to fear. I found a pleasant spot of soft grass with a waterfall nearby and fell asleep to the sounds of it."

John rubbed his face with a hand and took a great breath. "Alex, it's too cold for you to be sleeping in the open. We can talk about what happened later. Let's get you to some shelter and a warm fire."

She had to agree that she was cold and damp from sleeping on the ground. And thirsty. She was sure both she and her pretty mare were hungry and thirsty enough for some concern. That he still cared so much after what she had done to him made her feel like a wretch. He was probably cold and hungry too. "Yes, let's find an inn."

They continued west as the sun dawned pink on the horizon, the dark forms of the mountains surrounding them in the background. The road led through the small village of Selfoss that looked to be waking up for the day. The main road had a few businesses, one with a sign with a picture of a ram on it. It was the only place that looked like it might be an inn.

Alex dismounted, unable to look John directly in the eye, and followed him to the door. It was locked and the place looked dark, but he banged on it anyway. The owner, hair askew and still sleepy-eyed opened the door.

"Good day, sir. We are traveling through and are look-ing for some food and a place to rest for a few hours. Do you have such for sale here?"

"Yes, come in." He backed away and waved them inside and then showed them to the common room with assurance that breakfast would soon be ready.

Alex sat across from John, seeing his tired eyes and the tight lines on either side of his mouth. His coat was rumpled and he didn't look his usual dapper self. She wanted to say she was sorry, but that felt too small in the face of what she'd said, all that she had done. And anyway, what good would it do? He didn't want her apology. He wanted her for a wife and she knew, after pondering it the night through, that she couldn't give him that.

"Ah, here we are now." The innkeeper, introducing himself as simply Hans, came back scant moments later with two large bowls of steaming porridge and a pitcher of milk. "And whom might I have the pleasure of serving this fine day?"

Alex hurried to introduce them before John said they were married. "This is Lord John Lemon from Dublin, a dear friend of mine, and I am Lady Alexandria Featherstone."

"Featherstone!" The man reared back from pouring a mug of milk, sloshing spills onto the table. "Oh, dear."

"Is something amiss?"

"You haven't heard? You're the lady from England, aren't you? Looking for your parents?"

"Why yes, yes I am."

"The prince regent of England is looking for you! Haven't you heard? Soldiers everywhere." Hans woke up in an instant, eyes wide and swinging back and forth between them.

"Sir, what exactly are you saying?" John's blond brows lowered over his eyes and his voice turned low and serious.

"The king's soldiers are in Reykjavik as we speak, my lord. They have the town under siege searching for the lady here." He leaned in, fear lighting his eyes and clutching the milk pitcher to his chest. "There have been all manner of threats if the townspeople don't produce you. Of course, no one knows where you are, so how is anyone to obey?"

"They aren't…hurting people, are they?" Alex leaned forward and gripped the man's arm.

"Surely not." John scoffed at the idea, shaking his head. "Trying to frighten them, most likely."

But the innkeeper turned white. "The townsfolk there have been threatened for sure. People aren't leaving their houses. I found out from Gunterson, the man who brings the mail. They let him leave to spread the word in the neighboring towns."

Alex swallowed hard thinking of the Magnussons and the Johanssons. They had been so kind and helpful to her. She thought of her parents and the fact that she was at a dead end and didn't know where to go from here. She'd promised the duke that if she came to a dead end, she would come to him in London. And she couldn't deny that she wanted to see him again, to see if the feelings she was fighting were real or imaginary, to see if he was the same man of his letters. "We have to go back. I have to turn myself over to them."

"You would do that?" John's voice lowered into a harsh whisper as he leaned toward her. "Alex, the prince regent will put you under the duke's authority unless we are wed. Is that what you want?"

"I-I already told you." Alex looked up at the innkeeper. "Please, if we could just have two rooms, to rest up a bit and for our horses to be taken care of and rested, I will pay you well and then be on my way to Reykjavik and turn myself over to the king's soldiers. I give you my word. I do not want anyone to suffer on my behalf."

The man hesitated, looking from one to the other, and then nodded. "I believe you are the fine lady I have heard that you are. I will prepare the rooms and see that your horses are taken care of. Be gone by morning." He backed away with an odd stare and left them.

As hungry as Alex had been, she had little appetite now. John sat stiffly beside her making her feel even more wretched. She had used him. She had given him false hope and broken his heart. But what could she say? She reached over and put her hand on top of his. "I'm sorry," she whispered, feeling helpless. She held his pained gaze for a long moment.

John stood and bowed toward her. "As am I." He turned his back on her and left the room. She watched his tall, handsome form walk away with a lump of tears in her throat, not knowing where he was going or if she would even see him again.

God, forgive me. I truly have made a mess of everything.

ૹ ૹ ૹ ૹ

Hours later, a knock on her door woke her from a sound sleep. She sat up and ran her fingers through her tangled hair, having been too distraught to braid it before dropping off into a deep sleep. It was dark outside her window. She must have slept for hours. Hurrying to the door she opened it to find John, one hand against the door frame, swaying and glassy eyed.

"John, what are you doing? Are you all right?"

He shook his head in an exaggerated gesture. "Not aright a'tall." He stumbled toward her and jabbed a finger into her chest. His slurred speech came out in clipped staccato. "Why won't you marry me?" The last word was a near shout.

"Shhhh." Alex grasped his hand, pulled him into the room, and shut the door behind him. "You've been drinking!"

"Maybe…maybe I have." He swayed toward her and then straightened. He held out a cup toward her. "I brought you something."

"I don't want that. What is it?" Alexandria took the cup and smelled it. It didn't smell like any liquor she knew of. She took a little sip thinking it tasted like bitter tea. "Ugh. What is this?"

"That's tea for you, love. I've been drinking ale, of course."

"I'm not your love and I don't want it." Alex shoved the cup toward his chest.

"But I made it just for you. Come on, Alex…ander…ia…please?" He leaned closer and gave her a pout reminding her of a little boy. The smell of strong spirits on his breath took her breath away. He nearly fell against her. "Take a moment and chat with me, won't you? You owe me that, at least, don't you think?"

She sighed. Maybe if she drank some of his awful tea he would go and find his bed and sleep off the effects of his ale. From the few experiences she had had with drunken fools, she'd found it was better to go along with them when at all possible. She took a few sips from the cup, grimaced, and then set it on the bedside table. "It's awful. Did you make it yourself?"

"Yes! Yes, just for you. I badgered the whole kitchen down there for the right ingredients. Just like my mother used to make it. You have to finish it, love."

She shook her head and then sighed, picked it back up, and drained the cup in one long swallow. "There. Now, John, what do you want?"

"Alexandria..." His voice trailed off, his hand came up and brushed against her hair. "It wasn't just the money, you know. I really do love you."

The money? Did he think she thought he was marrying her for her money? Did he think that if he assured her he was not, she would change her mind? "John, I know you love me, but you need to go to your room, *quietly*, and sleep. We will talk about this in the morning."

He took a step closer and grasped hold of her shoulders. She tried to back away but he was too strong. His grip tightened. He brought her against his chest and mumbled, "So beautiful, you're so beautiful, Alex." His head came down and his lips crushed against hers.

"John." She tried to back away and talk against the pressure. "Stop it. You're not thinking clearly. Stop right now."

But he didn't stop. He nudged her with that sweet, teasing smile on his lips, almost gently, but too strong for her to get free, toward the bed. He leaned over her, swaying and smiling, kissing her face and then forcing her back, down on the bed. He landed on top of her with a whoosh of breath. "Mmmm, so soft and lovely," he murmured into her hair.

"John, I will scream if you don't get off me and leave this instant."

"No, no, none of that. Dearest Alex." His lips clamped down over her mouth, kissing her like he'd never kissed her before, deep and consuming, too consuming. She couldn't breathe! She kicked out and heard a little grunting laugh come from his chest. "I love you, Alex. Love you, only you. I'll be a good husband, I promise. We'll find your parents; we will together! That duke doesn't love you like I do." He moved over her until she could hardly draw breath, encompassing all but her arms. "Let me show you how much I love you."

Fear spiraled through her. He wasn't listening. "John, listen to me. Look at me. John!"

He looked at her, blinking hard as if to focus. Finally he sighed, seeming too tired to argue. "All right. We'll just lie here a moment 'til you feel better."

"Until *I* feel better?" Alex tried to squirm away. He pulled her back against his chest and, after a few minutes, started snoring.

Thank God. She would wait a few minutes, just to be sure he was sound asleep, and then leave him in her bed and go and find another.

It was a good plan. She meant to sneak away from under the tight grip of his arms, but a slow creeping lethargy came over her limbs, from her shoulders to her feet. She shook her head, trying to clear it. She lost track of time, floating it seemed, lying with her eyes half-closed as a wonderful warmth seeped into every fiber of her being. And then she drifted into a deep sleep.

Chapter Twenty

Gabriel woke with a jerk, rolled over onto his stomach, and reached for the ginger root hidden under his pillow. He closed his eyes against the pain of stretching the delicate, healing skin on his back, concentrating instead on chewing the ginger before he opened his eyes. He had found it helped, somehow, getting some of it in his stomach before he opened his eyes. A few minutes passed while he chewed on it and then Ryan entered the room. He was one of the few Englishmen on board the ship, used for translating and now nursing, though Gabriel still couldn't figure out how he had accomplished that feat.

Matter-of-fact and efficient, he bade Gabriel to sit up and hold his arms out while he unrolled the bandages, took a look at his back, and then spread some new salve on the cuts. He wrapped fresh bandages around him and then stood back and cocked his head to one side with a thoughtful look on his face. "Healing nicely," he mouthed clearly, taking Gabriel's chin and studying his eyes. "How's the rest of you?"

"Sick to death of this stinking hellhole." Gabriel felt the rasp of his voice against his vocal chords and knew, beyond a shadow of a doubt, that he would have died without this man. That God had decided to save his life with a song and a pragmatic Englishman.

Ryan chuckled and handed him a cup of tea and bread and then, when he'd finished that, a bowl of broth with some rice in it. Gabriel ate it slowly wishing he could really talk to Ryan, ask him questions about how he ended up with these madmen, but they wouldn't allow them a speaking book so they were forced to make do with short sentences.

He had learned a little about Ryan Wrothwood though, enough to know he'd been in the Royal Navy and was from Cornwall. He'd probably been captured on some port of call and pressed into Spanish service. A thin, stately looking fellow, not the typical brawny choice when searching for a good sailor, but he was a good communicator and someone must have noticed that and had him captured. If Gabriel ever got out of here, he was going to take Ryan with him. The question was, could he risk speaking the idea aloud?

"How long until we dock at Reykjavik?

Ryan held up two and then three fingers for days. "Depending on the weather."

So they were almost there. They had been aboard the *San Cristobel* for over two weeks, and while his back wasn't the constant fiery agony of the first few days, it was still sore and tight with new skin knitting the strips of torn flesh back together. His back would never look the same, that was certain.

"Do we walk today? I need to regain my strength." Every day he was allowed on deck for a brief walk, but the jeers and violent-filled hatred he received from the crew made him uneasy to be on the top deck alone. If Ryan was available to walk with him, he went. If not, Gabriel roamed his tiny cabin like a caged cat, padding back and forth with darting, suspicious green eyes, wondering if at any moment they would burst in with new reasons to harm him.

Ryan nodded. "One hour." He took the empty dishes and turned to go.

"Wait." Gabriel lowered his voice, hoping he could still be heard. "Escape is paramount. I plan to find a way. You are welcome to come with me."

Ryan's gaze darted to the door and then back to Gabriel. He nodded and then took something from his pocket—a very small piece of paper and passed it over to Gabriel. He pressed a companionable hand on Gabriel's shoulder, squeezed, and nodded again, turned and left, locking the door as he always did behind him.

Gabriel sat back on the bed and opened the note.

Your Grace, I sense in you a desire to escape if the opportunity presents itself. If you are reading this then you have confirmed my suspicions. If we should have opportunity, I am willing to take the risk and hopefully make my way back to England with you. I will be looking for opportunities when we dock. Let us pray God provides one. Please destroy this after you have read it. Your faithful servant, Ryan Wrothwood

Thank God. Someone on his side. He bowed his head and prayed that God would have mercy and provide them the opportunity and means of escape. Then he tore off a little piece of the paper and placed it in his mouth. He chewed with a grim smile.

Compared with some of the fare they'd been giving him since his capture, it wasn't half bad.

☙☙ ☙☙ ☙☙ ☙☙

The day dawned early when the *San Cristobel* docked on Reykjavik's shores. Three soldiers burst into Gabriel's cabin, filling the small space with their muscled bodies and dark, scowling faces, demanding he come with them. He barely had a chance to throw on his shirt before they hauled him above to the foredeck where Didacus, resplendent in the Spanish uniform of black coat with tails, red waistcoat with gold buttons, a golden sash, and dark breeches stood ready to meet him. His cohort, El Gato, made the uniform look less stately, more like a tomato with a tricorn hat for a stem, but his eyes were equally hateful as he glared at Gabriel.

The Spanish soldiers shoved him in front of the two men. Gabriel stood straight and lifted his chin, refusing to acknowledge the ill treatment, acting as if he had come here on his own accord, in full health, with the power of the St. Easton name behind him. It was a bluff. But a bluff was all he had at the moment.

"We will be going ashore now." Didacus motioned with his hand toward the shore.

Gabriel nodded briefly that he understood. The first order of business was to find out if the regent's army was still here. If so, and he wouldn't be surprised if that were the case, then they had yet to locate Alexandria and it would be up to him to find her. If they had departed for England, then she was on her way or already there. But he must not let the Spanish know of this possibility. If Alexandria was in the regent's care and protection, they would no longer need him. That fact would make him as good as dead. And if the regent had her safely in England, then his only chance for any kind of future would be escape.

Didacus motioned to Ryan who was ready with pen and paper. He spoke instructions while the man wrote. Gabriel pressed his heels together and waited, the wind blowing his hair into his face. It hadn't been this long since he was a boy. He didn't like it long; it had too much curl in it. Even though waving locks were the fashion for some, it wouldn't behave well enough to suit him. He liked it short. Manageable. Within the confines of a quick brushing or raking of his fingers. What he wouldn't give for a haircut and shave.

He looked down and almost chuckled at his thoughts. His clothes were filthy, in tatters, his body thin and battered. Alexandria probably wouldn't recognize him if she saw him like this. He doubted his own mother would.

Finally, the paper was handed to him.

Didacus says you will be given one day in Reykjavik to find out if Alexandria is in the town. You will be closely guarded and watched so don't do anything stupid. He will allow you to disembark with a contingent of six soldiers, and you are to report back to the ship by nightfall. Do you understand?

"Do these soldiers speak English?" Gabriel asked Didacus. "I should like Ryan to accompany me to help

183

translate and write in the speaking book so I may question the residents."

El Gato spit toward Gabriel's shoes, missed, and scowled at him, saying something Gabriel was glad he couldn't make out. Didacus rattled off a stream of commands at Ryan and then nodded.

"I am to come with you, Your Grace."

"I would also like funds to tidy my appearance and for food and other expenses for the day."

Didacus smiled a humorless smile, brows raised as if he found the request amusing. He looked down his long nose and nodded though, took a purse from his pocket, and counted out some coins. "Going to make yourself pretty for her, St. Easton? I suppose that is part of the trap, isn't it?" He handed the coins over to Ryan. "He will keep them for you and see that you spend them wisely."

Gabriel ignored the barb and shrugged. "When do we leave?"

"As soon as you can be ready."

"How about now?"

"Fine."

Didacus walked up to him, reached out a gloved hand, and took hold of Gabriel's chin. He squeezed it hard, lifting it so his dark brown eyes narrowed and stared into Gabriel's gaze. With as much intention as he could manage, Gabriel lifted his dark lashes and put his notorious green eyes to use, narrowing his eyelids until they were green slits of steel, mimicking the wild stare of lethal contemplation—a panther on the hunt.

Didacus let go of him and took a step back. "Don't try anything…"

Gabriel's lip curled. He lifted his chin and kept the steady stare on him until Didacus turned his back and strode away.

ஃ ஃ ஃ ஃ

The inn in Reykjavik was crowded with British soldiers, eating and drinking, laughing, some playing cards, some grouped around the fire, heads together in conversation. Their presence answered Gabriel's first question. They hadn't found Alexandria yet. It was as he had suspected.

As their group of eight made their way inside, the English soldiers eyed the Spanish soldiers with distrust and vice versa. Some of the soldier's eyes lit on Gabriel with brief curiosity, thinking him a prisoner perhaps from his appearance.

Gabriel stared each of them in the eye, hoping for a familiar face, and sat at a long table next to Ryan. "You must spread the word of who I am among them. Find the commander and tell him I am a prisoner and the regent's confidant in the matter of Alexandria Featherstone and that they would do well to help us," he whispered.

Ryan nodded once. The Spanish soldiers watched them, two of them edging closer to hear any conversation.

A serving woman came over, eyes fearful as she looked from one to another of them. "I am afraid we are low on provisions, sirs. I can bring you drink and a bowl of fish stew. That is all I have."

Ryan wrote down what she said and what the men around them were saying. They agreed to the food. She started to leave but Gabriel brushed her sleeve with his hand, stopping her. "Madam." He gave her his best self-deprecating smile as he brought her attention round to him. "Do you have a barber in this town? I have been seasick and on a ship for a very long time. I would like a haircut and a shave."

She shook her head and then stopped, studying him. Ryan wrote: *No barber, but she says she cuts her husband and son's hair and she would be willing to cut yours if you like.*

"Yes, thank you. Can we do that soon? Now?"

"Let me get the food first." She left and came back a short time later with a tray of bowls, putting the steaming stew in front of each soldier. She turned toward Gabriel and motioned him to follow her up the stairs to the second floor.

Gabriel directed Ryan to tell the soldiers where he was going and then ignored them and whatever reaction they might have. It was known that Ryan had coin for a haircut so let them fuss; he was getting this done.

The stairs led to the family's private quarters, a well-kept common room that was comfortably furnished. The woman directed Gabriel to a chair by the fire and went to fetch the supplies, coming back with a razor, scissors, a bowl of warm water, and a towel.

Gabriel leaned his head back and closed his eyes as she lathered his face, the smell of soap so welcome his eyes began to swim from behind closed lids. He pushed the emotion aside, determined to use this situation to whatever advantage he could find.

With deft scrapes of the razor that spoke of years of experience, she shaved weeks of beard from his face and neck. He lay back and let the muscles of his face relax, trusting her. She made quick work of it and then placed a steaming towel on his face, patting it, leaving it a moment before rinsing off the soap.

Heaven. The first real comfort since his abduction. She said something, he could tell by the vibration of her near him, but his eyes were too relaxed to open and try to make it out. She gave him a moment and then touched his shoulder. He opened his eyes.

"Your hair?" she asked, blond eyebrows raised.

"Short, if you please." He sat taller, looking aside for a moment. "I cannot hear you. Trouble with my ears." It was getting easier to say to strangers. He didn't have the strength to care what they thought about it anymore. She set to work, waves of black hair falling to the floor around him.

He took a breath and decided to risk it. "Madam, I would like to ask you a question. It's very important, and while you will have no reason to believe me, I need you to trust me."

She paused in clipping his hair, looked at him with a level glance, and nodded.

"I am looking for Alexandria Featherstone. As I am sure you already know, the British soldiers down there are looking for her as well. I have come with a troop of Spanish as their prisoner but I am British. I mean her no harm. I am a friend of hers…her guardian. I am the Duke of St. Easton."

She backed up, stared at his face, and then rushed from the room coming back scant seconds later with paper and pen.

Gabriel nodded toward the paper. "You must write quickly. My guards will not give us much time."

She dipped the quill and bent to the task, the pen flying over the paper. *Alexandria mentioned you. She left Reykjavik over two weeks ago, headed to the Dimmu borgir, the Black Castles, looking for her parents. I do not know what has become of her, but the British soldiers have searched all around this area and have not found her. They have spread rumors that they are being cruel to the citizens of Reykjavik in the hopes she would hear of it and come back to save us from further harm. I fear their plan may work as she has become a dear friend to us. Do you also want to take her back to England?*

Gabriel read it and then wadded it into a ball and threw it into the fire. "Yes, but under my protection. I will keep her safe and find a way to keep looking for her parents. Madam, she has no idea the depths of danger she is in. There are many countries that want to find her parents, powerful leaders, kings. I am here to protect her but I need help. I have to escape the Spanish and I believe I can with the British soldiers' help. Can you spread the word? We must make a plan to deal with the Spanish ship in the harbor. There are nearly fifty soldiers aboard it, and they will have no issue with destroying this town if they don't get what they want."

As he spoke her eyes grew wide with fear. "I shall do everything I can to help. Your Grace, Lady Featherstone saved my son's life. I would do anything for her."

Gabriel started to speak, but she sprang up and started cutting his hair again. He wadded the paper into a ball and shoved it up the sleeve of his shirt as three Spanish soldiers came into the room. The woman spoke to them. They glared at her and Gabriel and then went back downstairs. Gabriel winked at the woman. She finished his hair, set down the scissors, and brushed the hair from his neck.

She stood back and looked at him, surveying her work, a small smile playing across her lips. "You look much better."

"What is your name?"

She sat back down at the table and wrote. *Ana and my husband is Hans Magnusson. Tomas, our only son, was found by Alexandria. He had climbed into the church belfry and a beam of wood fell on his leg trapping him there for two days. No one would have noticed the white strip of cloth clinging to the stone from the belfry window. But Alexandria saw the piece missing from his pillow casing and thought he might have made a flag with it. We owe her everything.*

A flash of pride streaked through him upon reading what Alexandria had done. God love her; everyone who knew her did.

There was only one more pressing question he had to ask. "Ana, was there a man with her? Are they engaged to be married?"

"Yes. There is a man with her. John Lemon." She looked up from the words, pinning him with a glance full of understanding. "To my knowledge, she has not married him yet, but he is pressing her to do so soon."

Gabriel nodded.

He walked over to a small mirror hanging on the wall and raked his fingers through his hair making it stand on end. Who was this gaunt creature staring back at him? John's handsome face flashed through his mind.

If Gabriel got to her in time, would she even consider him?

Chapter Twenty-One

Alex opened her eyes against the pounding fog in her head and turned over with a groan. Why did she feel so wretched? She sat up to get out of bed, threw back the covers, and jolted awake at what she saw. John. Still asleep and lying next to her. The memory of the night before flooded back to her.

What had they done?

Her heart raced as her gaze flew over John's body. She had thrown the blanket off him too because it now covered only his feet. Panic rose to her throat as her gaze traveled up his naked form. Hadn't he been clothed when they fell asleep? She had her nightgown still on, but he could have easily lifted it... Why couldn't she remember anything? She closed her eyes and made a panic-filled sound.

"John. Wake up!" Her voice was a harsh whisper.

John blinked awake, reared up as Alex scrambled out of bed and stood near the door, keeping her eyes averted. "John, why don't you have any clothes on? What have you done?" Tears flooded her eyes as the cold air snapped her back stiff.

He rubbed his face and groaned. "Are you all right?"

"All right? Am I all right? How can you ask that?" She hissed the words too loud but didn't care at that moment who might hear. "Did you…?"

"I don't know. It would appear so."

A cry came from Alex's throat.

"Alex, no…please." He stood and reached for his pants. "I-I drank too much. I didn't know what I was doing… Alex come here."

"Don't come near me, do you hear me? Why would you do such a thing?"

He came around and tried to pull her into his arms, but she pushed him back with an angry grunt. *"Don't touch me."*

"We'll order you a hot bath. That'll make you feel better." He ran his fingers through his hair and looked longingly, lovingly at her. He looked sorry too.

She backed away from him, raging at him in a shattered voice. "Just stay away from me. I will never forgive you for this."

He stood in only his breeches, his wide chest, nearly hairless, moving in and out as if he'd been running, his blond hair a tousled mess, so handsome and so wretchedly deceiving. Had he planned this, or was it an act of desperation that sounded reasonable to a drunk man? Alex suspected the latter but it didn't make her feel much better.

"Alex, please. I thought that you meant to marry me now."

"I said nothing of the sort." She thought back, remembered how languid, how relaxed and happy she'd become. Her eyes widened. "The tea." She walked over, snatched up the cup from the bureau, and sniffed it. There were still brown dregs in the bottom giving off a sharp odor.

She walked over to him and pushed the cup into his bare chest. "There was something in this tea, wasn't there? You knew I would have never married you... you knew that so you drugged me. Of all the horrible, deceiving tricks." She hit him in the shoulder, her face crumpling.

John pulled her into his chest and wrapped his arms around her tight enough that she couldn't hit him any longer. "You don't understand. I love you, Alex. I need your money, yes. That was the beginning of it. When I heard you are the ward of the Duke of St. Easton, I knew that he would place a huge dowry on you, he's so rich. I swear I didn't know about your fortune until later, when I read that letter, but it doesn't matter. I love you so much. I couldn't just let you walk away."

He held her away from him and looked down at her with that boyish, blue-eyed sincerity that had always charmed her. "Please. I'll be the best husband. I'll do anything for you. We will travel the world looking for your parents. Or become treasure hunters ourselves. Anything you want. I'll protect you, Alex."

"Protect me?" she hissed in a broken whisper. "How can you even think that after this night? You...you are a monster."

His eyes hardened into blue flint. "You have no choice but to marry me now."

"Oh yes I do. I don't have to marry anyone—ever."

One hand tightened on her back while the other one came around and pressed against her lower stomach. "What if you carry my child? Would you make it illegitimate?"

"I'll get rid of it."

They both sucked in a shocked breath.

"No. I didn't mean it. I could never do *that.*" A shudder overwhelmed her and she collapsed against John's chest, sobbing.

"Shhh." He stroked her back, bending his head over her in a protective embrace. "Shhh. I'll love you my whole life. I'll give you everything you could ever want. Please. Alexandria. Please be my wife."

But I'm in love with someone else! She saw the duke's face against her closed lids and turned her face, her cheek lying wet with tears against John's bare skin. Maybe she deserved this. He wasn't a bad man, not any worse than she was, certainly. She had used John as a convenience when she needed him and he needed her, needed her money anyway. She didn't doubt that he loved her. She didn't doubt he would try to make her happy all her days.

She just doubted that he could.

"Alex, listen to me. As soon as you are…ready, feeling better, we'll leave for Reykjavik. But we must enter the town and go to the Magnussons without alerting the soldiers. I want to be married before we turn ourselves over to them, a small ceremony at the inn, do you understand?"

Alex nodded, a numb sense of nothingness lodged in her chest. What choice did she have?

"Good." He pulled her back into his arms and kissed the top of her head, holding her close and whispering into her ear, "Everything will be all right."

Then why did it feel like nothing would ever be all right again?

೩೪ ೩೪ ೩೪ ೩೪

Hours later, the sun riding low against the horizon in a glowing orb with pink-tinged clouds hovering around them, John and Alex trotted into Reykjavik. She wore her red cloak with the hood pulled up and hanging low over her face against the wind and the stares of anyone who might be about. John wore his hat low over his forehead as well. They had planned to avoid the main road and circle around to the back of the inn, and it was a good thing. There were signs of soldiers everywhere— more horses, noise, and people roaming the streets than when they'd been in Reykjavik before.

"Let's go to Svein's blacksmith shop first. It should be empty since he's gone, and the inn may be full of soldiers. We can send word to Hans and Ana from there."

Alex nodded, the tears that had been close all day rising to the surface again. The places that surrounded her heart and core of her being felt raw and ravished. As if she was no longer herself and didn't know who she was anymore. She turned her head away before John could see her eyes, wiping the tears off her cheeks with the back of her hand as soon as he looked away.

The blacksmith's shop was dark and empty as John suspected. They dismounted and led their horses to the back door. It was locked tight. "Here, hold the reins. I think I can pry one of the boards loose."

Alex shivered in the dim light holding the horses while John pried up some nails with a flat rock. After a few minutes, he had removed several boards from the door, leaving enough space for him to crawl through. From the inside he unlocked the door and swung it open. "Hurry. Bring the horses through here."

They worked together to light some candles and search the surroundings. Svein had two back rooms, one a living space for himself with a narrow bed, a table and chairs, a cupboard, and another smaller fireplace than the massive forge in the blacksmith-shop area. The other room was a narrow stable with hay and a water trough, though little water was in it.

John picked up a bucket. "I'll go to the well for water. The horses can eat some of this hay. See if you can find anything for us to eat."

Alex nodded, eyes downcast, and worked on lighting the fire in the living quarters. After he left she rummaged around in the cupboard hoping Svein had some food stores. She would leave some coins on the table for payment. Distracting her leaden heart with the domestic task of cooking dinner, she found some yams, a couple of turnips, and some salt pork and placed it on the table. She could slice the vegetables and when John returned with some water, throw it all in a soup pot to cook. The salt pork would give it a nice flavor.

As she was thinking this, she saw a small desk and chair in the corner. A thought streaked across her mind. What if she wasn't pregnant and didn't have to marry John? What if John had, for some strange reason, undressed but hadn't touched her? Neither of them could really remember. What if it wasn't too late to find out if her feelings for Gabriel were true and he might return them? What she desperately needed was time.

She rushed to the desk and rustled through the drawers for a sheet of paper and a pen and ink pot. Svein was disorganized, ledgers and shop notes in piles and bulging from the drawers, but she finally found what she needed. She dipped the pen in the ink and paused over the page. Dare she?

> *Dear Ana,*
>
> *I need your help, my friend. John and I are back in Reykjavik, and he plans to marry me before we turn ourselves over to the king's soldiers. I have decided I do not want to marry him, at least not so soon, but he is forcing my hand. He is planning to ask you and Hans to help arrange a secret, very quiet wedding, but I can't go through with it. I thought, perhaps, a sham wedding with a fake minister and papers. If you could arrange that, I would owe you a debt forever. Trust me, my friend, I have a plan. I know what I am doing.*
>
> *Yours,*
> *Alexandria Featherstone*

She folded the paper twice and then quickly began a second letter.

> *Dear Hans and Ana,*
>
> *John and I are back in Reykjavik and we need your help. We have heard about the calamities put upon the good people of Reykjavik because of me, and I would like to turn myself over to the king's*

soldiers as soon as may be. However, John thinks it wise that we marry before we do so. Can you arrange a special license and secret ceremony with a minister of the church? We are in hiding at Svein's blacksmith shop. Please hurry.

Yours,

John and Alexandria

A sound from behind her made her spin around in her chair.

"What are you doing?" John frowned down at her.

Alex hid the folded note under her hand. "I've written a note to Ana and Hans. Here," she held it out to him, "read it."

John eyes scanned the note. "I wouldn't have said it was my idea alone to get married, but I guess it will do. As soon as it is dark, I will take it to the inn."

"I will come with you."

"There is no need for that."

Alex stood and placed a hand on John's arm, smiling up at him. "If we are to be married, you must never forget what I am. I am not the sort of woman to be left behind on a middle-of-the-night mission." She raised her brows at him beseechingly.

John cracked a half smile and leaned down to brush his lips against hers. "You're right," he murmured close to her mouth, making her stomach curl with dread. "I shouldn't forget all the things I love about you."

Alex took a step back. "Did you find water? Were there many soldiers around?"

The distraction worked. He hefted up the full bucket. "Yes and yes."

"I'll take a little of that water for our supper before you give it to the horses." They went over to the table and Alex directed John to pour some into a pot she'd found and then turned back to the vegetables. "How many soldiers did you see?"

"At least ten. And interestingly, two of them were wearing Spanish uniforms."

"Spanish?" Alex stopped cutting one of the turnips. "I wonder if the Spaniards that were following us in Ireland have tracked us down here."

John's mouth turned down in a grim line. "It's possible." He looked over at the fire. "We really shouldn't be burning a fire here. Someone may notice the change. As soon as you finish cooking this, we should put it out. We have to be very careful now."

Alex nodded and hurried to chop the vegetables.

"I'll go and take care of the horses. Call me when it's ready, love."

She cringed inwardly at the endearment but only kept her head down. "Yes, John."

As soon as he left the room, she pulled the paper out of her sleeve and tiptoed to the desk. She folded the note John had seen into thirds and then slid the other note inside. Biting her lower lip and glancing over her shoulder, she poured a great puddle of wax on the fold and prayed that the inner note would not fall out at any time and give her away.

She shivered as she imagined John's anger if he saw it.

Chapter Twenty-Two

Back in the common room of the inn, Gabriel ate the fish stew, his gaze roaming over the faces of the British soldiers, hoping to see someone familiar. One man met his gaze and nodded an infinitesimal nod. Gabriel looked at Ryan, who also nodded. Somehow, Ryan had gotten word to the British soldiers of Gabriel's capture. He had to be ready for anything. And then he saw someone in the corner of the room who made him smile, almost laugh with joy, though he quickly squashed the urge—Montague. He'd finally come.

He didn't look at him overly long, not wanting to alert the Spanish that someone he knew was here. Indeed. He hoped Montague wouldn't see him and come over to talk. Gabriel sat down, facing away from his friend, and kept his head down as he ate, the Spanish soldiers seeming restless beside him.

His gaze swept the room looking for weapons. Swords and pistols hung from the British soldiers' belts.

There was a rifle hanging over the fireplace and an old broadsword propped up against a nearby table, heavy but effective. If he could edge over toward it…

As he planned his next move, a sudden commotion erupted from the corner of his eye. Two British soldiers were arguing with Montague and getting in his face. One threw a punch and then the other pounced on him. All the Spanish soldiers stood and pushed back from the table. Gabriel did as well, using the distraction to edge over toward the sword.

By the time he reached it, four men were flailing at each other, Montague's sword making elegant slashes toward his opponents but not harming them. It was a ruse. For a brief moment, a moment in which time seemed suspended, Montague looked straight at Gabriel and winked. Gabriel nodded back, a smile he couldn't help spreading across his face, and rushed toward the weapon.

Gabriel's hand clasped around the hilt of the old broadsword with a surge of satisfaction. He spun toward the nearest Spanish soldier hefting the heavy sword with a surge of energy. The room erupted as the British turned as one toward the Spanish, catching the rest of them off guard. The ruse had worked.

Swords clashed high and low, light glinting off the silver blades. Gabriel quickstepped around his opponent's thrusting steel, coming back with a long slash that rendered the man helpless. He kicked him to the floor and turned to see another lifting a pistol.

With all his strength, grunting with the effort, he swung at the man's arm with the side of the blade, knocking the pistol to the floor. Taking the hilt in both hands Gabriel reared back, the vibrations of a yell coming from his throat, and swung the mighty blade into the side of the man's head. He went down with a silent thud.

So weak. God help him. He was tiring already.

Across the room Ryan was backed into a corner, weaponless. Gabriel picked up the pistol, shouted Ryan's name, and tossed it to him. Ryan caught it, fumbled with clumsy, desperate fingers to aim it, and then shot. Gabriel nodded in satisfaction as the Spaniard went down.

Spinning around he saw one Spanish soldier heading toward the door, going for reinforcements. They could not let him escape to the ship and tell Didacus what had happened. Should the rest of the Spanish join the fight, they would be far outnumbered.

Gabriel sprang over two tables in pursuit. He pushed one soldier out of his way, which helped the British man fighting him, and then reached out and grasped the collar of the fleeing man. He turned and glowered at Gabriel. *Wonderful.* Big…and strong.

Gabriel didn't give him time to raise his sword. With a mighty heave and what felt like the last of his strength, he plunged the broadsword into his chest. The soldier fell to the floor, gasping his last.

When Gabriel turned back to the room, he saw they had won. The Spanish soldiers were being gathered up, some dead with pools of blood around their bodies, some alive and injured, held under the guard of several pistols.

Ana and a man who must be her husband stood in the far doorway with wide, horror-filled eyes. Gabriel hurried over to them.

"We don't have much time. I need all the weapons you can gather. Gunpowder too. And cannons. We have to bombard the Spanish ship before they find out what's happened and destroy this town."

He didn't waste time trying to decipher their response, instead turning to Ryan he ordered, "Help Hans gather the weapons from the townspeople." He strode over to Montague and the man in charge of the British. He clasped Montague on the shoulder. "I should have known you would show up just as I was most desperate to have you at my side. Well done, Admiral. I can't thank you enough."

Montague's blue eyes twinkled at him. "My shoulder is a bit stiff yet, but I found the strength to aid you, Your Grace. Have you found John and Alexandria yet?"

"No, I just arrived. The Spanish had me in a prison in Madrid. I convinced King Ferdinand that I could find her and he let me sail here, though they almost killed me on the journey. They have given me until nightfall to find Alexandria or what I can learn about her. I planned to use the hours instead for my escape. Thanks to both of you that just may happen."

He turned to the soldier in charge of the British. "Thank you, Lieutenant. You've done well. I have a plan to take down the Spanish ship. I would like to outline my plan to you both. Are you with me?"

They both nodded.

Gabriel led them over to the room's desk and took out the writing implements. He drew a map of the Spanish ship sitting in the harbor and their position.

"Your ship must be the one here." He marked out the spot. "It is not flying the British flag, but it's the only one in the harbor large enough."

The lieutenant nodded.

"Board it under the ruse of setting sail with a small contingent and hedge in the *San Cristobel* from here." He jabbed a place in the harbor. "Be prepared to fight. How many cannons have you?"

"Thirty." Gabriel thought he said.

"I need a few men to go aboard right now and get six of those cannons brought to shore. Another contingent will fire from land, here." He pointed at the shore in front of where the *San Cristobel* was docked. "We'll need to devise a way to disguise the cannons. Montague, think you can handle the shore assault?"

Montague lifted his gray eyebrows. "Doesn't look too difficult."

"Good. Next, I and five of your best men will borrow these Spanish uniforms," he gestured to the dead and injured, "and board the *San Cristobel* under disguise with a few homemade bombs I brought back the skill to make from my days in Jamaica. We will steal into the hold where there just so happens to be a large supply of gunpowder in the magazine. You will hold your fire until you see a signal from us that we have lit the fuses and are well on our way off that ship."

"What if you are caught, Your Grace? Shouldn't you remain here under our protection?"

Gabriel motioned that the lieutenant write down the statement, impatience humming through his veins. When he read it, his eyes hardened on the man. "I may be unable to hear, but I'm still capable of leading this mission. Do you doubt it?"

The lieutenant's face paled under the dark stubble on his cheeks. "Of course not, Your Grace. Forgive me." He bowed. "I will do as you've ordered."

"Whatever you do, don't let the Spanish see you or your men in uniform. They must not know that the British are here. Dress the men as fishermen and locals."

The lieutenant nodded his understanding.

"And hurry. I am expected back by nightfall. That gives us only a few hours."

The lieutenant turned toward the waiting soldiers to order the plan into motion. Montague clapped him on the shoulder and stared him in the eyes. "A worthy plan."

"Pray God it works." But Gabriel felt better, having the admiral's approval.

Within moments, all of the men, save for the small contingent left to Gabriel's mission of boarding the ship, had left the inn. Gabriel pointed to the uniforms.

"Let's see if we can clean these up a bit before we put them on, shall we, men? We don't want to alarm the captain of the *San Cristobel* coming back on board with blood all over ourselves. Bury the dead and place a guard on the living. They'll be thankful they were not aboard the Spanish ship soon enough."

They hurried to the distasteful task.

Gabriel sank down on one knee and leaned his forehead into his hand. *God help us. If this doesn't work we are all dead men.*

ঽ৺ ঽ৺ ঽ৺ ঽ৺

The light hovered in long, dusky shadows as Gabriel and five heavily armed Spanish-uniformed men walked across the shore toward the gangway that led to the deck. Gabriel and Ryan wore the same clothing they had left the ship wearing, knowing they would have to answer immediately to Didacus and his stout cohort El Gato. The soldiers dressed as the Spanish, weighed down with small bombs hidden under their clothing, had strict instructions as to what to do once they boarded.

The tension in the troupe was as thick as the swirling clouds overhead that moved like fingers of smoke over the light of a glinting half-moon. Gabriel looked straight ahead as they walked up the wooden planks of the gangway, his jaw taut, his gaze scanning the deck as soon as it came into view. Aside from the usual working sailors, only a few soldiers stood with Didacus. El Gato was nowhere to be seen. Problematic at best. The little man was as crafty as he was fat, and Gabriel would rather he was within sight.

At the top, he sprung over the railing, landing with a soft thud on the deck of the ship. He and Ryan strode forward, the soldiers seeming to lag quite a ways behind them as though tired, just as Gabriel had directed them.

"Didacus." Gabriel bowed his head, blocking the soldiers from view as best he could. Ryan stood shoulder to shoulder with him, doing his part.

"Such a story I have to tell you. Do you have the speaking book ready?" Gabriel made much commotion with his hands, waving and talking loudly. Didacus narrowed his eyes at him but made the motion to one of the sailors to fetch the book.

While they waited, Gabriel chuckled loudly and shook his head. "You will not believe it. Astounding really, what she has done this time." He walked closer and took up the man's full attention, glancing back only once to see with satisfaction that three of the soldiers had slithered away. Now, if they could just make it down to the hold and place the four bombs that each of them carried in the locations he had described to them...well, the fuses should give them all of four minutes to get off the ship before it blew to kingdom come.

"You know our Alexandria." He laughed again, feeling the desperate vibrations of it fill his chest.

They brought up a table and three chairs where Didacus indicated they should sit. "Oh, I could not sit, my lord. My excitement is too great. Ryan will sit and write it all down. Please allow me to pace about while I tell the story."

Didacus frowned, touching the upward curl of his moustache and then indicated with his hand and a bowed head that he should get on with it.

"It seems that Alexandria has foiled a whole British army. She came to Reykjavik over three weeks ago, spent some days in the town, and then took off into the high country to the north looking for more clues as to where her parents might have gone. The British soldiers have been here for weeks searching for her to no avail. There is talk she has slipped into a fissure of volcanic lava or disappeared in the Black Castles and caves thereabouts and disappeared forever. Or perhaps, some say, she boarded an unknown ship from a northern shore and headed to America where it is rumored her parents went next. America! Of course. Why did we not think of it before? A land of promise and possibility where anyone could hide anything without governmental hindrance."

Gabriel walked to the table, leaned into Didacus's face, and said in a low voice filled with the ringing tones of conviction and destiny, "What better place to hide the world's most valuable manuscript than in the new Promised Land." His voice lowered to a dramatic whisper. "Think of it. Protected by freedom."

He held Didacus's full attention for several seconds while the man digested the story, a story that Gabriel had just now made up. He must have done a decent job of it. Even Ryan appeared wide-eyed and believing.

Didacus said several lines, directing them to Ryan. When Gabriel reached for the page to read it, he winked at Ryan. "Tell Didacus of the kind innkeeper who made us the most wonderful fish stew."

Ryan seemed a little confused, starting to speak, stopped, and then started again, turning a convincing shade of red. Gabriel didn't care what he said as long as he kept Didacus's attention away from those stairs leading down to the hold. At any moment, if nothing had gone wrong, the three soldiers should appear at the top, moving quickly but casually toward the gangway—the signal to get off this ship.

Gabriel quickly scanned Didacus's words. *You seem to have it all figured out, Your Grace, but why should I believe you? You could be hiding her in that town as we speak.*

Gabriel looked up to see that Didacus had stood and wasn't paying Ryan any attention, instead watching him for his reaction. "What good would it do me to deceive you? As I have told you, and you refuse to believe me, I have joined sides with King Ferdinand on this matter. The king wants what I want—for Lady Featherstone to be able to continue her search for her parents. Admittedly we want the same thing for different reasons, as I don't believe in the importance of these mystical plans, but I do want Alexandria to find her parents—dead or alive— and put an end to her suffering. I will go to any lengths for her to know what's happened to them. Even casting my lot with the Spanish. Do you doubt that?"

Didacus peered into his eyes over the table. He took a breath to speak and then his eyes flashed toward something behind him. Gabriel spun around to see El Gato coming up on deck, pushing one of his soldiers in front of him with a flintlock pistol to his back.

God help them. They'd been found out.

Before he could act, Ryan stood, took hold of the chair he'd been sitting on, and crashed it across Didacus's head. *Good man!*

Didacus fell to the deck but Gabriel didn't have time to do anything with him. He could only hope Ryan would continue the fight if Didacus was still conscious and buy them a little time.

Lifting the pistol from under his coat, Gabriel swung it around to El Gato, rolled in a somersault across the deck toward them but to one side, and then knocked the man off his pudgy feet. Gabriel fired, wooden deck boards shattering and spraying splinters through the air.

El Gato fired back as he was flung to the deck, but his pistol only fired into the air. The British soldiers rushed toward him. "Hurry!" He read one man's lips. Someone grasped him and hauled him upright.

"Give the signal!" Gabriel shouted.

Spanish soldiers rushed toward them from the back of the ship as one of his men lifted a small flag with the pirate skull and crossbones of the Jolly Roger. It had been an old treasure of Hans and Gabriel had agreed that using it might confuse any survivors if word got back to King Ferdinand.

With a mighty heave he lunged toward the gangway with the rest of his men. "Wait! Ryan!" He turned back to see that Didacus was holding Ryan in front of him, a pistol to his head. Gabriel started to go back after him when one of the soldiers grasped his shoulders and spun him around to face him.

"There isn't time. She'll blow! She'll blow any minute!" His face was streaked with sweat and black gunpowder.

"No!" Gabriel fought to go back but the man was too strong. In his weakened state he was pulled along toward the edge of the ship.

A sudden burning smell accompanied a great explosion, soundless balls of fire erupting from the hold. Black curling smoke filled the air as the first bombs went off.

Gabriel's heart hammered in his chest, despair and tendrils of terror spiking through his body as he ran in earnest toward the gangway. The British soldiers around him flanked him, running alongside as fast as they could. They threw themselves over the railing as more blasts rocked the ship. Fire and burning wood exploded into the air, raining sparks and shrapnel and wood bits that could easily take a life. They plunged down the long gangway. Halfway down it, Gabriel felt it sway, crack, and give way, falling toward the cold Atlantic waters.

Gabriel clawed at midair as he fell, crashing into the water with a mighty gasp. So cold. The water took his breath away as he plunged under the surface. With every last sinew of strength he pushed himself up, cresting to the top of a wave with a deep inhale. Another wave crashed into him, sending him deep into the swirling waters. All silent, all dark, only the press of the water surrounding him and the press of his lungs starting to burn for air.

He opened his eyes and saw a few bubbles coming from his nose.

No! This would not be the day he died. He was too close. He would find her. He would not give up.

With a burst of energy he kicked with his feet and pushed the water down with his arms. His lungs threatened to burst, wanting so badly to take a breath. He restrained the urge with more willpower than he had, with the grace of God. He kicked and swam and broke free, taking giant gulping breaths as the water pushed him to the shore.

Within minutes he was swept onto the rocky beach. He crawled out of the water's greedy reach, so quiet he didn't know if the battle still raged until he turned and saw the fiery ship, sinking with men running to the highest point of the deck.

They saw him and the other soldiers who had managed to struggle to shore and took aim. Pistol shots peppered the rock all around him, silent but deadly, turning the sand into little tufts like an invisible person had tiptoed by leaving telltale prints of death, telling him that despite the utter quiet of this battle scene, someone wanted him dead. He crawled up the shore, one of the soldiers coming to his side and helping him up.

They ran together, a soundless bloodbath of carnage behind them.

A soundless and terrified town in front of them.

God help us. Had it worked?

Chapter Twenty-Three

The sky lit up from behind Alex's closed lids.

She tried to shake it away...a dream... She shook her head and covered her face with her pillow.

Boom! Crash! Cracks of thunder and flashes of bright light and then utter darkness.

She jerked awake and sat upright with a gasp. "John?" She looked over toward the other made-up cot in the room. He leapt out of bed, his torso glowing in the light from the window, pulled on his shirt, and reached for her hand. "It sounds like the town is being attacked. Come on!"

They bolted from the blacksmith's shop into the pale moonlight of the street, the sky lit up with streaking lines of fire, the sounds of bombs bursting with booming explosions.

Others from all around them were coming out of their houses and shops, streaming into the street and huddling in fearful groups. "What is it? What's happening?" Alex clung to John's side and looked up at his face, lighting white and then shadowed by explosion after earth-rocking explosion.

John leaned down toward her, his face tense and fearful. "I think we're being attacked." He shook his head. "I don't know. We should hide you. This might be—"

"No." The word came from someplace deep inside her. If she had caused any part of this, then she didn't know how she would bear it. She'd only been following her heart's cry to find her parents. How could such a noble goal come to this?

She took a step toward the shore and the burning, sinking ship. *Dear God, everything has gone so wrong. I stopped trusting You and listening to You when I took John's offer of marriage. I knew it wasn't right, but now I might have to marry him. How can we be married when we've done nothing but deceive each other? And now others are suffering because I've come here. What should I do?*

She took several more steps. A sudden thought rushed through her whole being, a certainty that pounded with her heartbeat.

"He's here." She said it so softly that only she heard it. "My guardian. You kept coming, didn't you? You're here, aren't you?" Tears trickled down her cheeks as she gazed at a shore on fire.

"Are you mad?" John grasped her and pulled her back. "Come back where you'll be safe."

She let him pull her back toward Svein's shop but she kept mumbling, "It's all my fault."

"Alexandria!" She heard her name amidst the cries of the people.

She turned to see Ana standing a little ways down the street outside the open door of the inn. She waved Alexandria over to her.

Had it been only hours ago that they had slipped the letter under the door? Had she read it? Alex found no stomach for such a plan now. She hurried over to her, John right behind her.

"Come inside!" Ana's hand shook as she grasped hold of Alex and pulled her inside the inn. John stayed just outside the door talking to Hans.

Ana pulled her farther away from the men and whispered in quick staccato, "The duke has come for you. He was a prisoner of the Spanish but he escaped. He and the British soldiers devised a plan to destroy the Spanish ship."

"The ship that is now on fire?"

"Yes, I haven't seen anyone since they left here, but it looks as if their plan is working. They are fighting them now."

"So it's true. He came for me."

Ana nodded. "I read your note, but so did Hans. He is not for such a plan and I confess I don't understand. Why would you marry John if you don't love him?"

Alex swallowed hard, her cheeks burning with shame. She looked away from Ana. "I–I may be with child."

She said it so low but Ana heard. "I see."

"I don't think you do. It was a mistake, an accident. He, I think he forced me, in a way."

Ana turned her face away. "Oh, dear. He seemed like such a good man. I can hardly believe it."

"I know. He is a good man. He just felt desperate…to have me…and my fortune. But in his heart, I know he is a good man."

213

"You have forgiven him then?"

"No…possibly…I don't know! I hardly know how I feel. But I have not been forthright in my dealings with him either. We have both done things to regret."

"If you can forgive him, then perhaps your marriage will be successful. Forgiveness is a cornerstone in any marriage, I think."

"But there is one other thing and it breaks my heart, Ana."

"What is it?" Ana took her hand and squeezed it.

"I think I was meant for another. I think I love another man."

Ana's brows drew together in the shared moment of heartbreak and then understanding dawned in her eyes. "The duke?"

Tears filled Alex's eyes as she nodded. "We've ruined everything."

Ana pulled her into her arms and patted her back. "We will pray and trust God. He will show you the way."

"I am unworthy of God's help."

"We all fall short. We are all unworthy. Only Christ was worthy, you know this?"

"Yes." Alex took a long breath and wiped the tears from her cheeks. "I confess my sin and have prayed for forgiveness for taking charge of my own life, for a lying and deceitful heart, for wanting my will at any cost, for demanding my own way over trusting God's way. And He has not forsaken me, Ana. I can feel His presence and His love for me, even when I went off the path and told John I would marry him."

"He hears you and forgives you. He will help you find a way through this with John. Just continue to trust

Him. Now, let us go back to the men and wait and see what happens."

Alex stopped her with a hand on her arm. "You said the duke escaped and is now with the British soldiers?"

"He is leading them. He came up with the plan to destroy the men who were looking for you. He was very weak when I saw him. These Spaniards that are after you…they have done terrible things to him. But he was very strong in spirit when he spoke of you, of finding you and protecting you."

"What if he is killed out there?" Alex whispered. "I could never forgive myself."

"I do not think he will fail."

"Thank you, Ana. For telling me this and being my friend. I think…I know what I have to do."

১৪ ১৪ ১৪ ১৪

Back outside Alex saw that the Spanish ship was engulfed in flames and sinking under the waves of the harbor. There was no more cannon fire, just an occasional distant shout that could be heard from the shore. Alex stood by John's side watching for Gabriel and the British soldiers to come back into town.

"Alex, come back to the blacksmith shop for a moment with me. I need to talk to you in private."

Alex looked up at John's frowning face. "All right." She was dreading the conversation to come, but she, too, had to tell John a few things and it would be better to tell him in a quiet place.

"Ana, we'll be back in a little while."

Ana nodded, her face tired and tense.

Once in the main room Alex turned toward the empty forge and stared into the cavernous, blackened hole. "Before you say anything, I need to tell you something. I have made a decision, John."

"What sort of decision?" John's voice was terse.

"I want to postpone our marriage, indefinitely."

"Until you know if you're expecting, you mean. Alex, please. You have toyed with my heart too many times already. I cannot abide these games you play."

"That's exactly what I mean to stop doing. From now on I promise to be honest with you."

"What do you mean to do? You aren't making any sense, love."

Alex turned toward him. "I believe that God has provided me with a guardian, a man who is willing to risk everything, even his own life, to protect me, and in return I have not obeyed or trusted him."

"You're in love with him!"

"No!" Alex wrung her hands together. "That is, I don't know. But as his ward I will go to him and submit myself to what he and the regent think is best." Her voice hardened. "It is more difficult than you know to give up my search for my parents. If I weren't at a dead end anyway, I don't know that I could. But we will let the Duke of St. Easton decide our fate."

"You would tell him everything?"

She looked at the floor as hot, pulsing shame filled her face. "Yes."

John took a step closer and then another. He gently grasped Alex's upper arms. "I can't let you do that."

The soft menace in his voice made Alex's gaze fly to his face. She took a step back, but he matched her step, his hands tightening like manacles on her arms.

"Think of it Alex. Think what he will do to me."

"You don't know— We aren't even sure anything happened!" She tried to wrench free. "Let me go!"

"He won't care. He'll have me thrown into Newgate or worse. Don't you think I saw the way he looked at you that day on Dublin's shore? He'll do anything to have you. That's why I had to drug you so I could seduce you. It was my only chance, love."

"Stop calling me that. If you're so afraid of him, you can leave. I won't tell him what you did. Just go."

"If only it were that easy." John came closer so his mouth was next to her ear. In a harsh whisper, his hands tightening so she made a noise of distress, he explained to her what he had really done. "Even if you are not carrying my child…even if you catch yourself a duke… don't you think he'll notice something is terribly wrong on your wedding night? Do you really think he'll want such…damaged goods?"

Is that what she was now? Spoiled, damaged, unworthy of any man's love? Alex fought back tears. "Stop it. I don't want to hear any more. Let me go. Please!"

"Not possible. I haven't gone to all this trouble to end up with nothing. Besides, I really do love you. If it takes the rest of our lives, I will make you believe it."

Alex shook her head back and forth, unable to utter another word, praying silently for help.

"Now. There's an attic I've discovered in this place. You will wait there while I determine what is going on and hire a ship to take us back to Dublin where we will be immediately married. No more talk of confessions and dukes, do you understand?" As he talked he dragged her over to the brick forge, picked up an object that was inside a jar, and brought it around.

She struggled against his strong chest as he hauled her up against him and shoved a cloth over her nose and mouth. Panic snaked down her spine and spread in prickles of terror. She kicked out, fought to breathe around the horrid-smelling cloth. She shuddered, her limbs growing ever heavy. *No, no, no.*

God help me.

Everything went black.

ৡ৺ ৡ৺ ৡ৺ ৡ৺

She woke to pitch dark and her head throbbing like she'd been clubbed. Thoughts flitted across her mind. Balls of fire, exploding bombs, a fiery sinking ship. John's face. Why was he so angry? It all flooded back to her as she sat up and rubbed her head. She was in the attic. He had snapped, lost his mind, and locked her in the attic.

She stood, her legs wobbly and unsure as she staggered around the room. There was a single window and when she pushed back the thin curtain, a little moonlight spilled across the wooden planks of the floor. She looked down at the street, seeing nothing—no movement, no people. Had they all gone to bed? What time could it be?

She turned around and fumbled about the room, finding a door that was locked from the outside and a few blacksmith's tools and creations strewn across the floor. Svein must use this room for storage. There were horseshoes, nails, shovels, and picks. She took up a pick-axe, went over to the door, and very quietly tried to pry it open. If John was sleeping downstairs, she didn't want him to hear her and come to investigate. He might use the cloth on her again.

After several tries, she let the heavy ax drop from her fingers and slumped to the floor. It was no use. Unless she attacked the door with the ax, splintering the wood and making a big enough hole to escape from, it wasn't going to open. Maybe later, if she watched out of the window and saw John leave, then she could make such a racket. It was the best plan she could come up with at the moment.

She walked back to the window, leaned her forehead against the cool glass, and closed her eyes. The pane she was leaning on moved, giving her a sudden idea. She raised the pickaxe and very quietly and slowly tapped at the square pane, wincing at the sound but thinking that John couldn't possibly hear it. After several hard taps the glass cracked.

Alex pulled up her skirt and grasped hold of the ruffled hem of her petticoat. With a mighty jerk on the seam, she ripped the fabric and smiled with success. Ripping the entire ruffle off, she had a long length of cloth that she wrapped around her fingers to act as a thick glove. With her hand protected, she pushed against the cracked glass until a piece fell to the ground outside.

With slow and careful movements, she picked out each piece of glass, some falling outside, but mostly she was able to grasp hold of the glass slivers and stack them in a pile in the corner of the room.

The opening was small, much too small to try to climb out of, but large enough for a white flag to fly from. If Ana saw the flag, like the one Tomas had used to signal for help, Alex was sure she would know what it was and devise a plan to rescue her. Thank God she had told Ana the truth.

Please God, let Ana see it and not John.

She tied one end to her wrist and let the other end flutter in the wind outside the window. She sat on the floor under the window, leaning her head against the wall and closing her eyes. She tried to stay awake. She meant to. But soon, she had slumped to the floor and was fast asleep.

Chapter Twenty-Four

The silence revealed a new horror.

Silent guns, silent cannon blasts, silent sailing bombs with their silent explosions—silent screams as men fell, flaming, from the deck of the ship. Vibrations all around, so loud in the silence, reaching into his core and making him feel the horrors of battle like never before.

His other senses, heightened from the months of his affliction, recoiled in anguish as he helped load the land cannons and fire them at the flaming ship. The hot burning smells of smoke and fire and burning flesh—the taste of gunpowder on his tongue. The feel of the searing bore of the cannon, the grainy gunpowder as they poured it into the bore, the soft wad of material and then the cannon balls filled with more powder and shoved in front of it all. A flash, a boom that he could feel in waves of vibration from the ground and air all around him, a cloud of smoke that filled his lungs until they spasmed, each breath an agony, and then the cheers he saw on the faces of the soldiers as it hit its mark. The gruesome sights of battle played out in slow motion, unreal and yet too real by the absence of sound.

Gabriel stood on the beach and watched the last burning embers of the ship sink under the surface of the water. His men spread out across the rocky beach, rifles ready in case any of the floating bodies decided to try to struggle up on shore. He fell to his knees and coughed, rubbing his face with blackened hands.

They'd won.

Alexandria was safe. He could take her home now. When he found her, that is. He should be thanking God for their victory. So why did he feel so wretched? Why did he grieve the lost lives of his enemy?

He stayed there, in the rocky sand, on his knees praying and grieving for a long time. The men dispersed, going back into town to celebrate, leaving only a small troupe to guard the area in shifts all through the night. Gabriel started to rise and go with them but found that he couldn't get up. His legs were too weak. He couldn't seem to move.

He sank back down to the ground and lay there for a while, resting and breathing, not caring if he slept the night through in the open or not. He thought of Ryan, grief stabbing at his stomach. How had the man, such a good man, gotten mixed up in all this? Bad luck? A senseless death added to all the other senseless things in this world around him. Gabriel prayed God would reward him in heaven. He prayed God's plan for every life really did make sense.

He felt a nudge and turned his head toward it. Montague stood over him, holding out a hand and motioning that he would help him up.

"Oh, very well." Gabriel let him, knowing that he needed water and decent shelter from the cold wind for the night if he was to survive.

He stood and took a few wavering steps. Montague reached out and started to support him with his arm around Gabriel's waist. "I can do it." Gabriel shrugged him off, embarrassed and harassed. "We'll talk tomorrow. I just need some rest."

Montague bowed, seeming to understand his need to be alone, but Gabriel could feel him watch his progression for a long time as he stumbled back into town.

With his head down he made slow progress toward the inn, thinking of a hot bowl of that fish stew, a bath if he could manage it, and then some long hours of sleep before he began his search for Alexandria.

Gabriel…Gabriel…Gabriel.

He blinked hard and glanced up. He'd heard his name. *Heard* it. Someone had said his name.

He looked around and saw no one. He clapped his hands feebly together, hearing nothing.

God?

Perhaps he was dying and God was calling him home. God knew he felt close to death. He looked at the sky. *Is that You?* The dark form of a bird flew by overhead. He followed it with his gaze, sensing…something. His gaze swept the sky and then the street ahead. Something white fluttered from the corner of a second-story window in the distance.

He blinked again as thoughts and ideas shifted through his mind, triggering the memory of the story of how Alexandria had saved that boy. Alexandria?

Could it possibly be her? Could she be right here in town? Right under their very noses?

223

And if so, was someone holding her against her will? Was she locked in up there, the flag her way of signaling for help? As the questions loomed his stride lengthened, the strength of fresh hope filling his muscles and pumping his heart.

When he reached the building, he saw it was the blacksmith shop. He peered into the front windows seeing nothing but pitch black. Pulling out the pistol he had shoved into the back of his waistband, he tried the door and found it firmly locked. If someone was on the ground floor, he couldn't afford to make any noise, not knowing how many there might be and how armed he might find them. No. He needed to be smart about this.

He peered through the moonlight at the smooth wood of the walls. No way to climb that. But the roofline was low on either side, with the second-story window directly in the middle of the building. If he could just reach the roof.

Further inspection of the area revealed a water barrel, half full, on the side the shop. With a grunt, he tipped it over and rolled it to the edge of the roof. Then he turned it back on its end and was able to climb on top and reach the eaves of the roof. He could reach the edge and hang from there, but he didn't know if he had the strength to pull himself up from that position. Better to jump and gain some momentum.

With that hope, he squatted a little in a bouncing movement…one…two…three. With a great breath and gritted teeth he sprang up, grasped the edge of the roof, and pulled himself halfway up, arms straightening, head and torso above the roofline but his legs still dangling below it. Without much of a pause he swung his knees up, bracing them on the lowest beam of the roof. One hand clung to the side and with his stomach pressed against the peat, he used the other hand to feel for the next support beam. Finding it, he lifted his foot, stretching the two-feet distance between each beam, and pulled himself up another notch. In this way he inched up the roof until he was even with the window.

He had landed with a thud and knew someone, especially the person in the attic room, might have heard him. On the other side of that window a pistol might be waiting for him. But no one came from the shop's door below, so perhaps he had only alerted the person inside the attic.

He peered around the corner as far as he could see, the white flag fluttering from a windowless pane. How to get inside, through panes of wood and glass, he did not know.

"Alexandria," he hissed in a whisper.

Nothing.

God, what now?

The wind kicked up a little. The flag fluttered closer and closer to his hand. If only he could reach it!

He stretched as far as he dared toward the fluttering cloth. The wind blew cold against his face. *Just a little more, please. Just a little farther.*

He stretched, his legs quivering with the effort to keep himself anchored to the roof while his arm stretched into thin air.

Got it.

His fingers curled around the edge, his body eased back a little. He pulled on the cloth. It wouldn't budge any further. It was tied to something…solid.

A sudden jerk on the strip of cloth nearly pulled him from the roof. He peered around to see a face appear in the window. She came as close as the glass would allow, her gaze following the length of cloth to Gabriel's arm. Her light eyes widened. Even in the dark, he would know those light blue eyes anywhere. He'd found her.

"Alexandria," he whispered. "It's me, Gabriel. Don't speak. Be very quiet. I mean to rescue you but I'm going to need your help. Hold your arm out the window and signal that you can hear me."

An arm came out of the window and waved.

"Good. Now see if there is any rope in that room. I need a long length of rope."

A few moments and then her arm came out of the hole with a rope, but it didn't look very long. It would have to do.

"All right. You need to hold on to one end and toss the other end to me. Don't let go in case I don't catch it."

He watched hoping against all hope that she wasn't whispering to him and wondering why he wasn't answering. She took the rope back inside and then one end came sailing above the cloth into his hand. He let go of the cloth and caught it.

"Good. I've got it. Now, I need you to *quietly* break enough panes in that window to get you out of it while I attach this rope to the rooftop."

Hoping she would obey he hurried up to the top beam on the roof, shoved aside the thick peat, and secured the rope on the end toward the front of the building. He tied the smallest knot he could without risking it coming apart when the weight of both of them was on it. Peering down he saw pieces of glass coming off in chunks and landing on the ground below them. He hoped she had the strength to break the pieces of wood that made up the panes, but one way or another, he would get her out.

Thinking to give them something to step on to help them climb down, he made several big knots in the rope at three-foot intervals and then tossed it over the edge. It dangled a good six feet from the ground but there was nothing he could do about it. They had to try. He took a deep breath, then lowered himself to the first knot, swaying on the thin line. With a tight grip on the rope, he lowered himself to the window.

Her face came into a view making his breath catch in his throat. The moonlight glimmered on her skin, her long dark hair unbound and falling in dark waves around her glowing face. Like a beautiful prize that his heart had been yearning for and had suddenly found, she smiled at him, her eyes full of warmth and joy. Her red lips said, "You came."

Gabriel leaned close, keeping his voice low and husky. "At last we meet…face-to-face…with nothing to separate us ever again."

"I want to believe you." He thought she said, her eyes turning uncertain and yet filled with hungry longing as they roved over his face. "Yes, at last."

He reached out and wrenched the remaining wood from the half of the window she had cleared of glass. "Come to me."

In a flurry of skirts she swung her leg out of the window and then squeezed her head and body through, straddling the windowsill with one leg still in the room. Waves of endearment, the only word he could think of for this overwhelming feeling of love, flooded him as she bit her lower lip and reached for the rope. "Put your feet on top of mine."

She did exactly as he directed. With one hand clinging to the rope he reached around her waist and hauled
her body out of the window and into his. He felt her
make a little noise as their faces came within inches
apart. Strength flowed through every muscle and sinew,
taut and quivering as he lowered them to the next knot
and then the next one.

A sudden head appeared above them, leaning down.
John Lemon, his face enraged and spewing something
from quick-moving lips. He started to come out of the
window after them.

"Hang on tight, my lady."

He let go of her, reached around to the back of his
pants, and pulled forth the loaded pistol.

Without pause…without thinking what he was doing
or anything to come…he cocked the firearm, feeling the
click within his palm, and raised his hand in the dim
light of the moon. With a speed that he didn't know he
had, he pointed the black barrel at the young blond man
leaning toward them, reaching for the rope to stop them.
With a neat twist of his wrist, Gabriel narrowed his eyes.
Then the Duke of St. Easton did his job as guardian.

He aimed and fired.

≈§ ≈§ ≈§ ≈§

Gabriel sighed, the heaviness in his heart so deep he
wished to sink down on the grass from the place where
he stood, hidden behind a tree. It was the next day. One
day after the shooting. Gabriel had overseen the plans
that would take them all to London and their audience
with the prince regent and then concentrated on the
details of the funeral. Now, he watched John's funeral
from a distance, watched Alexandria dab at the tears

flowing from her eyes and Montague putting his arm around her to brace her up.

What had he done?

Had it truly been necessary? The rumblings around him told him many of the townspeople didn't think so. John hadn't even been armed. Why hadn't he waited to see what John would do before firing? All Gabriel knew is he acted on instinct, protective, gut-wrenching instinct.

Would she ever forgive him?

He couldn't bear the thought of seeing her, seeing what look would be in her eyes toward him. Scorn? Hatred? Blame?

He couldn't bear the thought of trying to have a conversation with her either, asking her to forgive him and then needing the blasted speaking book to know how she felt. What would she think of him then? Her feelings toward him might change when she discovered his "affliction." He might never have a chance to win her love.

God, I just can't do it.

He could avoid her on the ship voyage home, but what of when she moved into his house as his ward? Seeing her every day, how would he manage then?

He didn't know, but he had to find a way to buy some time. Heal, look his best, get strong again, feel…normal again, in control and capable, not so weak and thin and ravished.

Lord, I will ask her forgiveness for John. And I will tell her I can no longer hear, someday, I promise. Just give me a little more time.

Or heal me and take this awful thing away.

Chapter Twenty-Five

London, England—1819

The wind whipped tangles through Alex's hair as she stood on the deck of the *HMS Destiny* and awaited her destiny. They had sailed for weeks from Reykjavik, finally coming to the Queen's Channel and wide mouth of the River Thames. The river narrowed, the water still a cold and choppy gray, as they sailed up into center of life in England, passing little towns and villages along the way to one of the largest cities in the world. February had passed and most of March too, and the cold drear of London's skies held the pale promising glow of the sun shining through the clouds. Spring was in the air.

But what did that mean for her?

She'd never felt so alone—so lost and alone.

She watched the sprawling city pass by in all of its glorious and squalid infamy. Where did the duke live in this vast humanity? Somewhere rich and fashionable she supposed. What would be expected of her there? *Where was he?*

Tears pricked her eyes as they rounded a curve and passed under the famous London Bridge. So much had happened since John's death. The memory of Gabriel's face the last time she saw him, so thin and stark and shaken, rose in her mind's eye. She had been too stunned to say anything or even look him in the eye.

What had he done?

What had *they* done?

She couldn't believe John was so suddenly, so completely...gone.

Gabriel's voice had been a low, terse, hollow sound. "I am placing you in the protection of Lieutenant Ardsley, my lady. You will stay here under guard with Ana at the inn until we are ready to sail."

He bowed then and left her, so gaunt and ravished, covered in streaks of black gunpowder, looking nothing like the man at the masquerade, and yet the inner man, the one she knew, was still strong, still everything she'd ever thought him to be. Just looking at him made her heart twist in a strange and frightening mix of ecstasy and agony. Why didn't he take her in his arms and comfort her? Why was he leaving her? Why did devastation follow them like the hounds of hell, their hot breath of destruction constant on their necks?

She had reached out and softly inquired at his retreating back. "What of John's body? Can't we arrange a funeral before we go?"

He hadn't answered, just walked away from her like he didn't care. And she hadn't seen him since, not once since he'd left her at the inn, though signs of him directing every move they made was evident and all around her.

Alex closed her eyes and allowed the day after John's death to heighten into flashing memories that played across her mind.

Montague had come. Dear Montague. Would he really forgive them?

They were preparing to sail, packing up her meager belongings when she'd come to John's bag. She had shaken out the contents onto the bed. Clothing, a shaving kit, a thin book of poetry, and little bottles and bags of herbs and strange liquids—bold reminders of his treachery.

She sniffed one bottle and quickly pulled it away, grimacing. This is what had sent her into a swoon when John pressed the cloth to her mouth and nose. The memory should have made her angry, but it didn't. With tears pooling in her eyes, she dropped the bottle, picked up his coat, and buried her face in the rough wool, bursting into sobs. Was he really gone forever?

Ana must have heard. She rushed into the room and pulled her into her arms. "Here now, Lady Alex. Shhh, shhh, it'll be all right."

"I know what he did was wrong, but he didn't deserve to die for it!" She backed away from Ana's comforting arms. "I caused a man's death, Ana. I wanted to find my parents at any cost…but I didn't realize. I didn't know it could come to this." She looked at Ana with shattered eyes. "It's all my fault."

"No. Those two men had something to do with it," Ana admonished in a harsh tone. "Don't you be taking the blame for everything."

It was well known that while everyone agreed Gabriel was within his rights to do whatever necessary to rescue and protect Alex, they all thought he had overreacted, especially after it was discovered that John had been unarmed. Of course, they didn't question a duke too closely when he had the regent's permission to do whatever it took to get Alex back to London and under their protection. But dark looks and plenty of grumbling followed wherever Alex went, making her feel more wretched than ever.

"Alexandria? What has happened?"

She had turned at the deep, familiar voice and saw Montague, healed and looking as good as new after his injury. The sight of his dear face wrung a wailing cry from her throat. She turned away, unable to see the look on his face when he was told, but she heard his booted feet come across the wooden planks of the room and felt his hands grasp her shoulders and spin her around.

"What is it, Alexandria? Tell me." His gray brows shot up and blue eyes implored her.

"He's dead," she whispered, blinking great pools of tears from her eyes.

"Who?" He shook her ever so gently.

How could she say it? John was his nephew. And Montague...like a father to her. He was more fatherly than her father had ever been. How could she give him reason to hate her? But she had to. She had to be the one to tell him.

With a great, shaking inhale, she shook her head slowly and let the weight of her head fall back, exposing her throat. "John," she whispered. "John is dead. Oh, Montague! I am so very sorry."

His grip on her shoulders tightened. "John's dead? What happened?"

"The duke. He came to get me. John had, well, he had locked me in an attic room at the blacksmith shop. He was forcing me to marry him. I'd—" She buried her face in her hands. "I had told him I couldn't marry him. That I didn't love him and he, he panicked, I suppose. When Gabriel found me he helped me escape from the window, but John must have heard us. He was coming after us and the duke...he shot him. Oh, Montague, it happened so suddenly! I still can't believe it. It's my fault. I should have never agreed to marry John in the first place and none of this would have happened."

Montague stared at her for a long, grim moment. "Have they buried him?"

"Not yet. I heard they will tomorrow, just before we sail for London."

Montague gave her a quick hug. "I need to see the duke. I will talk to you later, Alexandria. Get some rest."

After he left she collapsed onto the bed and became inconsolable for the rest of that day.

The memory caused fresh tears to course down Alex's cheeks, the wind from being up on the top deck drying them as fast as they fell. She looked down at her hand over her stomach. Would giving John a child be some recompense in a world that had spun completely out of control? But she wasn't sure yet and had no one to talk to about it. When would she know for certain? And even if she wasn't pregnant, not knowing if she was still a virgin or not was like a constant bag of bricks on her shoulders.

Lord, I need Your help with this. All she could do was try to place it in God's hands, but the guilt and shame wouldn't go away.

They'd had a brief funeral service and burial the next day. Montague, after hearing the full story from many of the townspeople, the soldiers, and the duke himself, had found her after the ceremony.

He pulled her tight into his arms and held her and rocked her in a small sway, back and forth, while she cried again. He spoke into her ear in a low voice filled with conviction. "You are not to blame for this, Alexandria. John made his choices. And the duke…he is devastated as well, questioning his decision and torturing himself. I insisted on accompanying you to London but St. Easton has demanded I do not."

With one hand on either side of her head, he pulled her back and directed a level stare into her eyes. "If you ever need me, I will be where you first found me—on the road to Whitehaven. Write or come and I will be there. Any day. Any time. Just find me, do you understand?"

She pressed her lips together, nodding, the solid stones of grief in her heart crumbling into humble thanksgiving. "I don't deserve you."

His lips curved into a smile and his blue eyes lit up. "No one does."

A tiny laugh burst from her chest to mix with the constant tears that seemed her life now.

They'd prayed together then. Praying for help when it was all too much to bear. Praying for forgiveness. Praying for strength.

The next day she sailed away from the Land of Fire and Ice a changed person. A woman grown up. Possibly a mother-to-be. A frightened daughter of the King of kings and a lonely exile, without friends or family or home.

Where are you, my duke? she'd asked in the weeks hence.

Was he on this ship? If so, why did he not come to her?

She looked for him, roaming the ship by day and dreaming of him by night. But no one would answer her questions. No one would speak with her above the instructions for meals and talks of time and weather. It was as if she were a ghost no one saw or wanted to acknowledge. So she clung to the rail and watched London pass by and wondered, hoping she was in God's hands, what her future might hold.

≈❦ ≈❦ ≈❦ ≈❦

Gabriel stood half hidden by the corner of *Destiny's* foredeck and watched Alexandria make her way down the ship's gangplank. She walked away from him, sure-footed with one hand grasping up the satin blue of her skirts, the wind blowing her hair loose from under her hat, her back straight, too straight. Like an arrow to his heart he watched her narrow shoulders, but then she stopped and turned her face to the side, as if sensing him. He took a step forward, seeing the uncertainty in her eyes, the way her gaze swept the shore as if she was looking for someone, as if she was searching for him. Wanting, needing him to come to her.

His heart leapt at the sight of her profile. Pure sweetness, a beauty that shone from her eyes in such a way that left him breathless, soul-stirring to his core. He wanted nothing more than to go to her and tell her everything was going to be all right, that the horror of John's death would fade and beg her to forgive him, but he didn't.

He grasped tight to the wood of the mast and gritted his teeth against the urge to call out her name. *Alexandria!*

He looked away. He couldn't bear it. When he finally looked toward her again, stepping from his hiding place, the wind brisk against his face, he saw her continue down the plank toward the awaiting carriage he had arranged to take her to St. James Palace. Her red cape flared out, her stride brisk as she followed the lieutenant to a duke's royal coach. Would she know it was his? Would she recognize his crest? If only she would turn around. Just for a second.

He took another step toward her, unable to miss the moment when she stepped inside his world, when his guardianship would begin in a new, more intimate way of everyday living with her. More steps and he stood at the railing, one hand curled around the iron bar, the other he forced into a fist, not allowing it to move and attract her attention. This was neither the time nor the place. He would face her, her love or her scorn, soon enough.

What would she think of him then?

The question had haunted him during all the long, seasick hours while he hid in his cabin. There were too many strikes against him here. And now, with John's death bloodying his hands... God help him, she had been so shocked, her face, her lovely face looking up at him with those wide blue eyes, questioning, horrified, grief stricken.

He couldn't endure that look on her face, so he'd done the only thing gut instinct had demanded. He hurried her away from him, back to the inn, back to a place where he couldn't hurt her any longer. And where he didn't have to face what he'd done.

His jaw clinched as the lieutenant, young and resplendent in his red-coated uniform, smiled down at her, bowed, and opened the carriage door. John's death flashed before Gabriel's eyes. He'd been wearing a red robe of some sort, grasping for the rope, pulling it and shaking it...his face full of angry astonishment and determination. It was that determination Gabriel had recognized in a millisecond. In an instant, a flash of time and gut knowing, he'd seen that John Lemon would not give up until he had Alexandria as his wife, conquered her completely.

Gabriel had snapped inside.

That's why he'd pulled the pistol out. It wasn't that a man was coming after them on a rope. No, it was a man coming after them as her husband. But he wasn't her husband and he wasn't meant to ever be that. Gabriel's act had been as if a wild beast had been after her, intent on taking her to his lair and making her his servant. John would wring her dry and leave crackling bits of her still alive to function as his wife; he just didn't see it yet. And while she might have a clue of it, a doubt that she couldn't explain, Gabriel saw it all, fully formed, in that instant.

And he acted as his role suggested he should. He pulled that trigger with no more than that moment's insight and instinct and guarded her from it all, that whole life she would have lived if he hadn't done his job.

But how to explain that to anyone? Even her?

Gabriel watched the carriage pull away and knelt on one knee at the railing of the ship. He leaned his face against the hands clasping one rail.

God, they don't understand. Only You know what happened in that moment. I don't know what to do.

The murmurs of the townsfolk of Reykjavik rushed back over him. Their take on it was that it was dark and he'd not been able to see whether John pointed a weapon at them, and with the duke unable to hear what John was screaming at them...well, they'd soberly nodded and said it was a misfortunate but necessary act. Not that that had made him feel any less wretched about it.

Then, seeing Montague at the funeral from where he stood afar off... *God, Montague! How can I ever explain it to him?*

Gabriel had walked back to the blacksmith shop and spent the next hour on his knees, praying for God's forgiveness, praying for Montague and Alexandria's forgiveness, hoping one day he would be able to explain it. That he had been doing his job as guardian in the only way he knew how.

Still grasping the railing like a drowning man, he looked up from his closed eyes and saw the carriage disappear around a corner. Someone touched his shoulder. He stood and turned to find the captain.

"Are you ready, Your Grace?" He enunciated clearly indicating the shore with a sweep of his arm.

Gabriel nodded, seeing the second carriage waiting for him. "I pray that I am." He clapped the captain on the shoulder. "Thank you, Captain. I hope to never board a ship again as long as I live, but that has nothing to do with your kind treatment."

The captain bowed his head and then reached into his pocket and held out a root of ginger, brows raised with a smile.

Gabriel chuckled, took the root from his hand, and hauled it back with a mighty throw. It landed in the

239

Thames with a splash. "Nor do I ever want to see that again."

The captain chuckled back, gray eyes full of shared amusement, and then gestured behind him toward Gabriel's lone bag. He laughed seeing it, remembering the enormous wardrobe and accoutrements he'd bought in Ireland to impress Dublin society and find his recalcitrant, lovely, wayward, irrepressible ward. Wonder what Meade had done with it all.

The thought of seeing Meade in the next hour brightened his mood further. With his stalwart secretary at his side, Gabriel might be able to face the regent and, God willing, the woman who held his heart in her hands.

Chapter Twenty-Six

Alex stood before a gilt-edged mirror in the opulent room she had been assigned for her brief stay at St. James Palace and sank into a low curtsy, trying not to stare like a backward country girl at the white gown embellished with blue decorations and trim. La! The lace alone, delicate and feminine, that adorned the bodice and then draped into a lace-trimmed train in the back was more elegant and lovely than anything she'd ever seen. The train was her favorite part—white satin trimmed in lace with a blue lining on the underside that gleamed like a blue waterfall when she draped it across her arm. The skirt was white satin, and adorning the bottom two rows of scrolling lace were blue flowers and blue velvet ribbon.

She wobbled, almost toppling from the weight of the enormous white feather hat, feathers waving from every direction in her periphery and up and over her eyes. What if it fell forward when she curtsied? The image of the hat falling onto her face before the regent caused a horrified giggle from her chest.

"No, no, no!" A woman led by two court pages charged into the room, her thin arms waving as if a great tragedy had occurred. Alex took one look at her frowning face, gaunt cheeks, and thick brows pulling down over her eyes and shrank back. "We only have a few minutes so do pay attention, Lady Featherstone!"

A few minutes for what? "Who are you?" Alex bolstered her courage enough to ask.

"I am Lady Wickham, one of the queen's ladies-in-waiting. I've been told you are to be presented to the regent and to make sure you are prepared. You must learn the proper protocol and that curtsy I just observed." She shuddered and turned her head away as if Alex had made the greatest faux pas imaginable. "Pay attention, Lady Featherstone. We haven't much time!"

Alex swallowed hard and nodded.

"Now," she lifted her skirt enough to show skinny ankles, "put your weight on your right foot and lift the left foot to the toe, slightly in front. Then with a graceful move," she lowered her head and glowered at Alex, "swing the left foot around until it is behind your right foot. Try that."

Alex lifted her skirt and copied Lady Wickham's movements.

"Only the toe of the left foot touches the floor!" the woman squawked.

"Oh yes, I see." Alex did the movement again with an inner roll of her eyes. With her skirts down, the regent wouldn't even see this movement.

"Now, sink down into a low curtsy with your weight on the right foot and tilt your head forward."

Alex sank as low as she could go without ending up sitting on the floor, feeling a bubble of laughter rise from her throat as the hat tilted forward. If she leaned forward any further, she'd be face-first on the floor.

"Don't tilt your chest forward so much! Just your head."

With a deep breath, Alex stood and tried again. It was difficult to remain upright and sink down so low, but she was determined to make this woman happy.

"That's better. Now, when you are down as low as possible, ever so slowly, without anyone able to tell, tilt your weight back onto your left foot and rise. This will free your right foot to take the next step."

Alex's eyes widened. How was she to rise on her left toe? A bead of sweat started at her temple as she tried the maneuver again and again. Her thighs were trembling in burning agony by the time one of the pages came back and motioned for them to follow him.

"It will have to do." Lady Wickham pursed her lips.

"Thank you for your help!" Alex gave her a quick hug, smiling at the look of astonishment that came into her narrowed eyes, and then turned and followed the page from the room.

After winding through corridors and passing suites of rooms, Alex stood just outside the entrance to the throne room, the splendor inside taking her breath away. Her heart sped up as she saw, across the vast space, a man clothed in a red robe with a suit of white and gold beneath them. His hair was dark brown and curling, his face pudgy but with an intimidating glare as he spoke to someone she couldn't see. She was suddenly very thankful for Lady Wickham's lessons.

A hush settled over the room as the Lord Chamberlain came forward and motioned her inside. She lifted her chin, straightened her shoulders, and walked as gracefully as her full skirts would allow to the place in the middle of the room where she had been told to stop. The Lord Chamberlain announced her in a booming voice just as Lady Wickham had said he would.

"Your Majesty, may I present Lady Alexandria Featherstone."

The prince regent beckoned her forward. Alex took a deep breath, walked slowly to the front of the throne on its raised dais, and sank into her best curtsy. Rising with as much grace as she could manage, she looked into the regent's eyes for the first time.

"So, Lady Featherstone, we finally meet. You've caused a great deal of trouble I'm told." His eyes narrowed at her.

Alex stifled a gasp as her gaze swept to the other inhabitants of the room. Her breath whooshed out of her as she saw Gabriel for the first time since the day of John's death. Dressed in an impeccable suit of dark blue, he was seated beside a man, both of them leaning over a book, off to the left side of the room. Why didn't he look at her?

"I beg your forgiveness, Your Majesty, if that is the case."

"Do you doubt my words?" the regent thundered.

"No!" Alex cast a glance back at Gabriel for help, but he remained focused on the book. Whatever could he be reading at a time like this? His dark hair was clipped short again, his face still thin though. Seeing him so close and yet he seemed so distant brought a pang of helpless longing to her heart. She needed to see his face, to see his eyes. "I beg your pardon, Your Majesty. I only meant that any trouble I have caused has been unintentional." She pleaded understanding with her eyes.

The regent's mouth softened and he looked at the duke. "You didn't mention how fetching she is, St. Easton." He chuckled. "I believe I have a better understanding of the situation now."

Alex cast another glance at Gabriel to gauge his reaction to those astonishing words. He read from the book and then looked at the sovereign and shrugged a shoulder in an almost bored fashion. "As you say, Your Majesty."

His deep voice reminded her of the time at the masquerade when he'd asked her to dance, sending a wave a warmth through her. She looked down, confused, unmoored. Wasn't he happy she'd finally come to him? It was what his letters had said he wanted, hinting at more between them.

The regent returned his attention to her. "Lady Featherstone." She looked up at his steady stare. "I demand you give up the search for your parents. It is time you face the truth, my dear." His tone softened. "They are lost to us. Think of them in heaven if you wish. I find it helps me with the queen's recent passing." He clapped his hands together. "Now, you will reside with your guardian, properly chaperoned by his sister, I am told. I will give you one season to find a suitable husband that has St. Easton's approval. You will cooperate, of course." He waved his hand. "Have your season and bring the ton's youngbloods to their knees, no doubt. St. Easton will see that you choose wisely among your adoring throngs." He steepled his hands and raised his brows at her. "Do we have an understanding?"

"Yes, Your Majesty." Alex sank into another deep curtsy, anger simmering in her heart. She still refused to believe her parents were dead, but she did acknowledge that she had little choice but to obey for now. She would find a way to continue her search, even if for a time that meant investigations from a London town house. What she needed was another clue.

Rising, she glanced back at the duke. He had risen and was bowing toward the regent. The prince started to say something to him and then shook his head and waved him away, appearing to change his mind.

Gabriel came up to Alex and took her hand, looking into her eyes for the first time.

A current of sparks seemed to leap from his fingers as they grasped hers. She took a little inhale, her eyes searching his eyes, roving over his face.

"Allow me to escort you home, my lady," his deep voice murmured.

Home.

Yes, home. She nodded, gripped his offered arm, and allowed herself to be led to her new life as the ward of the Duke of St. Easton.

≈≈ ≈≈ ≈≈ ≈≈

He couldn't look at her. Tight breath, sweaty palms, racing heart—it did things to his body that made his world tilt toward madness, leaving him reeling in senses gone awry. Instead, Gabriel kept his gaze on the passing view outside the carriage window as they made their way through London's streets toward his town house. He had one knee drawn up, an elbow resting on it, his fingers gripping his chin in what his close friends would say was a gesture of deep concentration.

Meade sat beside him and across from Alexandria, carrying the conversation for him, making Gabriel appear an arrogant aristocrat he supposed, but better than a deaf one. He couldn't bear to tell her or even look at her for longer than a moment. Not yet. Not until he had these emotions under control.

He glanced at Meade's animated, smiling face and a streak of pure jealousy and rage burst through him. That should be him sharing stories and making her feel at ease in her new surroundings. It should be his remembrances of their time in Ireland that were causing her to laugh, colors bursting through the carriage at the sound of her laughter so vibrant he had to turn away and stare out the window. He hated himself. Hated this blasted weakness. He balled his hands into fists and turned his head further away, closing his eyes.

The carriage finally rocked to a stop. Thank God. Gabriel sprang from the conveyance before it had come to a complete stop and bolted for the front door. He shouted directions to the household as he rushed through the hall and up the stairs to his suite of rooms.

"Lady Featherstone is here. Jane! Come take care of things. Mrs. Miller, make certain her room is ready; it has to be perfect. Dinner at eight."

Jane burst into the hall. "Gabriel?"

He swung toward her, his voice lowering. "I can't do it yet. No one is to tell her. Do you know what I am saying, Jane?"

Jane paled and nodded.

"Get her settled, will you?"

She nodded again, a pleading kind of sorrow in her eyes.

"Just give me a little time."

Just a little time to know what it might have been like.

He turned, swung away, and padded to his rooms. Once inside he paced, caged within a prison of his own making. He pushed back the heavy folds of the drapery at the windows and pulled them wide, letting in the westward sunlight. In a frenzy to feel the air he opened the sash, lifted it wide, and stood back against the sudden cool breeze, breathing it in and asking the question.

Why?

God, why?

Why give me this woman now, when I'm so weak and broken, when I'm not myself, when I'm so needy and… afraid. How am I to win her heart now? It would have been so easy before, when I was strong, when I had everything, when I thought I knew…everything.

He thought back on the life he used to have, how easy it was, how wonderful. He clinched his fists remembering how dull it had felt, how he'd had everything anyone could have imagined and it had tasted like dust in his mouth. The ennui that had haunted him was gone now, but in its place was searing emotion—pain, struggle, heartache, jealousy, rage, and on the other extreme, love, heartrending, besotted love that tore him apart.

She can't…she won't love me now.

He fell to one knee in front of his grand windows and lifted his face toward heaven. He asked for answers. He wanted answers and solutions and fixes to the emotional upheaval his life had become, the broken pieces of his life that lay at his feet.

His whole being cried out for relief, for…something. And then he heard a word, a single word. It made no sense, but it rang like a clanging bell throughout his entire being. The one thing that had always meant everything to him, his journey toward God.

Music.

Chapter Twenty-Seven

"This is your room." After a brief tour of the house, the duke's sister, Jane, who seemed very kind but weighed down with sadness too, encouraged Alex inside with a smile and an excited light in her eyes. She opened the double doors and led the way into the most astounding suite Alex had ever seen.

She walked into the middle of the main room, a sitting room and huge bedchamber in one, and looked up and up toward a ceiling within a ceiling of ornate plasterwork. There was no gold in this room, for which Alex was glad. No notion of kings and dukes and people who thrived on golden power. No, this room was in shades of sunrise, from pale pink and lavender to creams and soft shades of yellow.

The ceiling, where she couldn't tear her eyes from, didn't have one massive chandelier but twenty or so miniature ones in various lengths, hanging from high to low, their shapes from wide to narrow, some with many arms, some with a few, combining to make hundreds of dancing lights that flickered against the pearl essence of the ceiling.

The walls were lined with cream wainscoting and elegant molding around every window, doorway, and cove. The floor was pale marble, barely seen beneath thick carpets in lavender and cream, and farther across the huge space were two giant rugs swirling with pastel designs. She walked farther into the airy room. Beyond the sitting area, her personal drawing room, was the bedchamber. The bed was a huge four-poster with draping transparent curtains. Beneath it was a lavender-and-cream-striped counterpane, so thick she would be able to sleep on top of it from anywhere and not feel discomfort. She touched the softness, her gaze soaking in the hundreds of thought-out details.

There were window coves with deep cushioned seating areas, a pretty writing desk, little tables and delicate chairs, all done in pale yellows and shades of purple. Paintings and fresh flowers and sweet little knickknacks and delicate trinkets. She couldn't see it all, there was so much.

"Oh my." The sound escaped her.

Jane turned, a pleased smile on her face. "Do you like it?"

She looked at the duke's sister and shook her head, a feeling of disbelief taking over. "I've never seen anything like it. I didn't know places like this existed." Her gaze roamed over and over the gleaming furnishings, the paintings, the statuettes, the plants that must be real they were so thick and green.

Jane beckoned her further with her hand. "There's more. Come see this. It is my favorite part."

Alex followed her into an arched alcove, one of several the room held. They came into a smaller room lit from above by windows in the ceiling. Alex gasped as row upon row of colorful gowns, shawls and cloaks, shoes and stockings, petticoats and nightdresses, hats and bonnets—every wardrobe article imaginable met her eyes.

"He sent instructions for them to be made up for you after his visit to Holy Island." Jane pulled forth a gown of pale pink with a transparent overskirt in filmy white, rows of threaded white ribbon on the hem and sleeves. It seemed made of sunrise and mist. "Do you like it?"

Did she like it?

It was the most perfect dress she'd ever seen.

He'd done all this for her? And after finding her gone from Holy Island? She had supposed he must have been terribly angry when he found her missing. But there must have been something else he felt...to have done all this for her. The rooms, the gowns, the preparations— the time and thought he must have put into it.

She turned away before Jane could see the sheen of tears that rushed to her eyes as she stared, dumbfounded, at the lavish display. She blinked them back, touching another gown in deep red, trying not to crumble in a mass of emotion in front of his sister, trying to understand what was happening.

She took a deep breath and a step toward Jane and the dress. "How?" She held out her arm. "Why?"

Jane lowered the dress until it hung to the floor in a pink frothy pool around them. "You don't know?"

Alex shook her head, lips pressed down and quivering.

Jane leaned over and gave her a light hug. "You'll see. Just give him some time." She thrust the gown into

Alex's arms and turned to go. "Dinner is at eight." She waved over her shoulder and left Alex in the middle of a parade of color.

After Jane left, all the energy drained from Alex's body. She stripped down to her chemise and took the dress to the bed with her. She peeled back the mound of coverlets, slid inside, and spread the exquisite gown out beside her, clutching a tulle sleeve.

She drifted to sleep dreaming of green-eyed panthers and a man with jet black hair with a look that took her breath away. As she drifted down deeper the dream changed. She saw John's face blown to pieces and heard her cries and screams. She tried to stop the blood with the pink gown, but it only turned red and dark and then black. She woke with a strangled cry, clutching the dress to her face and panting so hard she couldn't catch her breath.

A sudden bell rang from somewhere in the house. What time was it? She rubbed her face. It was a dream. But a dream that had really happened. Her heart felt leaden, guilty because of the lavish rooms and the gift of a life John no longer had.

Dear Lord, I know he did some foolish, awful things, but I hope he is in heaven with You. I hope he believed in Your son for salvation. She wished she had talked about it with him and knew for certain.

She swung out of the high bed and landed on her feet. But it was too much to dwell on in the midst of so much change. She had to give this new life a chance, didn't she? Starting with dinner at eight.

Pushing aside the dark thoughts, she slipped off her clothes and dressed in the new finery. The pink gown fit perfectly. Going to the dressing table inside the dressing room, she sank down and searched through the drawers. Mirrors and powders, cosmetics, brushes, combs, hair bands, and tiaras—were those real jewels? And then in the middle, a wide drawer full of velvet-lined rows of necklaces, bracelets, rings, and earrings. Jewels glittered back at her in all shapes and sizes.

Was there no end to what had he done?

She lifted out a delicate diamond-and-pearl necklace, a large diamond pendant hanging from the center. With wide, unblinking eyes she lifted it to her throat. Dare she wear such a thing? There were earrings and a bracelet to match. In a daze she put them on, one by one, twisted her dark tresses into coils of curls around the delicate combs, and then looked at herself in the mirror. This was what he wanted. This was what was expected of a ward of the Duke of St. Easton. It was suddenly clear. This was her new life.

With a deep breath she took out a delicate fan from another drawer and experimented with fanning it. It was almost eight o'clock. Almost time for dinner.

Let it begin.

ॐ ॐ ॐ ॐ

Gabriel climbed the stairs to his private box at the Theatre Royal in Drury Lane and settled in for the evening performance. It had been a fortnight since he had installed Alexandria into his household. A fortnight of watching her from afar and directing her every activity—the dancing and music lessons, the commissioning of her portrait that she sat for at exactly ten o'clock each morning, the walks and rides in Hyde Park, the calls she received and the calls she and Jane paid, her first small forays into society with his sister at a musical soirée and a dinner party made up of his sisters, their families and some close friends.

He met with Jane and Meade each day and planned her debut with a military precision that left nothing to chance. She would know her options and she would choose what life she wanted; he would make sure of that.

The fact that she asked after him, according to Jane, wondered why he wouldn't speak to her, have dinner with her, see her at all, could not steer him from his course. Even with Jane's pleading and Meade's nervous head shaking, they didn't understand. Without the shield of distance and letters, he felt disfigured in her presence. But he could give her anything the world had to offer. He still had that.

Settling in his seat he returned to the place that always brought him comfort. He leaned his head back and closed his eyes. With practice he had discovered that he could tell when the music began through the vibrations of his wooden box. Then as he relaxed into the vibrating sounds all around him, he lost himself in the colors. They became a sort of prayer, a worshipful prayer he imagined only he and God shared. His being hummed with the vibrations, casting out his own colors up toward God, a living instrument of praise and worship.

It was a place of mystery and yet clarity—a place where he felt whole. Here being deaf was an advantage, being weak and broken brought the beauty of humility into his heart, and he could breathe deep and let go and believe and trust and bask in God's love for him. When the world and the voices around him said he was broken, he came here to find peace.

He no longer worshiped music itself; he used music as a tool to worship God.

୧ଞ ୧ଞ ୧ଞ ୧ଞ

A few hours later he returned to his town house. The place was lit up with lights from every window. A carriage stopped at his front door and let out four people dressed in the height of fashion. They paused outside his house and Gabriel stopped. Time slowed as he watched them adjust their hats and skirts, bowed toward one of them, and start toward the door.

He blinked. Looked again…Could it be?

Was that the regent? What was going on?

He hurried from his carriage and looked for Meade. There he was, standing close to Jane and saying something in her ear. Jane nodded and stared long at him, her face held a look that was something new. A look that took Gabriel aback. She looked happy again, happy and hesitant, like a fledgling flower, questioning her security but rising, growing under the bright light of his secretary's regard.

And Meade! He didn't appear to stutter so terribly now, though he still appeared overly flushed and pleased as he leaned toward her and listened to her thoughts. They nodded toward Alexandria and raised their brows in a laughing, happy manner.

Alexandria. His gaze took in the dress that moved like wisps of clouds around her. She looked up the moment he entered the room. She stopped everything she was doing, turned toward him, and lifted her gaze to lock on to his.

God help him, he couldn't take his eyes from her. And yet he must.

She had sensed him the moment he walked through the door. It had been like this every day. Whenever they accidentally ran into each other in the vast house, he'd bowed and tried to leave, ignoring the electric current between them, ignoring her imploring and confused eyes. Always that jolt of happiness in her eyes and then confusion and sadness as he turned to flee. Now she stared into his eyes, silently beckoning him, ignoring the small group of people in the circle around her.

He wanted nothing more than to go to her, place his hand at the small of her back and claim her as his, but then what? Pretend he could make out what was going on? Pretend he knew what they were saying? Their mouths moving unintelligible around vowels and consonants he'd learned as a child. No! Now was most certainly not the time to reveal his "condition."

Where was the regent?

Gabriel took a shattered breath and turned away from her, turned toward Meade instead and motioned for his secretary to follow him. They walked down the hall in silence, Meade behind him. The feeling that he was *behind* him, no matter what occurred, bolstered Gabriel's stride.

Once in the library, Gabriel snatched up the speaking book from his desk and thrust it at his secretary. "What's going on here? I don't remember there being a gathering scheduled for tonight. And was that the regent I saw walking through my front door? What is he doing here?"

Meade kept his head down as he made his way to the desk and sat down to write. Must be a lengthy answer since Gabriel could read his lips well enough for a short conversation. Gabriel read over his shoulder.

Sorry, Your Grace. We sent word to you at the opera. The prince regent sent a note that he would like an audience and that a dinner party would be appropriate as he was bringing some of his court to meet Alexandria. He seems to have taken a liking to her. We have been in a flurry of activity preparing for it these last hours. He also mentioned that he needs to tell you something. I believe he said, "He has news of great import for you."

Gabriel looked toward the dark window of his inner room, his brows coming together as he considered what that might be. News of great import. Could it have something to do with the missing manuscript? Had they found it at last?

"Please ask His Majesty if it would please him to come here to the library for privacy. I would like to hear this news before dinner, if he is so inclined."

Meade bowed his way from the room making Gabriel frown. Could Jane be falling in love with him? Everyone knew Meade loved her, had since the moment he first met her. Gabriel couldn't allow it, could he? Meade wasn't nobility; he was only a duke's secretary.

And one of the best friends Gabriel had.

He would have to devise a way for Meade to become knighted. Mayhap the regent would need a favor soon. A barony would be enough. With Jane's fortune from her marriage, it would be more than enough. But what would he do without Meade helping him navigate this silent world?

Gabriel shook his head. He'd never thought his life would come down to needing his secretary to get by in day-to-day living. He leaned a hand against the mantel and chuckled at himself. He'd never imagined needing anyone like he depended on Meade.

Jane couldn't ask for a better man.

He prowled about the room while the man who might someday be his brother-in-law delivered his message to the prince.

Finally the prince regent came through the door. Gabriel bowed low, counted to three, and then rose.

"Please, Your Majesty, won't you sit down." Gabriel indicated the best seat in the room. He waited while the copious man sat and adjusted his clothing for better comfort. Once the regent was comfortably settled, Gabriel motioned Meade toward the seat and speaking book beside him and sat across from the most powerful man in the realm.

"Meade says you have news, Your Majesty," Gabriel began, brows raised over slanted green eyes.

The prince regent smiled, his full cheeks florid, his eyes alight with mischief. "I do." He nodded and waved Meade and the book away as if unneeded.

He leaned in and said with clear lips, "The Featherstones have been spotted in Italy."

"You've heard from them?" He wanted it to be true, with everything in him, except that one part that said if they were alive she wouldn't need him...she wouldn't be his ward...or his anything.

The regent nodded again. "One of my spies saw them a few weeks ago. They said they were very close to finding the manuscript." He motioned that Meade write it down but Gabriel understood.

"Where in Italy?"

He shook his head. "I have sent trained investigators and some of the best Bow Street Runners after them. You will stay here with Alexandria. She is not to know

of this. We will keep her occupied with social events."
He rose to go.

"Your Majesty, please. Where are they?"

He pulled a paper from an inner pocket and flicked
it on Gabriel's desk, laughing. "Don't disappoint me, St.
Easton." He turned suddenly and glared at Gabriel with
a dark look. "I want that manuscript at any cost, and I
won't have the girl ruining everything by getting in the
middle of things. Get her married off—soon—to someone who can handle her." He paused with an intent look.
"Someone like you."

Shock spiraled through Gabriel as he watched the
regent lumber from the room. He had just been given
permission to marry Alexandria, not just permission,
a veiled order. He picked up the note and opened it.
A letter addressed to the regent, the words *Florence,
Italy* flowing from the spy's pen. So, it must be true. It
matched the location of the cryptic note the librarian
had given him.

A plan began to form in the corners of Gabriel's mind.

A wedding plan.

A honeymoon trip.

A plan she would not be able to say no to.

Chapter Twenty-Eight

"Latimere, come back here." Alex laughed in terrified glee as her white Great Pyrenees, recently sent for and delivered to her without the duke's knowledge, pounded down the hall, tail waving wildly and knocking over everything in his path. He rounded a corner with an enormous crash.

Alex hurried after him to discover a delicate table with a vase full of fresh flowers smashed into glittering pieces on the floor. She shrieked in horror. That vase must have cost a fortune! Oh no! "Latimere, stop this instant! Come back here!" She ran after him in a flurry of green-and-white-striped skirts and rounded another corner, sliding in her stocking feet along the marble floors.

Bam! She plowed into something very solid, came to a sudden stop, and then went down to land on her backside with a squeal. She looked up, brushing her long hair out of her face, to see the duke's scowl. Of course it would have to be him. She hadn't seen him in days and had even taken to haunting the halls around his suite of rooms to try to catch a glimpse of him, always looking her best at the time, with rehearsed lines of wit to make him smile.

She couldn't remember a single word of those lines as his deep green eyes impaled her. Oh, dear—he looked angry. He reached for her before she could say a word and hauled her up to stand, blinking in horror, in front of him.

"I'm so—" She started to say *sorry*, but he put a finger to her lips and cracked a half smile that was so devastatingly attractive, she felt her stomach slide and forgot to take the next breath.

"So you've managed to bring the beast to London." When she opened her mouth to explain, he shook his head in such a stern way she snapped her jaw closed. "Just nod *yes* or *no*."

She nodded yes.

"I suppose Meade had something to do with this."

She opened her mouth to explain that Meade had assured her the duke liked dogs and that Meade had been so kind, seeing how lonely she was, and had sent the duke's coach on a speedy weeks-long journey to Northumberland and back to fetch him for her. She didn't plan on mentioning the letter she had given the coachman for Ann and Henry, her aged servants on Holy Island, begging them to send any news they might hear of her parents to London. The duke needn't know she was looking for clues.

But the duke didn't let her say any of that! He narrowed his eyes at her open mouth and interrupted. "Uh-uh. Yes or no."

She sighed in frustration and nodded.

"Just as I thought." He looked up and down the hall at the damage as Latimere turned around and padded back toward them as if asking where his playmate had gone. Her pet squeezed around the duke as if he was just another inconvenient piece of furniture and buried his nose in Alex's skirts.

The duke glared at her giant pet, his lips in a grim line. "Keep that beast in your wing of the house. And see that he doesn't destroy everything."

Alex nodded "yes," wishing he would talk to her, or rather that she was allowed to talk to him. He seemed so formal now, so out of reach. Nothing like he'd been in his letters. He'd claimed to enjoy her banter and wanted to get to know her better. But if that were the case, then why did he avoid her as if she carried the plague?

She wasn't sure what she had expected living with her guardian to be like, but she hadn't imagined that she would feel like a pampered pariah. It was all so confusing. And, when she lay in bed at night and let tears of loneliness and despair drip into her pillow, disappointing. She had allowed her imagination to get away with her again and had imagined him half in love with her. Or at least *in like* with her. Especially after what he had said when he rescued her in Iceland. But he didn't seem to want anything to do with her and it hurt.

She looked up at him now, drinking in his beauty. She even swayed a little toward him, her eyes, she knew, too full of longing. The green of his eyes changed for a second, deepened, and looked searchingly into hers, but it only lasted a moment and then they hardened like emeralds. "Good day, Alexandria."

He gave her a short bow, patted Latimere on the head, who growled at him but he didn't seem to notice, and walked away.

As he turned the corner out of sight, she let out her breath, squatted down, and buried her face in Latimere's neck. "You must be good," she whispered at him. "I won't be able to bear it if they send you back."

Latimere nuzzled into the crook of her arm as if to say he would try. Standing, she grasped his collar and beckoned him toward the front door. "Let's get you outside for a while. I think a long walk would do us both some good."

≈≈ ≈≈ ≈≈ ≈≈

Gabriel burst into his study and shut the door with barely restrained force. That had been close. He had almost let that look in her pale blue eyes take over his sanity. He'd almost hauled her into his arms and kissed her silent instead of demanding on head shaking. He'd almost pressed his forehead against hers and told her everything.

But what if she recoiled from him? There was John's death on his hands. Could she forgive him for that? And his "affliction." He just couldn't risk her knowing the awful fact that he couldn't hear anything. What if she couldn't love him after knowing he would probably never be able to hear her voice…their children's voices…have a normal life, something she expected… *deserved*? He should marry her off to a normal bloke, the typical life of a lady of the ton.

The thought reminded him of the night before at a play. He sat in his box, as far from her as possible with ten guests in between them, and watched her from the corner of his eye. It had been her first real play on London's scale, and seeing her face soften and lighten, sadden and teary, the emotions of the performance registering on her face, well, he'd fallen deeper into this pit of love that had taken hold of his insides like a spreading infection.

Then Lord Basham leaned over and said something in her ear that caused her face to break into the sweetest smile. "Hush," she'd said while she tapped Basham with her fan as the tutors *he* had hired had taught her to do.

His heart pounded with the urge to pad over, pounce on the young hothead, and land a carefully aimed fist to his face. He wouldn't be so pretty when Gabriel was done with him. But then, Basham had proved only one of many suitors eager to find out what was so enthralling and original about Alexandria Featherstone. Gabriel had wanted to find her a husband. At least give her a good glimpse of what she could have. God help him, it was going entirely too well.

What if she did find someone else? The good Lord knew his behavior toward her hadn't encouraged any feelings toward him. What if despite the regent's sanction and his own desire to make her his wife, she fell in love with one of the youngbloods of the ton? He couldn't leave it to fate, and yet he was too terrified to do the one thing that would give his suit a chance—tell her everything.

The plan. He had to remember the plan. He prowled around the library for about an hour and then, when that didn't help, went to his fencing lesson with Roberé for the remainder of the afternoon. After exhausting his body, he went back to his bedchamber to dress for dinner.

Sometimes he attended dinner with Alexandria, but only if there were plenty of people in the house and he could confidently converse with Meade and Jane nearby with Alexandria as far down as possible on the other end of the table. It was rare that he attempted it with only the four of them. Jane had said that Alex didn't think it strange that his secretary ate at the table like family most times. She had always eaten her meals with her two servants. Alexandria thought Meade was wonderful, Jane blushed when she told that morsel, obviously agreeing.

Walking into his dressing room, he shrugged out of his coat and waistcoat and untied his cravat. Laying that aside, he unbuttoned several buttons on his white shirt and strode to the wardrobe. George, his valet, was usually on hand to sort through what he would wear, but Gabriel had sent word through the butler that he would do it himself this night. The encounter with Alexandria still left him rattled and he wanted to dress alone.

He changed his boots for more formal ones, then walked over to the wide window and opened it, letting the spring breeze cool his face. His eyes blurred and he saw her face again, looking up at him, distraught by the mess her beast had made but not afraid of him, even when he'd scowled at her. He saw that sparkle in her eyes when he'd pressed his finger against her soft lips and demanded her not to speak. She'd clamped her lips together and met his gaze, unafraid, her blue eyes roving his face, seeming like…she loved him.

He blew out a breath and turned from the window, blocking the thought that if he threw his hat in the ring for her heart, she would reject him and then the ennui would come back like nothing he'd ever known. This agony was better than that.

As he turned he saw something white on his pillow. Frowning, he strode over to it and picked it up. Lavender and mint wafted to his nose. He turned it over and saw the Featherstone seal in pale pink wax.

She'd written him a letter.

He opened it and swallowed hard at the first line.

> *Dear Gabriel,*
>
> *I only call you by your given name in my mind, when you aren't around and I imagine you won't mind. Do you mind? You seem to mind so much now that I am here.*
>
> *I must confess some things as they are too heavy on my heart to remain there unsaid. Firstly, when I learned that my guardian was a duke, I thought you would be old. And fat. And have the gout or some sort of quizzing glass to make you eccentric and impossibly dukelike. But then when we started to write one another, I thought maybe you were not so old, mayhap just a little intimidating and wiser than I. When I saw you at the masquerade ball (you know the moment when I discovered it was you), I confess to being shocked and intrigued. You were nothing as I imagined and everything I could hope for. I was confused and told myself that I had to keep the mission to find my parents the most important thing in my heart and mind. Nothing could come between me and finding them. I still pray every day that they are alive and that I will see them again someday soon. Do you believe they might still be alive? I long to talk with you about them. I would do anything to find them, which brings me to my next confession.*

I did not love John Lemon. I liked him enough to think we might match, and he promised to help me find my parents. And you seemed determined that I not find them, that I come here to London with you, so I did a rash thing and said I would marry him. But I couldn't. I wouldn't have done it. His death was more my fault than yours. He believed me when I said I would marry him and he loved me, in a way I now see was desperate and very wrong. It cost him his life, and I can't begin to sort through how wretched I feel about that. I wish we could talk about that too, together. Why won't you talk to me?

I live with you and never see you. Why? I miss you.

Yours,

Alexandria

P.S. I know I'm not to speak of Latimere, but I promise he will be good. You should walk with us some day and get to know him. If you will only give him a chance, I know you will love him as I do.

She missed him. Gabriel looked up at the ceiling. She didn't love John, never had. She wanted Gabriel to walk her dog with her and talk to her. She missed him.

And she was writing to him again, taking a great risk to tell him what was in her heart and hoping that letters would break the icy silence between them.

He walked to the desk and took out paper.

Dear Alexandria,

Of course you may call me by my given name, I prefer it from you, but only when we are at home. Elsewhere, as my ward, it would only be appropri-

ate for you to address me as "your grace." We don't want to set the gossips' tongues to wagging.

Listen to me, my dear. You are not responsible for John's death. I am. And he is. He decided to travel with you throughout Iceland. I wish you had known that I was prepared to do the same. I was coming to the shore at Dublin that day, not to take you back to London, but to go with you to Iceland. I had decided to defy the regent and join you on your search for your parents, but that giant friend of yours success-fully forestalled me. You may be wondering why it took me so long to come to you. Let's just say I was waylaid by the Spanish, the same ones who were following you in Ireland. When I finally arrived in Reykjavik, it was too late. We were both caught by the king's soldiers and had to come back. You ask if I believe your parents might be still alive. Yes, I do. But we must wait and pray as the regent is keeping a very close eye on us both.

This brings me to another issue. You have done everything I've asked from the lessons to attending all the social events of the season. Next week, we will host your debut. The regent is demanding you choose your husband soon. Choose wisely, my dear, for you are what any man dreams of.

Yours,
Gabriel

He dripped the wax onto the folded letter and pressed it with his seal. Then he knelt on one knee, pressed his fist against his forehead with eyes closed, and prayed for courage.

Chapter Twenty-Nine

"No, no, no." Her dancing instructor, Mr. Wilson, shook his head as he rose from the pianoforte and came over to her, arms waving in the air like a featherless bird. "Like this." He stood beside her and showed her the intricate steps to the second figure of the quadrille. It was the tenth time that morning he'd demonstrated them.

"I'm sorry, Mr. Wilson. It seems I cannot concentrate today." Alex looked down at his feet and tried to pay attention, but all she could think of was the duke's letter. He'd written her back. And so soon.

She had gone to dinner to find that he had left the house again, gone to some play or the opera, his favorite pastime. Or maybe he was dancing with beautiful women at a ball—a thought that made pricks of pain score her heart. That's what she had been thinking when she'd entered her bedchamber and with despondent fingers helped Clarissa, her bossy, chatty maid, unbutton her gown. The gown she had carefully chosen for the night thinking that after reading her thoughts, he might be there and finally speak to her, acknowledge her. But he hadn't been there at all.

She made her way to her bed and crawled into the dark, warm covers to hide and cry, only to hear the crinkling of paper. Her frenzy as she opened it made her heart race. She read it twice, lay back, clutched it to her chest, and then reread it several more times. She had already memorized every line:

Of course she might call him by his given name, he preferred that she did.

He was coming to the shore at Dublin that day, not to take her back to London, but to go with her to Iceland. He had decided to defy the prince regent and join her search for her parents!

She would have her debut next week and he wanted her to find a husband soon. Was he offering himself as a candidate? He did say, *"he thinks her a woman that any man would dream of."*

Did he mean that? Any man? Even himself? Then why didn't he pursue her? But the letter was a start. He sounded like himself, the one she knew, in his letter. And he thought her parents were alive!

"Lady Featherstone!" Mr. Wilson barked. "The ball is a mere week away. You must pay attention!"

She jerked toward him, her face burning with embarrassment. "Sorry."

"Please pay attention!" He took her hand and held out her arm in an elegant position.

The door to the drawing room suddenly opened and Gabriel stepped inside. He was here! Was he looking for her? She stared at his face, willing him to look at her. He appeared torn, eyes downcast and holding his hat as if he didn't know how it had gotten there. He turned as if he would leave.

In a panic, Alex rushed over to him, touched his arm with a brush of her fingertips, and hurried to say, "Please stay. I cannot seem to concentrate on my lessons today."

He was looking at her lips so she smiled encouragingly at him.

"Perhaps I can be of some help," his deep voice rumbled.

He gave a dismissive wave to the dance instructor and turned Alexandria into his arms. His hands fit perfectly around hers. His body snapped into the pose to dance, shoulders back, chest up, chin up, but looking down at her. "You know the waltz. We danced it at the masquerade. Shall we practice that?" Without waiting for her answer, he turned his head toward Mr. Wilson. "The waltz, if you please."

They waited while he seated himself and found the music for the song. They waited, facing each other, so close Alex could feel his breath against the top of her hair, his hand clasped in hers, holding it with just the right amount of pressure—not too tight or too loose, his other hand lightly at her waist, causing warmth to spread down to her knees. She was so attuned to his nearness that she dared not speak and break the spell.

He seemed to feel the same. He stared down into her eyes, so intent, so unguarded for these few heartbeats in time…as if a shield had lowered and he stood before her as bare and utterly beautiful as God had made him. The sudden notes from the pianoforte made her jump and then they were moving.

It was like the last time. She didn't need lessons when she danced with him. The simple steps came easy.

She stepped into his world and he guided her through it with a twirling masculine grace that made her heart light with joy. She was smiling so big that she suddenly laughed. She couldn't hold it in, this joy. He tightened his grip on her, his eyes lighting with equal pleasure.

On and on around the room they turned and floated, every now and then he would pull her tighter to him so their chests almost touched. It was scandalous, the way he held her and made her feel, but she didn't care. She didn't want him to ever let go.

The music came to a slow stop but they kept dancing. Around the room again they went until a sudden, strange look came into Gabriel's eyes, a mix of irritation and embarrassment. He stopped them and looked at the dancing instructor, "you may leave us," then quickly back to Alexandria.

"How long ago did he stop playing?" He gazed down at her with such a look of anger, she couldn't begin to understand what had happened to change his mood so abruptly. The door shut behind Mr. Wilson.

Alex took a step closer to him and pressed her hands against his chest. "Only a little while ago. It's all right," she said in a soft voice. "I didn't want to stop either."

He grasped hold of her hands, hard. He was staring intently at her lips. Did he want to kiss her? She leaned toward him and closed her eyes.

"I hope you'll not offer yourself so easily to any man who dances with you."

It was like a slap in the face. Alex reared back as heat flamed into her cheeks. Of course she wouldn't. He wasn't any man. The memory of the times she had let John kiss her filled her with shame. Perhaps he was right. Perhaps she was a wanton woman with no principles. Perhaps she would like kisses from any man. It wasn't true though! It was *him*. Tears sprang to her eyes.

She turned to leave but he caught her and pulled her back into his arms. "I'm sorry." He pressed his cheek to her temple. "Forgive me. I—I, Alexandria." He took a long breath that she felt against her chest. "There is something I haven't told you. Your guardian...I...I cannot hear...anything anymore. I can't hear you when you speak to me. I couldn't hear when the music stopped."

He let go of her then, looked one time into her eyes, and then pushed away from her and hurried from the room. Alex stood staring at the slammed door, stunned, unable to move or think. Her duke was deaf?

♍ ♍ ♍ ♍

What had he done? Gabriel rushed toward the dark recesses of the house, to the blue salon that was so rarely used, his grandmother's salon, where he could be alone with the wretched feeling that he'd ruined everything.

Oh, God, what have I done?

He felt like hitting something. Instead he took long, deep breaths and prowled around the room. Finally he stopped and made his way over to the grand piano. It was the best instrument in the house and, sadly, never played. He sat on the bench and poised his fingers over the black keys. He plucked at them, head hanging over them, feeling for the vibration through his hands and feet, trying to remember a song he had once played. With a straining in his heart for some solace, he closed his eyes and played a chord and then another. No colors yet. Nothing but a silent emptiness that filled his whole being.

He felt a sudden hand on his shoulder.

It was her. He knew it. He felt her particular gentle strength coming from her hand, chasing away the despair that was devouring him. Without opening his eyes, he began to play the song in earnest. It flooded back to him and through him, her hand on his shoulder giving him strength. Slashes of blue and green streaked across the darkness of his closed lids and then turned to droplets of vibrant color, notes that floated up and away. A shower of yellow when he played the higher notes and dots of purple on the lower scale.

He played like he had never been able to play before. With the colors guiding him, it was as natural as breathing. With her hand on his shoulder, anything seemed possible. The song ended. His eyes flew open and he turned his head to find Alexandria looking at him with big, questioning eyes that did, as Meade had said when he first tried to describe her, perfectly match this room.

"It doesn't matter," she said slowly.

Her lips were easy to read, like Meade's, her face an open book of compassion and love. He turned on the bench and wrapped his arms around her waist, burying his face in her stomach. Her hands, hesitant at first, touched his hair, running her fingers through it and then down the sides of his face, a gentle caress.

"What of John? Don't you hate me for what I did? I killed the man you were going to marry." He looked up at her, tears on his cheeks.

Her thumbs wiped away his tears. "I forgave you for that a long time ago."

Oh, God, thank You. I've been such a coward, but You knew all along, didn't You?

He pulled her down onto the bench beside him. With his thumbs he wiped away her tears and then leaned down to kiss her.

ᏰᏣ ᏰᏣ ᏰᏣ ᏰᏣ

His lips came down on hers. A mere brush of softness and breath held against a wild tenderness. She could feel it, his tenderness toward her, and that thing that lay deeper, an unleashed power that lurked, that said he could devour her if he chose. But he didn't choose. He undid her slowly, with painstaking intent that had her breathing shallow and her heart thudding, caught in his spell. She couldn't move, her hands splayed across his wide chest, feeling his heartbeat underneath her fingertips, trapped by tenderness.

He changed, ever so slightly, his arm around her waist pulling her as close as her trapped hands would allow. He demanded more, coaxing her mouth open, delving inside, the wildness he held in check beating against her palms and pulsing through her body—the panther, as they called him, surfacing. He would take her over, if they continued. Brand her forever his. And she wanted that, didn't she? She wanted this.

The thought of what John had possibly done made her suddenly sick to her stomach. Excitement turned to dread. What if she got what she wanted? This glorious man as her husband. He might find out that she wasn't a virgin. He would demand to know what had happened, and she wasn't even really sure what *had* happened, how much of it was her fault, how much she had led them to. Gabriel might be unable to hear, but she was quite possibly something far worse.

She might be pregnant with another man's child.

Chapter Thirty

He was frightening her. Gabriel pulled back and saw the confusion in her eyes. He'd let too much of his feelings show and would scare her off if he wasn't careful. *Get control.* She stood and backed away from him.

"Alexandria, would you like to go riding in the park? I hear you are a very good rider."

She hesitated and then nodded.

"I can read your lips if you talk slowly and distinctly." He cocked up one brow with a self-deprecating smile. "Some of the time anyway."

A look of compassion came into her eyes. He never thought to use his inability to hear as an advantage, but with her he would do anything to make her feel comfortable with him again.

"That would be nice." She took a step back, then took a deep breath, seeming to gather herself. "I will go and change." She pointed upstairs on the word *go* and then gestured toward her dress.

"Meet me at the entry in an hour?"

She nodded, turning away.

"Alexandria."

She turned her head back toward him.

"Thank you."

She blushed and looked down and then hurried from the room.

ᘒᔏ ᘒᔏ ᘒᔏ ᘒᔏ

An hour later they were mounting their horses in front of the stables for the ride in Hyde Park. Alex didn't know where Gabriel had heard that she was such an accomplished rider, but it certainly wasn't true. She had only ridden on a few occasions since coming to London, with Jane and Meade to Hyde Park and once with Jane to the new shops at the Burlington Arcade on Bond and Piccadilly where they had found the most splendid bonnets.

Hyde Park had been illuminating, to say the least, with Jane and Meade pointing out personages of interest such as the famous Viscount Petersham who they assured Alex was a great dandy and most elegant dresser. He had a brown carriage, brown horses, and all of his footmen wore elaborately golden-trimmed brown livery. Jane said he was a friend of the prince regent and that they enjoyed taking snuff and drinking imported teas together.

They had also seen Beau Brummell, the most fashionable man in London, with a razor-sharp wit that one did not want to be on the receiving end of. They had directed their driver to stay clear of him.

There had been so much to see—Dalmatians riding with their owners, a gentleman and his poodle looking remarkably alike with their curling blond hair, ladies parading in the height of fashion, some waving to Jane and looking curiously at Alex, others looking at Alex with green-eyed jealousy once they learned she was the Duke of St. Easton's ward and lived with him at his town house. There was more than one arched brow, but Jane did her best to smooth things over.

"Her parents are daring treasure hunters and they've come up missing. Isn't it the greatest tragedy?" Or "She was all alone on that dreary Holy Island in the wilds of Northumberland. Can you imagine? Why she hardly sees the duke, of course, but I have a new best friend."

Jane proved deft at deflecting anything that might make for a nasty rumor all the while making Alex seem like the most interesting, exotic thing to happen to the ton in a great while. And the callers they'd had after that day in the park! Well, Jane had somehow, magically, launched her before her official coming-out ball.

For the first time ever, Alex found herself in the sweet solicitude of a woman's friendship. It was one of the many unexpected joys she'd found living in London and sometimes, even though she squashed the thought feeling strangely disloyal when it came to her mind, made the idea of going back to Holy Island rather dismal.

Alex looked over at Gabriel's ruggedly handsome profile with his high cheekbones shadowy with stubble, his jet black hair worn shorter than any other man she'd seen but so perfect on him, square chin and wide shoulders that any girl would think attractive and made a quick decision. She didn't want to ride in the park with him on horses; she wanted to be in a carriage so they could finally talk, though she wasn't sure how successful that would be without paper and so little experience. But she wanted, *needed*, to hear him tell her things about himself and his life.

What had happened to him? When did it happen? So much had clicked into place when she learned the truth—the day in front of the regent when he kept looking at the book Meade was writing in, the avoidance of her in the house, not wanting to have dinner with her. Was it any wonder he was so different in person than from his letters? But why hadn't he told her? Did she seem so shallow that she would care less for him if she knew? She hoped not and she planned to somehow find answers to these questions.

They were both mounted but close enough that she could reach him. "Gabriel?" She reached over and touched his shoulder. "It is hard to talk," she put her fingers to her mouth and then took them away and toward him, "while riding. Might we go in the carriage instead?" She made hand gestures for riding and a carriage. He seemed to understand, eyes narrowing at her hand gestures and looking at her lips.

"We might."

Alex smiled at him and then burst into a laugh. "I don't know who told you I am an accomplished horsewoman," she motioned to the horse and shook her head, "but it isn't true!"

Gabriel cracked a smile and came around to help her down. She thought he would reach for her hand but he didn't. He placed his hands around her waist and brought her to the ground in front of him as if she weighed no more than a feather pillow. He held her waist for a moment too long, taking a long inhale of her hair.

She was suddenly glad she'd worn the lavender water she'd made up last week. She was wearing her best riding habit in dove gray with dark blue velvet collar and cuffs and light tan gloves. Her hair was done up in the back with a small hat made from cork and a few dark blue feathers at a rakish angle. His eyes held a light in them while he stared down at her that made her think he liked what he saw.

"Your carriage awaits, my lady." Gabriel swept his hand toward a fashionable high-perch phaeton. "Allow me to help you up." With the same ease, he took her hand and helped her ascend. It was a high seat and thrilling; she could see everything from here.

They went up Piccadilly and then the short distance to the entrance of the park. Alex didn't attempt to talk yet since Gabriel was busy driving the team of matched grays, so she looked around, taking in the sights instead. The sun was warm and there was a light spring breeze. She smiled, inhaling the fresh air as they turned into the park. They made their way down Rotten Row, and Alex let several moments go by, gawking at the fashionably dressed people who were laughing and talking, greeting friends. She imagined what it would be like, not hearing this scene.

Like silent, animated dolls, like a frightening nightmare.

She shivered and turned to him. "How did you lose your hearing?"

He flicked the reins taking them down a side path that was quieter and away from the throng. "It was the day I learned of you, actually. The day I learned I was your guardian."

"Oh." That sounded sad. "What happened?"

He shrugged as if it was of no consequence but his cheeks reddened. Alex placed her hand on his out-stretched arm. "Please, tell me."

He launched into a long story about going to the opera, being handed a note from the prince regent about his guardianship, and then having his head explode. The weeks afterward where he learned to live with it and then when his hearing had seemed to be coming back as he traveled to Holy Island to fetch her. There was a catch in his voice when he spoke of that. "I thought I would be able to hear you when I first met you. I thought I was better."

The grief and longing in his voice was a stab to Alex's heart. He wanted to be normal for her. He wanted her to accept him, love him? "But it went away again?"

He nodded, his face harsh as he turned it away from her, the late afternoon sun making the sharp planes of his cheeks, his eyes both shadowed and harsh. "It hap-pened suddenly, something popped inside…and it was gone again. I haven't given up all hope that it might return and that someday I might find a cure, but I don't know if that will ever happen. I don't know whether to hope for it or accept it." He turned toward her, his dark brows low over emerald eyes. "Alexandria, I have tried everything I can think of thus far and I might have to live the rest of my life without sound."

"Is it…difficult?" She sighed, everything in her want-ing to reach out and hold him, comfort him. "I can only try and imagine what it is like." She placed her hand on her heart when she said difficult and then two fingertips to her mind taking them off and circling them when she said the word *imagine*.

"Yes, it is difficult. The most difficult thing that has ever occurred to me thus far. This is what I referred to in my letters about needing your prayers. I hated God for a while after it happened. I thought Him unfair."

"But you don't now?"

He shook his head. "You gave me hope that He still loved me and had a plan for me despite this, *with* this affliction. I don't know how He can bring good out of this, but I believe He can and will. I have faith that He will. Your prayers have helped more than you know." He took her hand and squeezed it, leaned forward and kissed her knuckles, then bowed his head over her hand. "I want to ask you questions too but it is too difficult here. We will need the speaking book." He looked over at her with a half smile and teasing light to his eyes.

She imagined them alone, huddled on the settee in front of the fire, heads close together over the speaking book. No, she wouldn't mind that at all. She looked down, shy, and then remembered that she couldn't look down if she wanted to say anything. She had to hold her face up for his full regard so he could see everything she spoke to him.

"I like talking to you." She pressed on her chest for *I* and then put her fingertips to her mouth and then away toward him as she said the word *talking*.

He looked at her hand signals with a curious light. "Meade sometime makes hand signals, but you are much better at it. I can tell what you are saying without reading your lips sometimes. How do you know this?"

Alex shrugged and then smiled. "We will practice and soon have our own special language."

ૡૢૺ ૡૢૺ ૡૢૺ ૡૢૺ

Their own special language. Why hadn't he thought of it before? Had anyone? Gabriel turned back to the horses with an intense smile. "I do believe you have struck upon something brilliant, my lady. Something that may help people without sound function in society again." His voice cracked with emotion; he could feel it in the catch in his throat. "Come." He glanced sideways at her in a teasing, lighthearted way to restore the feeling of a normal drive through the park. "Let's go back to Rotten Row and I will tell you the little-known facts of our illustrious members of the ton."

Chapter Thirty-One

His mother was here. She had finally agreed to meet Alexandria.

Gabriel opened the door to the newly favorite salon, the blue one, and ushered his mother and three sisters in, their husbands and children in tow filing through the door in a solemn procession, settling like ornate birds onto the perches of the room. He watched the silent process, knowing each of them well as head of the family, knowing their strengths and weaknesses, their trust in him that he would always see to their needs.

Mary and Charlotte sat down with his mother on the settee; Lord Wingate and Lord Easley leaned against a high cabinet and the mantel respectively; Jane and Meade sat in chairs close together. The servants saw to the refreshments, everyone seeming a little higher strung in their actions than usual. Not that getting the family together wasn't always without its drama, but today they would meet his intended duchess. None of them knew that, of course, not even Jane, though he was sure she had her suspicions, but this was his way of saying it might happen. Of introducing her to his world in its most intimate manner.

And demanding their approval. His eyes roved each of them, communicating with a penetrating look his desire for their absolute compliance.

Meade motioned to him with upraised eyebrows and a glance toward the door.

She was here.

He turned, thinking he was prepared...he wasn't. She walked in, resplendent in a deep blue gown of flowing satin, jewels glittering from her throat, her dark hair pulled high from her face in a crown of its own. Her face... He had to look down for a moment, catch his breath and recover. He caught her eyes, so happy to see him.

She seemed to see it, a duke brought to his knees; she knew her impact on him in an instant, and as if deciding to have mercy on him, she shot him a smile across the room. A lovely smile, her eyes so warm and laughing. Her chin tilted toward him, suppressing laughter, just for him to see, so obvious and yet so private in front of everyone. A shared moment where she jested with him, almost daring him to go through with this.

He nearly laughed out loud.

Turning away, he hid his smile and nodded toward his mother. If Alexandria could win her over, she would have the world at her feet.

"Alexandria, my mother, the Duchess of St. Easton."

He took Alexandria's hand and led her over to the dowager. She curtsied low, almost as low as she had to the regent. "An honor, ma'am."

"I've heard much about you." His mother gave her a regal nod. "Not all of it good."

The room sucked in a collective breath.

Alexandria gave her a small smile. "I have an interesting story, I suppose." She quirked a perfectly groomed brow. "Would you care to hear the truth from me?"

Society was not so forthright when challenging someone of Gabriel's mother's status. Had no one told her? Eyes swung to Jane. Jane gave a small smile and shrugged. Gabriel tried to keep up with what was happening but he couldn't. Were they being rude to her? Ridiculing her? He couldn't bear not knowing.

He swung toward Meade with demanding brows raised.

Meade shrugged and gestured toward Alexandria.

What was going on?

"Mother, Alexandria is…" He grappled with the words. He swallowed around them, his arm out and gesturing to the party. He felt a fool in a room of scholars. "Mother."

Jane jumped in. She chattered and bade Alexandria to sit near her. She gestured and shot a calming glance at Gabriel. He tried to keep up with what was happening. He tried to understand if they were accepting Alexandria or taking her under in the sea of social etiquette. He felt adrift, as if the sea had risen and waves were flinging him up and then drowning him until he didn't know what was right-side up.

He clung to Alexandria's face, watching for signs that she needed his help, his rescue. But she didn't look at him. She nodded and talked and turned to whoever spoke and nodded and talked. She seemed to be doing all right, but he couldn't shake the notion that they were interviewing her, testing and trying her...and he couldn't help. He had to stand by and watch their fast-moving lips and her face, studying her face.

He hadn't thought it would be like this, Meade unable to write everything such a large group said and he so at sea. There was nothing he could do to help her but pray God gave her grace.

She faced his family alone.

ಇಳ ಇಳ ಇಳ ಇಳ

Alex took a long breath and stood before the wide-open windows of her room. She wrapped the silken folds of the dressing gown around her, hugging her arms together, thinking of his family and all their concerns.

They were so afraid for him. For themselves.

Didn't they know? Couldn't they see his strength?

She leaned into the breeze coming from the window, smelling the flowers from the garden below. She knew the duke far less than any of them, and yet why was it that she could feel his strength running a straight line toward her, holding her up and giving her the courage to face their questions?

His mother, so elegant and stately, just as a duchess should be. She studied Alex in a way that made her want to squirm in her chair, though she didn't. The sisters less so, though Charlotte frowned a lot. The brothers-in-law seemed hungry, eager for a misstep from her or Gabriel. She was particularly careful when answering them. Finally Gabriel had gestured her over. She took his arm, smiled serenely up at him, and allowed him to escort her into dinner.

It was the first time she was seated beside him, at his right side. She had kept her head down, too pleased and not wanting to show it, as he seated her at that place beside him that said she was someone special to him. His hands had lingered...at her elbow, her lower back, her waist, finally grasping her fingers for a tiny second as he pulled out her chair and seated her, leaning near her ear to whisper how lovely she looked before pulling away, as if he'd said nothing, and seating himself at the head of the table.

She could hardly bear to look at his face. He was too stunning in his dark evening clothes and his slick black hair and emerald green eyes—he took her breath away too thoroughly. The food came, course after course, tasting of grit and sand, her throat swallowing but her heart being so attuned to his that she could have been eating saddle leather and she wouldn't have known the difference.

"Alexandria, tell us. What did you do with yourself on that dreary island of yours? It must have been terribly lonely," Charlotte asked from down the long table.

"Oh, not at all. At least, it was the only life I knew then and I was quite content in it." Alex turned to Gabriel and said, "Charlotte wants to know what I did on Holy Island."

"Sheepherder." Gabriel barked out with a laugh.

Alex smiled over at Charlotte. "Yes, he is quite right. I have a small herd that took up much of my time. We also fished and hunted rabbits. I learned to cook, experimented with recipes. Ann, that's our maid of all work"—Alex nearly laughed at such a description of the woman who was like a harping grandmother to her—"she only knew a few dishes, and we grew so tired of them that I began experimenting with herbs and spices. Of course that led to my recipes for hair tonics and cosmetics. I will have to make up a batch of my lavender water if you like. Jane seems to like it so much."

"Oh, I do!" Jane nodded with enthusiasm. "She has taught me how to make so many things. I think my favorite is that hair tonic. Charlotte, it makes the dullest brown hair fairly shine and smells so good." Jane shot a glance over at Meade. "She even taught me a recipe for men that Mr. Meade was willing to try. I daresay it was… very appealing." Jane looked down, pink in her cheeks as Meade swallowed hard and stuttered, "Q-q-quite nice." He nodded, hurriedly taking another bite.

Alex laughed, turned to Gabriel, and said in a voice so quiet only he could hear, "They are extolling my tonics and perfumes." She smelled the part of her inner wrist where she had applied some lavender water earlier and then held out the spot for Gabriel to smell.

It didn't seem inappropriate at first, just something she would do to help communicate, and yet when he took her arm and held her wrist in a gentle grasp to his nose, his lips just touching the delicate skin of her inner wrist, her body flooded with warmth and her heart sped up.

Gabriel didn't seem to care whose eyes were on them. He gave her that half smile and green-eyed look from beneath thick lashes that devastated her and then leaned toward her ear and inhaled at the spot just below it, his lips close and whispering, "I believe I like it here as well."

It was all she could do to breathe and nod for her next course to be served.

Gabriel's mother cleared her throat, loudly, making Alex's head jerk up. Good heavens, she had to gain her composure before she did something worse.

"So the regent has given you one season to find a husband, Alexandria. Have you met anyone of interest thus far?"

It was a deliberate reminder of her duty to look among the ton for a husband. Of course, Alex could most definitely think of one person, but she couldn't tell the duchess she was quite certain she was falling in love with her son. It was up to Gabriel to pursue her, which he had in the blue salon when he'd kissed her, but then he'd also said she was to look for a husband, which was confusing. And then there was the very great matter of the possibility that she was pregnant. She wasn't sick or weak or even tired, as she'd heard was often the case, but she hadn't had her monthly time in over two months, though it never came in regular intervals. When would she know for certain? If only she had her mother here to talk to. She'd never needed her more.

Her throat tightened with the thought of what Gabriel would do and think and feel when he discovered the truth. But she mustn't think of that now in front of everyone. She might burst into tears. "I haven't met very many eligible bachelors yet, Your Grace."

"Yes, well that will be remedied after your ball. I daresay this house will be full of callers."

Gabriel made an impatient movement, probably not able to see his mother so far down the table to keep up with what she was saying. Alex turned toward him, not sure what to say. "She speaks of finding me a husband."

A flash of irritation and heat hardened his eyes. He took up Alex's hand, rubbing her fingers with his thumb where no one could see, and said in a loud voice, "Alexandria will have the opportunity to meet any man I deem acceptable, rest assured, Mother."

"Let us hope there are a few that fall into that category," his mother said in a dry tone.

Jane looked to be suppressing laughter. Charlotte rolled her eyes and Mary looked afraid for her.

Meade intervened. "Oh yes. His Grace and I have drawn up a list of names. I believe Lady Alexandria has met two of them already, Lord Basham and Kit Harington."

"Kit Harington is very nice," Mary spoke up, "so dashing and handsome." Mary's husband glowered at her and she shrank back, making Alex feel sad for her.

"Oh, I like Basham better. He's a smart fellow and doesn't gamble. Hard to find one of that age who doesn't dabble at the tables." Charlotte put in.

"I daresay Basham would make an excellent husband if he should be so inclined to be shackled," Charlotte's husband, Lord Easley said, his voice haughty with a nasal edge that made Alex press back a smile.

"I do believe he would welcome Alex's shackle." Jane laughed. "He was tripping all over himself at the play trying to impress her."

"I've changed my mind about Basham," Gabriel boomed from the end of the table, frowning at the lot of them.

"Whatever could be wrong with Basham, Gabriel?" His mother challenged with raised brows and a puckered mouth. "He is of the right age and a decent enough fellow." She shouted as she spoke, making Alex feel embarrassed for Gabriel. It was obvious that his mother did not know how to communicate with her son.

"I don't approve of the way he looks at her." There was an angry frustration coming from Gabriel that Alex could feel rising to an alarming degree. He was guessing at what they were talking about and seeming desperate to grasp a foothold in the conversation.

291

Alex looked at him and gave him a gentle smile. "I didn't like the way he looked at me either," she said softly.

He took a long breath and seemed to gather himself.

"Well, I doubt it is so different from the way you look at her," the duchess intoned, chin up.

The table gasped, all except for Gabriel who hadn't made out what she'd said. Alex looked with pleading eyes toward Jane to do something, which she did, turning the conversation to her mother's favorite topic, her charities.

~ ~ ~ ~

What a long and tiring night. And yet, as Alex looked out the window toward the garden below, she couldn't sleep. There were too many questions, maddening mazes in her mind, and worries. What if someone like Lord Basham did offer for her? What if Gabriel pushed her toward one of the men of the ton? She would have to tell him about that night with John. Would he believe her, even accept a baby not his own? Who might she meet that would be willing to do that?

And what of Gabriel? Since telling her his secret, they had felt so close. He had kissed her and touched her and gave her every indication that he returned her feelings… but what would he do if she told him? And what of how she felt? A part of her, a very small part wanted to give John the legacy of a child. It would make up for her part in everything that had happened, a little.

She leaned her forehead against the pane of wavy glass and closed her eyes. She couldn't seem to think about it…it seemed, still too unreal. If only she knew for certain. She shook her head against the glass and concentrated on God's love for her, shying away from the cold place inside that terrified her.

Chapter Thirty-Two

Gabriel stood on the threshold of his ballroom at his town house at number 31 St. James Square and gave a sound of satisfaction, a rumbling from his throat like the purr of a cat. It was perfect—every detail polished and bright, a thousand candles lighting the gilt and blue room. In another hour the guests would begin to arrive and Alexandria would have her ball, her special night, her coming out from girl to woman. And he would be there for every moment of it.

He thought of the beginning. A letter from the prince regent who had decided on a whim that Gabriel would be the best choice for Alexandria Featherstone's guardian. And then *her* letters—letters he cherished, still held in a secret place bound by green Irish ribbon. Letters that had saved him during the darkest time of his life. Letters that had led him to this moment.

And letters that had led him to love.

He thought of his plan and chuckled, a rumbling deep in his chest. He would kiss the prince regent square on the mouth if given half the chance. His sovereign had given him more than a guardianship. His sovereign had given him the love of his life and Gabriel thanked God for it.

"Your Grace." Meade touched his shoulder, snapping him from his reverie.

Gabriel turned, brows raised. "Yes?"

"A letter from the regent, Your Grace." Meade's face was somber, a hint of unease resting in his eyes.

Gabriel took the missive and flipped it over, seeing the royal seal. A feeling of déjà vu came over him. He tried to shake it off as he pried up the wax with his fingernail. He flipped open the letter and quickly read:

> *St. Easton,*
> *There has been word of a capture. No details as yet, but it appears the Featherstones have been taken, no one knows exactly where. I have search parties looking for them, but the political climate in Italy is always tricky in the best of times. We have found few in power who are willing to speak of anything concerning the manuscript or the Featherstones. I hope you have heeded my warning and not mentioned to Alexandria that we had sight of her parents for I fear the worst. If they are still alive, it may not be for long.*
> *Another thing. King Ferdinand sent word through a special envoy that he is none too happy at your success in dispatching the San Cristobel and some of his best men to the depths of the sea. If I don't release you and Lady Featherstone over to him, he*

is threatening war. Of course I plan no such thing, for now, at any rate, and sent the man packing with gifts and empty promises. But you should bolster your guards. Be ever wary, St. Easton. Until this business is done, neither of you are safe.

And quit dallying and marry the chit. It's the only way you can really keep an eye on her, and besides, I saw the way you look at her. Get over this deaf problem if that is what staying your hand and make her a contented woman. Contented women are much easier to manage, didn't you know?

HRH George IV

The last of the letter made Gabriel want to laugh— but the rest of it was too serious, too real. Thank God the regent didn't just pack them off to Spain and wash his hands of them. But what of Alexandria's parents? He closed his eyes and imagined them captured. *Who, Lord? Who has them?*

It was time to put the plan into action and with all haste. And it was time to make Alexandria his. He would keep her safe.

He was her guardian, after all.

ᕮᔙ ᕮᔙ ᕮᔙ ᕮᔙ

Alex stood alone in the room with her eyes squeezed shut. She couldn't look in the full-length mirror before her. It was too fragile and frightening, too new, and yet foretold. She had become everything they expected her to be.

It was the night of her debut ball, the time to be presented like a barely bloomed flower before society. Her time to bask in their acceptance or, heaven forbid, their scorn. She had been bathed and powdered, cinched into a beautiful dress, tutored and groomed, reassured and rehearsed for every moment to come. And yet she couldn't look at that ethereal creature they'd made her in the eye. The mirror showed a perfection that she had never known and she wasn't sure she wanted to know it.

They'd made a sheepherder into a fairy-tale princess.

She opened her eyes a crack, grimacing, heart pounding. *Lord, is this who You want me to be?* She blinked wider seeing the light blue gown with a semitransparent overskirt in fine silver mesh that floated around her, a darker silver sash, a white bodice with tiny cap sleeves that fit tightly over her slim shoulders, slippers of silver on her feet, and a tiara that sparkled with a hundred diamonds from her dark hair.

She tried to imagine what Ann and Henry back home would say and choked out a laugh. They wouldn't believe it. They would tell her to get off her high horse and help with the latest leak in the roof.

She tried to imagine what her parents would say and swallowed around the lump in her throat. The truth was, she didn't have any idea what they would say or think. Would they love her like this? Take notice and time? Would they finally be proud of her?

She felt sick thinking of it.

With a deep breath to calm her stomach, she straightened her shoulders. She should only care what God thought and He had led her here to this place. She'd made a conscious effort since John's death to listen and obey the voice of God. And she was sure, well mostly sure since she hadn't had much choice, that for now He had led her here to the duke's house in London. It was just all so new—a new kind of challenge she hadn't known existed.

With another deep breath she curtsied to herself in the mirror, which made her laugh out loud, then turned away with a swish of silver skirts. She made her way down to the ballroom. At the end of the stairs, she closed her eyes for a moment, concentrating on the sounds of the crowd. Then she opened her eyes, intent and determined to pretend she couldn't hear anything for the first minutes of the ball.

It was an instant challenge. She came to the doorway where a liveried footman bowed and murmured something she tried not to hear. The music...the dancers... the roaring crowd—she stood on the threshold of the glittering ballroom and tried to block them out, seeing only the whirling bodies and straining instruments, the laughing faces and swaying bodies.

Oh, dear God, it's so horrible. How does he do it?

She was breathing too fast, seeing it as he did. And then a stern voice crashed into her imaginary world.

"Where have you been?"

She turned to find Gabriel, dressed in immaculate evening wear of black and white, frowning down at her.

"I...I lost track of time."

He took in her dress with an appreciative glance. "Never mind. You look beautiful." He raised a brow and gestured to the watching crowd. "They are eager for an introduction. Shall we?"

She took a deep breath and nodded. With him by her side she would make it through the night.

He took her to one group and then another, introducing her, keeping her on his arm, watching her speak to them, noticing the moment she was bored or adrift and then whisking her into another crowd. A sea of faces and names, a few she knew but many she did not. How was she to keep them all straight? And so many men, young and old and in between, looking at her with speculation, interest, and even a few with a feverish besotted look in their eyes.

As she'd been told countless times, with her rich fortune and pretty face the offers would not take long to come in. Already she'd had one young man hint at a proposal and three others ask to call on her the next day. An older gentleman, though quite distinguished and handsome, even asked if she would care to ride later in the week. She'd not known what to say and looked to Gabriel for help answering. He seemed to be growing more and more impatient and angry, looking red and flushed and barking out comments to any man caught talking to her.

She felt him strain to understand, sometimes at sea as well in the conversation, sometimes keeping up. She found herself helping, turning toward his face with clues on her face or lips or moving her arm in a subtle way that said they should move to another group in the crowd. She couldn't tell if the night was going well or not.

The dancing was as bad. Gabriel glowered at them when she danced with anyone other than him, which was several times. She found herself acting too tired and out of breath to avoid making him so angry even though she loved to dance. Anyway, when she did dance, she couldn't really concentrate on what her partner said. Her mind, and gaze, wandered to where Gabriel was standing, who he was speaking to, and how he was faring. One gentleman called her out on it.

"I see that your heart has already chosen, mademoiselle."

Her gaze shot up to meet the dark brown eyes of Count Fallourd from Paris. "Whatever do you mean, my lord?" She must appear cold and uncaring, but she couldn't seem to help it.

He gave her a slow smile and dramatic sigh, his gaze darted to Gabriel and then back at her. "It is convenient at least, no?"

She felt her cheeks warm. Were her feelings so obvious?

By the time the midnight supper was to be served, she was exhausted. Gabriel came over to her, she thought, to escort her into dinner. She turned and shook her head at him. "How do you do it? It's so tiring." She looked up into those piercing green eyes. "I see your world…a little."

He leaned down and spoke to her, his warm breath with a smile in it in her ear. "I have grown accustomed to it, I suppose. You are not enjoying yourself?"

"I am when I'm with you." The words slipped out before she had time to wonder if she should say it.

Happiness lit his eyes making her glad she had spoken them.

"I have a surprise before supper that might, I hope, make you very happy." He looked at her in such a way that the crowd disappeared and it felt like just the two of them stood in the ballroom. He took her hand and placed it in the crook of his arm, leading her onto the middle of the dance floor.

The crowd parted as they made their way to the center. There was no music; it had stopped the moment the musicians sensed their host had something special in mind. That he could command them all so easily, his very presence commanded a crowd with a flick of his wrist and a simple nod. What was he up to? Her heartbeat quickened as the crowd grew still and quiet.

He took her into his arms, nodding to the orchestra, as they all watched. Her jaw flexed in determination, nervous for him that he start in time, but he knew just when the music began. The song was unknown and yet...strangely familiar. Alex smiled up at him as she realized it was the song he had played for her that day in the blue drawing room. He had played so beautifully, so passionately. It was the loveliest song she'd ever heard. They swirled around the space the guests made, watching them. Like the time at the masquerade, it was as if they had stepped into their own private world of oneness with the music and with each other.

He leaned down and whispered into her ear, "Do you trust me, Alexandria?"

She narrowed her eyes in curiosity and some hesitation. What was he up to? But she nodded that she did.

At the end, he leaned her back into a sweeping move that surprised her. She hung suspended by his arm, having to trust him. Her body was in his control and it was frightening and thrilling at the same time. He pulled her up toward his face and she gulped in air, biting her bottom lip and staring into those deep green eyes.

They were making a spectacle of themselves. She laughed. In his arms. In front of everyone. Not caring what anyone thought. Just happy to be with him.

He set her away from him and then did the most astonishing thing. He knelt, on one knee, in front of her and everyone. Alex gasped along with the crowd. He pulled something from his pocket. The crowd hushed as he held the sparkling object toward her. With a deep and confident voice, he asked, "Alexandria Elise Featherstone, will you be my wife?"

Her eyes widened. She stared at the glittering ring. Dare she? It was all she wanted and yet there was still so much between them, things he didn't know, things she didn't know how to tell him. But she loved him. She wanted him, for her whole life, to be hers and she, his. What should she do?

The silence lengthened as she stared at the ring. The crowd began to murmur.

"Alexandria?" His green gaze impaled her, questioning and delving into her very soul. Oh! Why had he done it here? Now? When she couldn't explain and he couldn't take it back if he learned the truth about her and changed his mind. What should she do? *Dear God, what shall I do?*

She felt a nauseous wave of gut-wrenching sickness like she'd never felt before. The room started to buzz and swell around her.

"Alexandria!" Gabriel stood and clasped her around the waist just as she let out a breath and collapsed.

≈ ≈ ≈ ≈

The room went wild with speculation. Gabriel saw their eyes—greedy, gossipy, shock, some sad for him but many gloating as he scooped her up and carried her, shouting orders to his staff and hurrying from the ballroom.

"Bring smelling salts, water, to the blue salon."

He took her to their private place as he now thought of it and laid her on the brocade settee. She was so pale. It made his heart race. Why hadn't she said *yes?* He was sure she loved him. He placed his ear against her chest and felt for the thud, thud of her heart, then leaned into her face.

"Come back to me, my sweet. Alexandria, wake up."

The servants entered with the smelling salts. Gabriel placed them under her nose and called her name. After a few moments her eyelids fluttered open and those sky blue eyes roved over the ceiling. She turned her head and looked at him, her cheeks flushed. "Oh dear. I fainted, didn't I? In front of everyone."

And rejected me, in front of everyone.

She slowly sat up and arranged her skirts with nervous hands. "I—I—" She looked up at him and swallowed hard. "I was just so shocked. I've ruined everything, haven't I?"

He wasn't sure what she said and it made him angry. Turning from her he found a speaking book and writing implements and brought them to her.

He held them out to her. "Do you love me, Alexandria?"

She looked at the paper, then up at him, bit her lower lip, and nodded.

"You were just shocked then? Tell me."

She took the book and set it in her lap, dipped the quill in the ink pot he held, and poised it over the paper. Tense and sickly white, she just kept looking at the blank page. Why wouldn't she tell him whatever this was about? Gabriel sat beside her and took her face gently into his hands. He turned her toward him and began to speak.

"Alexandria, listen to me. I have it all planned. I was going to tell you on our wedding day, as a gift to you, but perhaps you need to hear it now. We have had word that weeks ago someone spotted your parents. The regent and I think you are right. We believe your parents are still alive."

He didn't mention the regent's letter. He didn't tell her they had been captured and might not, indeed, be alive. He needed her hope. There was no reason to worry her beyond giving her that hope.

Her eyes widened. "Where are they?"

"In Italy."

"Italy?"

"Yes. The regent has already sent the very best investigators to find them. He has ordered me to keep you here and not to tell you, but I know how important it is for you to find them yourself. I wanted to give you that chance."

"But how?" She looked close to tears.

"My dearest Alexandria, do you know where the bride and groom go after a wedding?"

She shook her head.

"On a honeymoon trip. It would be expected that we leave the country, and after a brief visit in France to throw off anyone who might be watching us, we'll end up in one of the most beautiful places in the world." He gripped her hands. "Florence."

She nodded and then leaned forward and wrapped her arms around his neck, clinging to him. "Yes," she said into his neck, kissing him. "Yes." She clung to him, saying it with her whole body. "I will be your wife."

His heart soared with happiness. He hadn't bribed her. Of course not. She was about to say yes anyway. Of course she would be his wife. He'd been subconsciously planning it since her first letter. He'd been conscious of it since the masquerade. And she'd accepted him, loved him despite everything that had happened to him in the last year. He shoved the thoughts aside and kissed her more deeply, losing them both in the world of touch.

They *would* be happy together.

He would make sure of it.

Chapter Thirty-Three

She wasn't pregnant.

The banns had been read. The white dress trimmed in pearls and aquamarine stones, the color of her eyes, lay perfect in every way on the bed ready to slip into. The church overflowed with thousands of waiting guests, and the streets surrounding it thronged with Londoners eager to get a peek of the Duke of St. Easton's bride. And thanks be to God, *she wasn't pregnant.*

Alexandria Featherstone stared at her family crest on the stationery from home that said Ann and Henry couldn't make the journey and represent her only family for the biggest event in her life. Her thumb brushed across the wax seal, reading the Featherstone motto on the banner over the lion and eagle's heads:

Valens et Volens—"Willing and Able."

Was she?

Clarissa, the maid assigned to her since coming to Gabriel's household, burst through the door. Alex had always been thankful that Clarissa wasn't the shy sort who held Alex in any kind of esteem. No, she was the chatty, gossipy friend sort who had helped Alexandria navigate the household and instructed her about the duties of a duchess. And today was no different.

"Gracious me! Look at the time, my lady. We have to get you dressed and into the carriage within the hour." When Alex didn't move, she glowered at her and shook her head. "Come now, no time for bride's nerves. Bless the saints, at least we have your hair done. Come, come."

Alex let her chatter wash over her and calm her nerves. She had had her woman's time two weeks ago, days after her engagement became official. The relief had left her reeling with both happiness and shock. And even though that news had been welcome, she had felt a surprising stab of sadness that John would die without legacy. She could have given him that, at least. Still, she was terrified of her wedding night. What would Gabriel discover? Would he be horrified if he found out she was no virgin and hadn't told him? Any normal man might be.

She took a shaky breath and turned as her maid directed. There was no backing out of it now. She loved Gabriel. He loved her, as he'd told her several times over the last three weeks during which the reading of the banns occurred. They would work through it together. She would tell him, just not yet. Not today! She couldn't ruin their wedding day. But something kept whispering to her that this was the only day left. The last day he could change his mind.

She had been trying to get up the nerve to tell him every day since agreeing to marry him, but she froze every time she thought of it. She just couldn't seem to get the words out of her mouth. And now, she couldn't stop thinking about what would happen on her wedding night. He would discover the truth on his own, wouldn't he?

She stepped into the white gown and stood rigidly as Clarissa buttoned the row of pearl buttons. "Now, there isn't any reason to be so nervous, my lady. Why, the duke is happier than we've ever seen him. He left for the church an hour ago with that handsome friend of his, Lord Albert Bartrom. Why, his lordship and the duke were joking and laughing and having a right good time all the way into the carriage, both of 'em looking so dapper in their uniforms."

She turned Alex and began straightening the folds of the sleeves and the skirt. "And the dowager duchess is all smiles." Her voice lowered in a grumble. "And we know how often that occurs, almost never." Her voice brightened again. "Lady Jane is teary eyed, happy tears, you know, and so pretty in her pink dress as your attendant. They wanted to come up, but I said to give us a minute to get you in all your glory and they've listened for once. Mr. Meade keeps talking about that time you shot him." Clarissa leaned back and eyed Alexandria with laughing hazel eyes, her brown curls bobbing on the sides of her cap. "I still can't fathom your sweet self shooting any-one."

"It *was* an accident," Alex interrupted.

"Yes, well he's taking credit for endearing you to us. And the duke's other sisters are said to be at the church already. Have you heard about the crowds? Why all of London has turned out in the streets, and we don't know how we're going to get you to the church on time."

Alex had heard about the crowds and it only made her more nervous. A sudden knock at the door gave her a jump.

"There now, that'll be the dowager and Lady Jane." Clarissa rushed to the door and flung it wide. True to her words, Gabriel's mother and sister came inside.

"Oh, Alexandria. You look so beautiful! Doesn't she, Mother?"

"She does." The dowager, having softened toward the idea of their marriage in the last three weeks, saying she was glad her son had finally found someone and could get to the business of producing an heir, looked as misty eyed as Jane.

Jane came forward and took Alex's hands. "I'm sorry your parents couldn't be here to see you, Alexandria. You must miss them terribly today."

Alex nodded and bit down on her lower lip with sudden tears in her eyes at the thought of it.

"Good heavens, Jane. Don't bring that up," Her Grace admonished.

"Oh, I'm sorry." Jane squeezed her hands and then backed up. "We've brought you something borrowed and something blue." She held out two wrapped packages.

Alex smiled, telling Jane with her eyes that she wasn't upset at her for the comment. "That was so kind." She sat in one of her bedchamber chairs and unwrapped the first gift. Inside, on a bed of white velvet, lay two teardrop-shaped earrings with large, blue topaz stones and diamonds surrounding them. Alex could only stare at them for a long moment. "They are amazing."

Jane nodded happily. "They match your eyes and the gems sewn into the dress." Jane handed her the second package.

Her Grace lifted her chin and spoke with pride. "This has belonged to the Duchesses of St. Easton for over two centuries. Until you are pronounced husband and wife, it is still mine and can be your item borrowed. After today, you will be the Duchess of St. Easton and it will belong to you until your firstborn son marries when you will give it to his wife."

I am about to become the Duchess of St. Easton.

For the first time the impact of what that meant struck her. Her stomach quivered as she took the small package and carefully unwrapped it. There, in a pile of tissue paper, lay the most delicate tiara she'd ever seen. Small and dainty but with hundreds of diamonds mounted on what looked like spun silver. "I can't," Alex said. Just the thought of picking it up made her nervous. What if it snapped in half?

"You must." The dowager insisted. "Let me." She came and took the piece in her gloved hands. There were tiny combs along the edge that she slipped into Alex's hair with practiced ease.

"Alexandria, it's perfect. Come see." Jane took her hand and led her to the mirror.

Alex looked at her reflection, shock and joy and terror warring within her. Was she really about to get married?

They heard bells from afar. "The church bells!" Jane shrieked eyes bright with panic and laughter.

"Saints preserve us!" Clarissa clapped her hands as if leader of an army. "We have to get her to the church!" They all laughed, Gabriel's mother even cracking a smile.

Alex let the excitement of the day wash over her. Gabriel would be her husband soon!

Her husband.

When she thought back to that simple girl on Holy Island, waiting…wishing her life would hurry up and really begin, praying God would send her on her own adventures, so much longing, so much hope—well, she'd never in all her daydreaming dreamed of this. She had found love and to a man unfathomable to that girl. She had grown up and found her place in the world. A shot of joy pulsed from her spirit through her soul and then sent tingles through her body.

This was no time to worry about the bad things of the past, nor the mystery that was the future. This was the time to live the moment where all her dreams were coming true.

With that thought, she pushed her worries aside and rushed with her new family from the room.

ॐ ॐ ॐ ॐ

After what seemed hours of being clogged in the horrific crush around the church, the guards Gabriel had insisted accompany them flanking their carriage from every side before and behind, they finally arrived.

Alex stepped from the duke's glossy carriage and walked, guarded all around and so overwhelmed she was numb inside, into Westminster Abby. She was greeted by splendid pages in the duke's royal blue livery, looking like young princes themselves. They bowed and scraped as she passed by as if she was already the duchess. They opened the massive doors for her and stood like rigid statues, chins up and looking only forward. Alex nodded her thanks and swept inside.

All of her confidence drained away as she stopped inside the grand, echoing entrance and inhaled. The church was like nothing she'd ever seen—gothic with a rich, ancient air that sent goose bumps up and down her arms. She looked up at the vast, vaulted ceilings that looked like row upon row of stone fans as far as she could see. The ceiling was upheld by fluted columns with massive stone bases attached to the pale marble floor. The walls held the paintings of kings and saints, twice her height, and farther down, past the entry and into the main part of the church, were rows of colorful flags.

She peered forward, down the long aisle toward the altar, visible but small from so far away. She looked for Gabriel, noting the people in their best finery and hats seated ahead through the arched entries, but couldn't see him. There were so many people, murmuring people on rows of elegant benches, a thousand faces she didn't know. She felt too small to move…too insignificant to be here, too stained with sin to remain standing. She felt the presence of God in this place.

It took everything in her not to run away or fall on her face and weep. She stood frozen, more afraid than she'd ever been in her life.

"Alexandria, do not even think of fainting."

She turned around to the familiar voice. "Montague!"

A broad smile swept his face and joy shot from his piercing blue eyes. "Come here, child."

His face brought back a deluge of emotions—joy, sorrow for John, his nephew's death. Sorrow for a moment that she couldn't tell him she was pregnant and that they would yet have a part of John with them. Relief—both that she wasn't pregnant and that he was here for her. And *love*, mostly love, the kind she would feel for a father. If she couldn't have her parents with her, then Montague was the next best thing.

You are so good to me, Lord. Her heart cried out the prayer as she smiled at this man who had been her protector, her friend.

He met her halfway. Her legs wobbled and she had to clutch the heavy skirts up, but she managed to make it to his side and into his arms. He held her for a moment and then pushed back to see her face. His voice was quiet yet strong, echoing across the ceilings of the ancient church. "I've come to walk you down the aisle if you will have me."

She pressed a hand against her mouth, tears threatening. "How did you know?"

"That you are marrying the duke?"

Alex nodded. "And that I needed you."

"He asked me to come. Well," Montague chuckled, "commanded is the better word for it. Sent a fancy carriage for me loaded with food and drink and ten outriders. As if I needed all of that." He looked at her intently. "Is this what you wish, Alexandria? I thought it might happen this way, but I need to hear it from you. Do you love him?"

"I do." She nodded, missing her parents and yet so glad he was here and she didn't have to do this alone. "But how can you bear to be here...after all that's happened? After he...shot John?"

Montague gazed deep into her eyes. "How can *you* bear it...after all that's happened...after he shot John?"

"I've forgiven him." The words rushed out and she realized it was true. She had forgiven him, more than she'd forgiven herself, for everything that had happened.

311

"And so have I." Montague's deep voice echoed across the cavernous antechamber. "People say one can forgive but they cannot forget, and yet forgiveness is that very thing—forgetting, trusting again as if it had never occurred, and trusting God to take care of us when people fail us. That's how God forgives us, as far as the east is from the west, that's how far He has removed our transgressions from us."

Gabriel loved her. He would be like that. He would understand. When she told him the whole story, he would forgive her too.

Alex kissed Montague's cheek. "Thank you for coming, Montague. I am ready now."

He chuckled and took her arm. With a signal from some unknown person, the notes of an organ swelled into life. Jane hovered behind her, spreading the train of her gown, and then followed after them as Alex began down the long white aisle toward her future.

ᝍ ᝍ ᝍ ᝍ

Waves of vibration started up Gabriel's legs and filled his body with a humming roar.

The organ had begun to play.

He turned, straining to see her down the long aisle, heart pounding with hope that made him feel alive, lighting inside in vibrant white glowing streaks of pure joy. *Come to me, my beloved Alexandria. Come and marry me.*

When her face came into view, the room filled with colors. Streaking and dancing, shooting across the wide space and dissolving before he saw the full form of it. The silent room lit up—alive—the air moving and glowing, surrounding and encircling her. He could hardly bear it, it was so powerful. It nearly drove him to his knees.

And then she was beside him.

He leaned close, closed his eyes, and smelled her special lavender water she'd made herself, driving his household to distraction looking for all the ingredients she needed. He inhaled and nearly laughed out loud with the pure joy of it.

She was about to be his forever.

His wife. His other half. His forever on earth.

He opened his eyes and said a silent prayer of fervent thanksgiving. He'd never been so thankful for being who he was and what he had—her. If he'd had to lose his hearing to have her, then it was worth it. As hard as it had been, he would choose this path again and thank God for it.

He took a deep breath and concentrated on the ceremony. It was practiced. He knew his cues, when to say "I do" and when to recite his vows. He read her sweet pink lips as she recited her vows, the loving, happy look in her eyes melting him inside. They were one now.

He turned at the right moment and met the stares of the people, some friends, some family, some acquaintances, and even a few who thought themselves enemies. He met their stares with a wife beside him and felt that together they would manage anything that came their way.

Together, with God as their foundation, they were whole.

☙ ☙ ☙ ☙

Gabriel touched her arm and Alex jumped.

"Don't be nervous." He leaned over and whispered into her ear, the throng of people his mother had invited to the reception at her town house nearly crushing them. They hadn't had a single private moment since the ceremony, and her husband seemed to be getting more and more anxious to leave. She'd already begged for a little more time. She'd already eaten and danced and circulated the room, sometimes even leaving him to fend for himself.

Finally, Jane came over and took her hand. "Let's get a bit of air, shall we?"

Alex followed her out to the terrace and breathed in the uncommonly cool summer breeze.

"It was a beautiful ceremony, don't you think?" Alex leaned against a scrolling stone railing.

"The most beautiful I've ever seen." Jane smiled a gentle smile. But there was something in her eyes, some questioning thing that Alex steered away from.

"Alexandria." Jane came closer and her voice lowered. "Please forgive me if I am overstepping, but your mother isn't here and...well...you seem so nervous. Do you know what to expect tonight?"

Alex shook her head, tears—tears she despised—rushing to her eyes. She *didn't* know what to expect.

"Well, no wonder." Jane leaned against the rail with her. She took hold of her hand and squeezed it. "I was afraid too. Poor Matthew. I was practically in hysterics when he came into the room." She laughed in a fond way. "Which makes them more nervous, so try your best to hide that."

"Hide what?"

"Oh, dear. Your nervousness! I'm sure Gabriel knows what he's about. Just...trust him."

That sounded very hard indeed.

"I know I'm not really helping, but we'll laugh about this later. Can you believe that?"

She couldn't but she nodded anyway. She'd never had a sister and Jane would be such a wonderful one. She kissed her cheek. "Thank you, Jane, for everything."

Jane squeezed her hand. "Thank you, Alexandria. Gabriel was devastated after he lost his hearing. Having you has given him his life back. You don't realize the change in him. You are such an answer to all our prayers. I'm so happy to have you as a sister."

They hugged.

"Is my wife—?" Gabriel cut off the sentence as he saw them. "We should go."

His features were drawn into a serious look that made Jane laugh and scurry away. He came up to Alex and enveloped her in his arms. "I want to take my wife home. We leave for France in the morning, but we still have tonight."

Alex wondered that he couldn't feel the pounding of her heart against his chest as she clinched her eyes shut, clinging to him, and lifted her face for a kiss.

She kissed him with everything, all the love and passion inside her, knowing that soon everything could change.

"We've tarried long enough. Let us go home, beloved," he murmured against her lips.

She took a deep, sudden breath at the endearment. She had never trusted anyone the way she was entrusting this man with her heart. If he stopped loving her she would shatter into a million pieces.

He took her hand firmly in his and led her away.

She pushed down the fears, the tears…tried to slow the frantic beating of her heart.

It was time to find out what the Duchess of St. Easton had in store for her future.

Coming Soon:
A Duke's Promise

"I am not afraid to die." Ian Featherstone gripped his wife's hand for as long as he could, his fingers reaching and then slipping as they pulled him away.

"Don't give up, my darling," Katherine rasped out after him. "She is coming, I promise. Alexandria will find us."

Read the conclusion of Gabriel and Alexandria's story in *A Duke's Promise*, the third and final book in the Forgotten Castles series, as the Duke and Duchess of St. Easton travel to Italy to find Alexandria's parents. Fraught with danger on all sides, they must learn to work together and fight together. The mysterious key is within their grasp, but they have yet to recognize it. It will be a journey of faith to find this happy ending. And sacrificial love.

Coming from B&H Fiction in September 2012.

CPSIA information can be obtained at www.ICGtesting.com
Printed in the USA
LVOW100157030412

275782LV00001B/2/P